A Mother's Choice

By Kristin Noel Fischer

The best way to keep up with my new releases is by subscribing to updates at my website.

Other books by Kristin Noel Fischer

Anna's Courage

Jillian's Promise

Forgiving Natalie

For Joe and our six beautiful children
Frankie, Joey, TJ, Ben, Beth, and Sarah.

And

For my parents – Phil and Jeanne Smith

Chapter 1

Seattle — 1961

*I*T WAS RAINING *the day I fell in love with Jude Kingsley, and whenever it rains I can't help but think about that February day in 1961, my junior year of high school.*

My best friend Ruby dashed across the parking lot as a light drizzle escalated to a downpour. I scrambled to keep up but found running impossible in the high heels I'd bought for the Valentine's dance. I despised my freakishly large feet, so I was willing to sacrifice comfort for shoes that made me feel pretty and sophisticated.

Ruby and I joined the other girls in the bathroom and crowded around a single foggy mirror, where we attempted to fix our hair and makeup before venturing out to the stuffy gymnasium. On the stage, a local band played an old Frank Sinatra song, but nobody danced. Rock 'n' roll had been outlawed at our little private school after the archbishop of Chicago had publicly condemned it. My parents, especially my ultraconservative father, agreed with the decision, insisting school dances should be kept innocent and pure.

Ruby scanned the gym. She'd been distracted all week, and while I suspected it had to do with my seventeenth birthday, I didn't know for sure.

I tugged on her sleeve. "Why are you acting so strange?"

She twirled around and gave me an innocent look. "I'm not."

One of our teachers passed by and wished me happy birthday. I thanked him, then placed a hand on my hip and grinned at Ruby. "And how did he know it was my birthday?"

A sly smile played on her lips. "I don't know. School records?"

"Oh, school records," I repeated, with a smile of my own that called her bluff. Ruby and I were close like that. We always knew what the other person was thinking, and we never kept secrets.

All that changed after the accident, of course, but I'm getting ahead of myself.

Ruby had befriended me in the second grade when I'd moved to Seattle from Texas. All the kids had made fun of my southern accent, especially pesky Tim O'Connor who always tried to imitate me. Ruby, however, had brought me into her fold, insisting she'd have her father arrest anyone who bothered me.

"Okay," Ruby said, threading her elbow through mine.

"If you wouldn't mind closing your eyes for a moment—"

"Closing my eyes? What's going on?"

Ignoring my question, she covered my eyes with her hand. "Come on. You'll find out soon enough."

She guided me across the gym where voices erupted with shouts of "Happy Birthday, Nadine!" I opened my eyes to see all our friends gathered around a table that held a small pink and white cake with seventeen candles.

"For me?" I said, feigning surprise.

Ruby hugged me. "You knew, didn't you?"

"No, of course not. This was completely unexpected."

We laughed at the absurdity that either one of us could keep a secret from the other. "Attached at the hip" was what people used to say about us.

Annoying Tim O'Connor sidled up beside me. "How about a birthday kiss, sweetheart?" He waggled his thick brow and puckered his lips.

I smacked him on the arm. "In your dreams."

Everyone laughed except Tim, who rubbed his arm, offended. Over the years, I'd grown fond of him. He was funny, although many people didn't like him because he often went too far with his teasing. Nevertheless, he had a good heart and had become somewhat of a friend. Part of me even thought he was kind of cute with his curly red hair, bushy eyebrows, and ruddy Irish complexion.

Ruby lit the birthday candles and led everyone in sing-ing Happy Birthday. *Before blowing out the candles, I* looked around the room, taking it all in. Nobody had ever given me a surprise party before, and I was overwhelmed. Smiling, I blew out the candles, making a wish that every birthday would be just as memorable.

When I looked up to thank Ruby, I found her talking to Jude Kingsley, an absolutely divine boy with intense green eyes and thick black hair that swept across his forehead. Jude sat next to Ruby in art class and behind me in world history. He'd just moved here from Boston, and both Ruby and I thought he was gorgeous, although until now neither one of us had worked up the courage to talk to him.

Tim grabbed my arm. "Come on, Nadine. Dance with me."

I pulled away, my eyes glued to Ruby and Jude. Something odd settled in my throat. Jealousy? A premonition that everything was about to change? Or maybe just a desire to reach up and brush Jude's hair off his brow.

My stomach clenched as Ruby took Jude's hand and led him toward me.

"Nadine," Tim said.

"Not now. I'll save you a dance when they play Elvis."

"Elvis! That's never going to happen. Elvis is a horrible dancer, and according to Sister Hildegard, the devil incarnate."

I scowled at Tim. "Elvis is the greatest musician in the world, and he served in the Army, which is more than you can say, Tim O'Connor."

He batted the air and shook his head. "That's it, Nadine Greene. I'm crossing you off my list." Although he was joking, he turned abruptly and headed toward another girl.

Ruby nudged my shoulder. "He's such a dweeb."

I shrugged. "He's okay."

Jude stared at me with his beautiful green eyes, and I felt a thrill skitter up my spine.

"You like Elvis, Nadine?" he asked.

My stomach did a little flip flop. Jude Kingsley knew my name?

Ruby answered for both of us. "We love Elvis." Although she was no longer holding Jude's hand, she continued standing close to him.

Jude nodded approvingly. "I'm going to sing Jailhouse Rock *at the talent show next month."*

I laughed, convinced he was joking. "Sister Hildegard has outlawed rock 'n' roll. I'm certain she won't allow you to perform a song by Elvis."

Jude's gaze didn't waver from mine. His lips tugged upward in a conspiratorial smile. "True, but I have a plan, and if you'll help me—"

"Me?" Heat burned my face. For the first time, I allowed myself to really study his eyes. In addition to being the most incredible shade of forest green, they contained shards of amber that caught the light as he spoke. I'd never noticed that detail before, not that sparkling shards of amber were something easily noticed during fifth period when our history teacher was droning on about the Bolshe-

vik Revolution.

"So, will you help me?" Jude asked.

I wet my bottom lip. "Sure. What do I have to do?"

"Just play the piano. You can sing if you want, but Tim said you're a talented pianist."

Nervous laughter squeaked out of my mouth. Ruby gave me a disapproving glare, but Jude didn't seem to mind. He reached his hand toward me. "Come dance with me, and I'll tell you about my plan."

I hesitated a moment, too shocked to move. I liked Jude. Really liked him, but so did Ruby, and I wasn't going to let a boy—even a boy as cute as Jude Kingsley—get in the way of our friendship.

Ruby shrugged. "Go ahead. You're the birthday girl, after all."

Her tone held a layer of irritability, but before I could address it, Jude clasped my hand and led me to the dance floor. I glanced back at Ruby, relieved to see her talking with another boy. Maybe she didn't like Jude as much as I thought.

Jude smiled and gestured toward my heels. "Can you dance in those things?"

"I don't know. I've never tried."

He chuckled, the sound rumbling in his chest. Then he pulled me close, and I ignored everything except my body against his. I closed my eyes and rested my head on his solid chest. My insides tingled from my toes to the top of my head.

Lowering his hand, he pressed it to the small of my back. "Is this okay?"

I nodded and held onto the moment. The band played Earth Angel, *and my heart burst with elation because from that moment on, I knew I would love Jude Kingsley forever.*

I just wasn't prepared for what that love would cost me.

Chapter 2

Texas – 2014

NADINE'S HANDS SHOOK as she held the envelope postmarked Seattle. She sank into her desk chair and cringed, wishing she could run Tim's letter through the shredder without reading it.

The last time they'd spoken on the phone she'd hung up on him. Not the most mature action for a grandmother her age, but he'd made her so mad with his self-righteous insistence that she revisit the most painful time in her life. Why was he bringing this up? Why now?

Using the gold letter opener, a gift from her deceased husband Jude, she sliced open the envelope with one swift, decided movement and removed its contents.

My Darling Nadine,

I'm sorry I upset you when we last spoke on the phone, but it's time, sweetheart. Time to tell them the truth. Time to tell them about the choice you made, and the choice I made to help you.

I know you're afraid, but you don't have to do this alone. I love you, and I'm here for you.

I wasn't able to tell you this on the phone, but Ruby's daughter is trying to find you. She's planning a party for her mother's seventieth birthday, and she wants both of us to be there.

I have no doubt this beautiful and capable woman will succeed, even without my help. That's what I was trying to tell you before we were ... disconnected.

I know you're angry and scared, but please don't shut me out. Please don't ignore me. I'm not the enemy.

All my love,
Tim

Fear gripped Nadine. She crumpled Tim's letter and threw it in the trash, wanting it out of her sight. She tried to slow her breathing and get ahold of her emotions, but her heart hammered.

Ruby's daughter was looking for her!

No wonder Tim had been so relentless. Standing, she paced the wood floor and prayed for guidance. Outside, a gusty winter wind caused the trees to sway so hard she wondered if this time they'd actually snap in half.

They didn't, of course, and she breathed a momentary sigh of relief. She'd bought this house nearly thirty years ago because the enormous live oaks reminded her of being in a tree house, and who wouldn't want to live in a tree house?

Thirty years ago, it had been easy to run away. There'd been no internet, no Facebook, and no 24-hour news coverage. Thirty years ago, she'd simply piled the kids in the car, left Seattle, and escaped to Texas. These days, however, technology made escaping impossible.

Her children and grandchildren constantly badgered her to join various social media sites. She always feigned disinterest, but truthfully, she didn't want to connect. Didn't want her high school and college classmates to find her.

Didn't want Ruby to find her, even though they'd once been best friends.

She missed her best friend so much. If only they could see each other again. Talk about their lives, husbands, and children. But that was impossible. Nadine had made her choice long ago, and she was determined to do everything in her power to keep that choice a secret.

Bending over, she scooped the letter out of the trash and carried it to her bed where she sat and smoothed out the crumpled paper.

Loud pounding up the wooden stairs outside her bedroom interrupted her thoughts. Four-year-old Zane, clad in shorts, a red jacket, and black fireman boots, barged into the room. "Grandma, Grandma!" He held up a plastic dinosaur in each hand and launched himself onto the bed beside her. "We're coming to your house *tonight* for dinner."

Nadine quickly shoved the letter into a book on her nightstand. "Oh, I'm so happy." She tickled Zane's wiggly body and reveled in the simple joy of his laughter. "Where's your mother? I didn't hear you come in the house."

"She's in the kitchen," Zane said, prancing the dinosaurs across the striped comforter. His older brother Logan had gone through a dinosaur phase as well, but now Logan was obsessed with machines and how things worked.

"Hi, Mom," Autumn said, entering the bedroom.

Nadine jumped in surprise. "Goodness, I didn't hear you sneak up."

Autumn laughed and pulled back her long red hair. Her cat-like green eyes danced with amusement. "I didn't sneak up, so ... maybe it's time to consider purchasing a hearing aid?"

She said it in jest, but Nadine accepted there was

some truth to her youngest daughter's words. Standing, Nadine tried to usher Autumn out of her room and away from the letter. "Shall we go downstairs and see if we can find some cookies?"

"Yes," Zane shouted, bashing his dinosaurs against each other.

"Hold on." Autumn moved toward the bookshelf. "Zane and I have to pick up Logan from school in a few minutes, but I came over to return your tablecloths. I figured you might need them for the family dinner tonight."

"Thank you, sweetheart."

Autumn studied the bookshelf. "Do you have anything new I can borrow?"

Nadine loved to read and had hired a carpenter to build an enormous bookshelf that ran the entire length of her bedroom's north wall. She'd often lie in bed at night, looking at all the books she'd read over the years.

Reaching past her daughter, Nadine retrieved a well-worn paperback. "Here, I think you'll enjoy this."

Autumn read the back cover. "It looks fabulous. Thanks." She kissed her mother on the cheek and tucked the book under her arm. "Sorry to leave so quickly, but I don't want to be late picking up Logan. Thanks for the book."

"What about my cookie?" Zane asked.

"You already had three at Aunt Darlene's, you don't need another one from Grandma."

Zane pouted and Nadine leaned over to hug him good-bye. "I'll see you soon, okay?"

He nodded, waved good-bye, and ran down the stairs after his mother. Nadine stepped into the hallway and watched her daughter and grandson leave before returning to her bedroom and locking the door. With four adult children and seven grandchildren living nearby, she never knew who would stop by unannounced. Not that she ever minded. They all had a key and were welcome to come and go as they pleased.

But what Nadine had to do right now required absolute privacy.

Hidden at the back of her dresser drawer, she found the journal she'd bought years ago when she'd gone in for foot surgery. At the time, she'd thought it might be wise to write down her story in case she died. She hadn't died, of course. Nor had she written down the story, but it wasn't for lack of trying. Hours spent searching for the right words to explain her long-kept secret had yielded nothing but a brief entry on the day she fell in love with Jude.

Returning to her desk, she opened the journal and wondered how to continue. Explaining her choice wasn't going to be easy, but she needed to do it before

Ruby's daughter found her.

She picked up her favorite pen and began by addressing her grown children.

Dear Angela, Eleanor, Dan, Michael, and Autumn,

I need to tell you something that will change how you feel about me...

She reread her words and froze. Unintentionally, she'd included Angela's name.

Angela.

Fighting back deep sorrow, Nadine ran a finger over the name of her firstborn. Angela had been gone nearly thirty years now, yet Nadine thought about her constantly. Her stubborn daughter had the most beautiful green eyes, the same green eyes both Jude and Autumn had.

The pen in Nadine's hand shook, but she gripped it tighter. Instead of erasing or crossing out Angela's name, she pressed on, struggling with the story of her life and how to explain what had led to her fateful choice in September all those years ago.

Chapter 3

2014 – Autumn Anderson

$\mathcal{S}$ TANDING AT THE kitchen sink in our small rental house, I watched the rain beat against the window. Kyle had promised to be home in time to drive to my mother's for dinner, but now he was late.

The only reason I hadn't gone ahead was because he was leaving for Haiti in a few days and would be gone for an entire month.

"Autumn, please wait for me so we can go together," he'd asked. "I promise I'll be home by six. I don't want to take two separate cars."

Glancing at the clock on the kitchen wall, I saw it was already eight. I'd texted Kyle at seven, and he said he was on his way. So where was he now? Stuck with a patient or a doctor or someone more important than his family? I knew that wasn't fair, but I was frustrated.

Wasn't I smarter than this? Didn't I know by now not to depend on him? Clenching the scrub brush, I attacked the pan of baked-on macaroni and cheese that had been soaking since yesterday. I was angry my husband made a promise he couldn't keep, but even angrier with myself for believing him.

Right before Kyle started medical school, a doctor's wife had pulled me aside and asked if she could give me some advice. I was newly married and unexpectedly pregnant with our first child. It was an overwhelming time, but I was thrilled to begin this new stage of my life with Kyle. He'd always dreamed of becoming a doctor, and I was determined to help him succeed.

"I'll take any advice you have," I'd said, eagerly.

Smiling politely, she'd adjusted her diamond tennis bracelet. "If you don't want to be constantly disappointed in your marriage, don't expect anything from your husband. Ever."

"Excuse me?"

"For the next ten years or so," she'd continued, "it's going to be all about him. His tests, his patients, his sleep, and his needs. You have to carve out your own life. A career in medicine is demanding. Your husband will forget birthdays, anniversaries, and all other important events he promised to remember. When sleep deprived, he'll even forget how to be a decent human being. The best thing you can do is pretend you're a single mother with a horrible roommate and an occasional lover."

I'd stared open-mouthed at this woman, thinking she had a terrible attitude. Kyle and I were best friends. We did everything together. Sure, I knew medical school would be rough, especially after the baby arrived, but I prided myself on being self-sufficient. I was an independent woman with a degree in speech pathology. I was even planning on applying for a master's program in a few years.

Unfortunately, that doctor's wife had been exactly right. Once medical school began, I lost Kyle to an alien world filled with unfamiliar jargon, tests, and other students. Determined to keep my sanity and my marriage intact, I made a decision to be happy. I didn't place any demands on Kyle, and I trained myself to believe he was doing his best, even if he forgot to pick up his son from preschool like he offered.

Life with a husband in medical school wasn't easy, but we survived. We even purposely had another baby, wanting our children to be close in age. Plus, everyone said having a second baby during medical school was easier than during residency.

The boys were three and one when Kyle walked across the stage at graduation and accepted his diploma to become Dr. Kyle Anderson. I'd never been more proud or happy in my entire life.

Internship nearly broke us, but Kyle was now in his last year of residency. Both of us were looking forward to the day he joined a practice, and we could begin paying off our credit cards. "Five more months," I told myself. "I can do anything for five more months."

The boys wandered into the kitchen, wearing their jackets and brandishing light sabers in anticipation of leaving for my mom's house.

"When is Daddy going to be home?" Logan asked.

I wiped down the counter with a towel and tried to keep the frustration out of my voice. "I'm not sure."

Zane, our youngest, tucked his light saber under his chin and did a karate kick. "I think Daddy is late, and we're going to be late for Grandma's house."

I'd already called my mom and told her to go ahead and eat without us. At this point, she and my siblings were probably done with dessert. I sighed and made an executive decision. "You know what guys? We're going to skip Grandma's house tonight. Go put on your pajamas while I make some popcorn for dinner. Then we'll pile into my bed and watch one of the movies we checked out from the library."

The boys scampered off to change, arguing about which movie to watch and who got to hold the popcorn bowl.

Although disappointed, I told myself Kyle was helping someone in need. Besides, he'd been offered a clinic job starting in the fall, and that meant regular hours with no hospital call. "Five more months. Five more months."

Both boys were sound asleep in our bed by the time Kyle came home. When he leaned over to pick up Logan, I caught a whiff of beer on his breath. The hair on my arms stood straight up. "Did you go out tonight?"

His latte eyes twinkled as he flashed me his irresistible smile. "I just grabbed a quick beer with Dr. Forman. He needed to talk to me about something."

I scooted off our bed and glared at him in disbelief. "We were supposed to go to my mom's house for dinner tonight. My brothers and sister wanted to wish you good luck in Haiti. Darlene made you her famous Red Velvet Cake."

Alarm flashed across his face. "Oh, Autumn. I'm so sorry. I completely forgot."

"Didn't you get my text at seven?"

"Yeah, but I wasn't thinking."

I inhaled sharply and held back the angry words that threatened to spill forth. This was no big deal, I told myself. My family got together for dinner all the time.

"Don't be mad," he said.

I scooped up Zane. "We missed having dinner with

my family because you were out drinking with your mentor. Of course, I'm mad. Why didn't you call?"

He looked at me with innocent eyes. "Baby, I forgot." Reaching over, he took Zane from me and held both boys in his strong arms. "I'll make it up to you. I don't have to work tomorrow, so I'm all yours. Whatever you want to do, we'll do."

I lifted my chin in defiance. "I have to go to the grocery store and clean the bathroom. Are you telling me you're offering to scrub the toilet?"

He smiled. "Yeah, it'll be fun. I'll let the boys help."

An image of Logan chasing Zane down the hall with the toilet brush sprang to mind, and I shook my head. "It's not going to be fun."

Kyle winked. "Will you at least let me try?"

I hid my smile. This was why I loved Kyle. Why I knew, in the end, everything would be okay, even though he could make me so mad.

He carried the boys down the hall and put them to bed; then he seduced me into taking a shower with him. I loved the feel of his hands over my body as the hot water poured down on us. Loved how amazing he tasted when he kissed me.

After we made love, we lay in each other's arms, and I told him about the new subdivision being built near his future place of employment. The boys and I had toured the model home, and all three of us could imagine living there. "We can plant flowers in the spring, build a tree house in the summer, and hang Christmas lights in December. Maybe we can even get a dog. What do you think? Wouldn't a dog be nice for the boys?"

Kyle didn't seem too interested in my fantasies of home ownership, but he was tired, so I let him sleep. In the morning, we took the boys to the donut shop before heading over to the grocery store. Zane and Logan were hanging off the sides of the shopping cart, having the time of their lives, when we turned onto the coffee aisle and spotted Dr. Forman himself.

The handsome Australian was a divorced obstetrician who'd taken Kyle under his wing a few years ago. In addition to having a soft spot for my Meat Lovers' Lasagna and Sopapilla Cheesecake, he adored Logan and Zane.

"Hello, Andersons!" He pounded fists with the boys, patted Kyle hard on the back, and gave me a chaste hug. "Sorry I kept your husband out so late last night, but we had to celebrate the big news. Isn't that right, mate?"

"Big news?" I removed Logan's hand from the coffee bean grinder. Even though he was six and old enough to know better, Logan was obsessed with anything mechanical.

"The fellowship," Dr. Forman said. "Your husband got the OB fellowship. Isn't that fantastic?"

The air grew tense, and a muscle in Kyle's jaw clenched. He shot Dr. Forman a warning look. "Autumn and I haven't had a chance to talk about it yet."

The obstetrician raised his brow. "No worries. You're going to take it though, right? It's the chance of a lifetime, and I had to pull some strings to get you accepted."

My gut tensed. Now I understood why the good-looking physician was divorced. Before either Kyle or I could respond, the coffee grinder sprang to life with a high-pitched whirl. Logan leapt back, knocking into the cart and claiming he hadn't done anything.

I grabbed my son's arm and forced a smile. "It was nice seeing you, Dr. Forman. I'm going to take the boys and wait in the car."

"It was wonderful seeing you, too, Autumn."

Kyle said nothing as I snatched my purse and escorted the boys to the car. By the time he came out to the parking lot with the groceries, I was livid.

"Can we at least talk about it?" he asked, sliding into the driver's seat.

"You're not thinking about actually doing it, are you?"

"It's an amazing opportunity."

I curled my hand into a tight fist and thought about punching the window. All the patience I'd had with his career over the past seven years vanished. "What about your job offer from the clinic? What about regular hours and no hospital call?"

He started the engine and thrummed his fingers on the steering wheel. "It'll be there after the fellowship, if that's what I still want. Or I'll get a better job."

"No," I shouted. "Absolutely not."

"It's just one more year."

"One more year? Are you kidding? What about our plans? What about my master's program that I've kept on hold for the past seven years?"

"Mom?" Zane called from the back seat. I seldom shouted or even raised my voice, so I'm sure my hostility alarmed him.

"Sorry, boys." I popped my feet on the dash, hugged my stomach, and glared out the window. How could Kyle have applied to a fellowship program without telling me? Did he think he could make such a monumental decision like this on his own? Was I that much of a pushover?

And why did a divorced obstetrician know more about my husband's ambitions than I did?

Chapter 4

*T*HE FIRST TIME *Jude and I practiced at my house for the talent show, my mother stayed in the laundry room where she could keep an eye on us. Jude sang Ave Maria— our decoy song—while I attempted to accompany him on the piano. I say attempted because between my mother's supervision and Jude's heavenly voice, I could barely concentrate. I must've messed up a million times, but even my mistakes couldn't diminish Jude's performance.*

"That was divine, Jude. You have a remarkable voice," my mother said, clutching one of my father's dress shirts to her chest. Her face was flushed, and I wondered if she was having another one of her menopausal symptoms.

"Thank you, Mrs. Greene," Jude said with a confident smile.

My fifty-year-old mother practically melted, and I real- ized I wasn't the only one with a crush on Jude.

The next time Jude came over, my mother gave us a little more space, supervising from the kitchen and only passing through the living room a few times.

When she was out of earshot, I asked Jude about practicing Jailhouse Rock.

He gave a slow smile that danced through my entire body. "Just be patient. We have plenty of time."

During the third visit, my mother vacuumed. My heart pounded as Jude imitated Elvis by thrusting his hips back and forth. Something inside me came undone, and although I worried about getting caught, I couldn't stop admiring the way he moved. When he finished, his gaze lingered on my mouth, and I almost fainted. My insides tingled, and my pulse raced just like the women in the steamy romance novels my mother kept hidden under her bed.

"Well, what'd you think?" he asked.

"You were amazing."

He grinned. "You were amazing, too, Nadine."

I allowed the way he said my name to linger in the air. How in the world did I get so lucky to have Jude Kingsley in my living room?

"Nadine," my mother snapped, jerking me out of my trance.

"Yes, Mother?" When had she turned off the vacuum, and how long had I been staring at Jude?

"I'm going across the street to talk to Mrs. Foster. I've left two pieces of carrot cake and some lemonade on the kitchen table."

"Thank you, Mother."

"Thank you, Mrs. Greene."

She eyed us suspiciously, as if doubting her decision to leave us alone. I held my breath and waited for her to walk out the door, but she continued watching us.

Jude knocked on the piano and winked at me. "I think we should practice one more time before we take a break, what do you think, Nadine?"

I held back a smile. "Yes, I agree." I turned my attention to the sheet music and began playing Ave Maria, grateful for something to do.

When my mother finally left, Jude sank onto the piano bench beside me. His gaze dropped to my mouth. Was he going to kiss me? I stopped playing but kept my hands on the keys.

"We're going to forget about Elvis and just perform Ave Maria," Jude said, his voice serious.

"Why?" My heart pounded. He was so close I could smell his shampoo—a woodsy, inviting scent that sent a shiver through me. "The way you perform Jail House Rock is amazing. It would be a shame not to perform it."

He smiled. "Thanks, but I was kind of a troublemaker at my old school, and my dad keeps threatening to send me to boarding school if I misbehave again. My mom would never let him do it, but ... mostly, I don't want to get a sweet and innocent girl like you in trouble."

I noticed the small scar underneath his earlobe, and I had the craziest desire to touch it. "I'm not that sweet and *innocent. And for the record, I'm not afraid."*

His brow lifted, and he slid down the bench until he was so close I could feel his body heat. I yearned to reach forward and run my hand through his hair.

"What if I kissed you right now?" he asked. "Would you be afraid?"

My pulse jumped, and I couldn't speak. I'd never been kissed before, unless you counted Tim O'Connor in the third grade, and I definitely did not, since that had been more of a dare than true love.

Jude removed my hand from the piano keys and entwined his fingers with mine. Then he slid even closer.

With his free hand, he brushed back my hair, tucking it behind my ear. I held my breath as he gently pressed his lips to mine. The touch was so light, so tender, but everything inside me exploded. He kissed me softly for a long time, and when he pulled away, I found myself wanting more.

"That was wonderful," I said, sounding way too polite for the heat burning in my belly.

Jude grinned. "Guess what?"

"What?" I asked.

"I think I might be falling for you, Nadine."

I smiled so big my cheeks ached. "Really?"

He nodded. "Yeah. Really."

Chapter 5

KYLE INSISTED MY negative reaction to the news about his fellowship was unwarranted. "I've only been accepted," he claimed. "I haven't made a commitment yet."

"The fact you didn't tell me you'd even applied feels like a betrayal."

"A betrayal? It's not like I cheated on you!"

We were in our kitchen, trying to keep our voices down as the boys dug for dinosaur bones in the back yard. Every so often, Zane would call, "Eureka! I found one." But then Logan would point out it was just a rock, and they needed to dig much farther to find an actual fossil.

I leaned against the kitchen counter and folded my arms across my chest. "Maybe you didn't cheat on me, but applying for the fellowship probably took a tremendous amount of time and effort. You probably had to pay for the application fee. I'm hurt you kept that from me. It's like you didn't even think twice about locking me out of your life."

He groaned, completely dismissing my feelings. This wasn't a new problem in our marriage. Kyle had been raised in the foster care system and sometimes seemed incapable of true intimacy. Of remembering I was his partner, his family, his wife.

"We're married," I continued. "We have children. You can't go off making important decisions without me."

"Okay, I probably should have told you," he conceded. "I'm sorry, but can we talk about the fellowship? Can you tell me why you're so opposed to it? It's just another year, then I'll be able to get a better job with higher pay."

I slammed my heel into the bottom kitchen cupboard. "I don't want you to get a better job with higher pay. I don't want to continue living like a single mother who has extra laundry to do. You're never here, Kyle, and when you are—"

"When I am, I don't spend enough quality time with you," he said, throwing words from a previous fight back into my face.

As if to prove the point, his phone buzzed with a text, and he automatically glanced at it. "I've got to go to the hospital."

"I thought you weren't on call today?"

He shrugged. "I'm not, but I told Alex I'd help if he got stuck. I'll be back in an hour, then we can finish our discussion."

"No," I said, my voice resentful. "You're not going to get back until late tonight, then we'll be busy with dinner and bathing the boys and—"

"I'll be back," he said. "Soon."

My blood boiled, but I said nothing as Kyle went into the bedroom to gather his things before leaving.

INSTEAD OF WAITING for Kyle, I went to my mother's house. From past experience, I knew an hour at the hospital could easily turn into two or five, and I didn't want to stay home, waiting for my husband's return. I was sick of waiting behind everyone else who demanded his attention.

At my mother's house, we ate lunch on the back porch under the live oak trees. It was unseasonably warm for late February, and I embraced the sunshine, knowing the Texas weather could change any minute.

Usually, my mom asked all sorts of questions about work and school, but today she seemed distant and distracted. Her eyes were red rimmed as if from crying, and she kept coughing.

"Are you okay?" I asked after the boys excused themselves to inspect the perimeter for invaders.

She rubbed a finger over the wooden picnic table. "My allergies are bothering me, but other than that I'm fine, sweetheart. What about you? Is everything okay with you and Kyle?"

"Of course." I swallowed the lump in my throat. I hadn't even mentioned my fight with Kyle, but somehow she knew, just like I knew she wasn't fine.

She touched the sleeve of my emerald-green sweater. "I love this color on you. It brings out the color of your eyes."

"Thanks. Kyle gave it to me for Christmas." I hugged my chest and rubbed the sleeves of my sweater.

"Hey, Mom, look at me," Zane hollered from a lower tree branch. "I'm going to climb all the way to the moon."

I smiled. "Just be home in time for dinner."

"What if an alien asks me to spend the night?"

Logan joined his little brother in the tree. "I'll make sure he comes back."

"I'll send my spaceship to get you if it's dark," my mother added.

Both boys grinned. "Cool."

"Thanks," I told her, feeling content. I'd always found being at my mom's house comforting. I loved how she took care of me, cooked for me, gave me books to read, and often let me take a nap while she watched the boys. Instead of being a responsible wife and mother, I could relax without worrying about anything.

Logan had been such a fussy baby, and at one point, my mom suggested Kyle and I move in with her so she could help. I'd jumped at the offer, but after talking it over with Kyle, we both agreed it would be best for our family to stay in our little rental house next to the medical school and hospital. Today, I questioned that decision.

My mom stacked the plates, but instead of carrying them into the kitchen, she remained seated. "Did I ever tell you about the horrific fight your father and I had before you were born?"

"No, tell me." I tried not to sound too eager, but she seldom talked about her past, and certainly never spontaneously like this. Perhaps my melancholy mood had triggered her memory.

Everything I knew about my father came from my older sister Eleanor. She'd told me his name was Jude Kingsley, and he was a handsome man, very much in love with our mother. They'd built a good life in Seattle, but shortly before I was born, he was killed in a horrible car accident along with my oldest sister Angela. After that, my mother moved our family to Texas in order to be closer to her parents and start over.

Scooting back on the picnic bench, she smiled. "Well, the fight was awful. We yelled and screamed and didn't talk for hours."

"What was it about?"

She shook her head. "It's not important now, but we worked it out. I didn't think we could …"

"How did you resolve it?"

Her eyes lit with mischief. "Your father finally realized I was right."

She said the last part as a joke and I laughed. Hopefully, Kyle would realize I was right. This fellowship was a terrible idea.

She squeezed my hand and stood. "I'm playing golf this afternoon, so I better get going. If you want to stay for dinner, there's leftover seafood pasta in the refrigerator, but I'm going out and won't be back until later."

"Who are you going out with?" I asked.

She gathered the plates, placing the silverware on top. "Oh, just some friends from golf. No one you know."

There was a faraway note in her voice. She didn't elaborate, and I didn't ask her to. After she left, the boys and I went inside, and I helped them set up my old wooden train set. I'd been somewhat of a tomboy and had collected several thousand train pieces over the years, including my beloved ferryboat and suspension bridge. There were now enough track pieces to construct a large circular path that ran through the kitchen, living room, and dining room.

While the boys played, I went into the living room and pulled down several photo albums from the bookshelf. As a child, I'd spent hours on the couch, paging through family albums while my mom taught piano lessons in the other room.

Opening the first album, I smiled at a picture of my parents on their wedding day. My mother wore soft pink lipstick and a beautiful, white lace gown. My father looked young and gave an expression of wonder, as if he couldn't believe this gorgeous woman was actually marrying him.

The edges of the picture had yellowed, and I vowed once again to scan all my mother's photos into the computer to make a digital file. I'd helped my brother's wife, Darlene, do the same last summer, and while it was time consuming, it hadn't been difficult.

Turning the page, I found a picture of my father holding a newborn baby. "Angela and Jude," the caption read. This was my father and oldest sister who'd died together. I often wondered how different my life would've been had they lived. Would my parents have stayed in Seattle? Would they have had more children after me?

Several pictures were missing from the album. My

mom explained they'd fallen out during the move to Texas thirty years ago, and she'd stuck them in a box for safekeeping. Maybe I should start my digital project by scanning those loose photos before addressing the pictures already in albums. I was pretty sure the photos were in a box at the back of the attic; the worst place in the world for photographs.

Deciding there was no time like the present, I climbed into the attic and made my way past the Christmas decorations, old furniture, and clothes. I used to criticize my mother for having so much clutter, but once I became a mother myself, I understood how difficult it was to throw away your preschooler's macaroni masterpiece of Abraham Lincoln.

As a teenager, I dreamed of turning the attic into my own private sanctuary like I'd seen in several teen movies. Unfortunately, my mom never agreed to the idea, and I was forced to live in a conventional bedroom with heating and air-conditioning like the rest of my middle-class subdivision.

At last I reached the back wall, and sure enough, the box was exactly where I thought it would be. I peeked inside, relieved to see most of the pictures were still in good shape.

I laughed at a picture of my mother with Angela and my brothers—all wearing red, white, and blue bicentennial button-down collared shirts. I'd never seen anything so tacky. Scrawled on the back of the photo were the words, "July 4, 1976. Happy 200 years, America!" Had my mom sewn these shirts? Had she made one for my father? What about Eleanor? I couldn't imagine my finicky sister wearing something so atrocious.

I continued digging through the photos, overwhelmed by how many there were. How would I ever organize them?

I found one of the many handmade postcards my father had sent my mom during their courtship. Eleanor told me he'd written hidden messages in them, but I couldn't see any secret message. Maybe if I used a magnifying glass I'd be able to read them.

I continued looking through the box, laughing at all the various fashion trends. Some of the things my brothers wore were hysterical—plaid pants, sweater vests, and wide collars. Dan had a plum-colored velour sweater he was quite fond of, and Michael didn't seem to go anywhere without his red tracksuit. No wonder neither one of them had any fashion sense to this day.

My phone buzzed with a text from Kyle. "Where are you?"

"At my mom's," I typed back.

I watched the cursor blink, wondering if he was mad or actually writing something. Finally, his text came through. "Come home … please."

Chapter 6

*J*UDE UNEXPECTEDLY SHOWED up at my house on *Saturday evening with a sheepish grin and two pairs of ice skates slung over his shoulder. "A pretty girl like you probably has plans for Saturday night, but—"*

"No," I practically shouted, too excited about seeing him again to hold back the eagerness in my voice. I hadn't been able to stop fixating over the way he kissed me during our practice the other day and what he'd said about falling for me.

He shifted his weight from one foot to the other. "Would you like to go skating? I don't know if you have your own pair, but I borrowed these from a neighbor."

"Wonderful. I've outgrown mine." I gestured awkwardly at my enormous feet, then cringed, fearing I'd frighten Jude. If he noticed, he didn't seem to be bothered.

My mother came to the door and invited Jude inside while I collected my coat, hat, scarf, and mittens. Daddy came out of his office to say hello, but he kept his distance and scowled at the way Jude's hair hung over his brow.

"We'd better get going," I said, worried my father might suggest a barber or offer to cut Jude's hair himself.

Outside, I exhaled with relief and watched my breath dance in the cold air. It had snowed all morning, transforming the trees and rooftops into a magical kingdom. Our feet crunched on the sidewalk as we walked down to the park.

At the outdoor skating rink, we sat on a bench underneath the large evergreen tree decorated with hundreds of little white lights. As we laced up our skates, our legs casually brushed against each other, delighting me each time.

Finally, I stood, excited to join the other skaters on the ice and show off my skills. "Ruby and I used to come here all the time. It's one of my favorite places in the world."

"Then I'm glad you agreed to come with me." Jude remained seated, looking up at me with a vulnerability I didn't understand. "I should probably confess I've never skated before."

"What?"

He nodded. "Tim suggested I take you ice skating, but now that we're here, I don't know what to do."

I laughed, both surprised and touched. Holding out my mitten-covered hands, I pulled him to his feet. "Come on. I'll teach you."

His ankles flopped back and forth as we walked to the ice. "You won't let me fall, right?" he asked, sounding like *an adorable little kid.*

"Falling is half the fun," I insisted. "Besides, it doesn't hurt that much."

I stepped onto the slick ice, and he followed, gripping my arm with his left hand and flailing wildly in an attempt to catch his balance with his right. I'm sure we looked like Laurel and Hardy, tripping over each other until we suddenly fell hard, my back landing against his chest.

"Are you okay?" I asked, worried I'd hurt him.

He laughed and so did I. The ice was cold on my legs, but my back and neck felt warm against Jude's body. He squeezed me tight. "All right, superstar, let's try again."

Blushing, I stood and brushed off my pants before helping Jude to his feet. Then, holding his hands with both of mine, I skated backwards, gently pulling him forward. We both stared at his shaky feet as we circled the rink in an awkward dance. He didn't seem to be improving, and I wondered if skating was one of those skills you had to learn as a child. Maybe it was too late for Jude.

"Wait a minute," he said, interrupting my thoughts. "I think I can do this."

He straightened and released his grip. Then he shocked me by striding across the ice as if he'd been skating his whole life. I stood in awe, watching him expertly glide forward, knees bent, head up, and torso straight. He easily turned one direction, then the other. Beaming, he raced back toward me before angling his blades to shave the ice and come to a full stop.

"Jude Kingsley," I shouted. "You tricked me! You're an excellent skater."

He laughed. "I guess I did play ice hockey for five years back in Boston."

I tried to swat him on the arm, but he spun out of my reach and took off across the ice. I sprinted after him, chasing him around the rink several times. We both laughed until our bellies hurt.

"Will you forgive me?" he asked when I'd finally caught up with him. "You can't blame me. I just wanted an excuse to be near you."

I softly elbowed him in the ribs, and he put his arm around me. He didn't need an excuse to be near me, but I wasn't going to tell him that. At least not yet.

We continued skating together, talking and flirting as if we didn't have a care in the world. On a distant radio, I heard Elvis singing Are You Lonesome Tonight. Jude squeezed my hand and winked. Lonesome? No, I wasn't, thank you very much.

Afterward, Jude bought two hot chocolates from a street vendor, and we leisurely strolled home, talking about books, blueberry pancakes, and architecture. Jude was obsessed with large structures, especially the Empire State Building, which he told me had 103 floors and 6,514 windows.

"That's a lot of windows to clean," I said, trying to be

funny.

His gaze met mine. "I'm sorry. I'm talking too much. It's just so easy to talk to you, Nadine."

I smiled. "It's easy to talk to you, too."

On my front porch, Jude kissed me goodnight for a long time. His kiss grew more urgent, and without warning, he placed both hands low on my hips and pressed me against the wall. I let out an involuntary moan of pleasure. Oh, Lord. Is this why the nuns spent so much time warning us about boys and their lustful desires?

Running my hands through Jude's thick hair, I pulled him closer. Kissed him harder. Held him tighter.

Then Daddy yanked open the door and told me it was time to come inside this very instant. Jude practically jumped off the porch. With a startled wave, he said goodnight and disappeared down the street.

"Goodnight, Daddy," I hollered, racing up the stairs to my bedroom.

"Nadine!"

Heat burned my face, and I imagined my cheeks were red from Jude's rough whiskers. "Yes, sir?" I turned around slowly, praying he hadn't seen me in the mist of passion on the front porch.

His eyes narrowed. "You be careful with that boy, do you hear me?"

"Yes, sir," I replied. Then I hurried down the hall, certain that "careful" was the last thing I wanted to be with

that boy.

∿

ON THE NIGHT *of the talent show, my stomach fluttered with nerves. Ruby came over to my house to help with my hair and makeup.*

"Are we okay?" I asked as she teased my hair into a beehive that rivaled Audrey Hepburn's. I was worried about our friendship because lately, I'd spent a tremendous amount of time with Jude. I hadn't meant to neglect Ruby, but every day after school, Jude and I studied at the library while Ruby worked at her grandparents' grocery store. Sometimes she'd join us after work, but most of the time she was too tired.

Ruby picked up a bobby pin from my bathroom counter. "Of course we're okay. Why wouldn't we be?"

"Well," I began, nervous about her reaction, "I'm worried things aren't okay because of Jude."

Her face flinched. "You mean because I liked him first?"

I wanted to argue that I didn't know she liked him first. I thought we both liked him at the same time, but I knew that wasn't the point.

"Do you want me to stop seeing him?"

She sighed. "No, you two are perfect together. I'm just jealous."

I released the breath I'd been holding. "Don't be jealous. He could never replace you. You'll always be my best friend."

She pressed her lips together. "Too bad he doesn't have a brother."

I smiled. When Ruby and I were kids, we talked about marrying brothers so we could be real sisters and spend vacations and holidays together. "What about Tim O'Connor? Jude and Tim are good friends. They're practically brothers."

Ruby made a face. "Tim O'Connor? No way."

"You were laughing with him yesterday."

Her face reddened. "Okay, I admit, he's gotten kind of cute, and he isn't as annoying as he used to be, but ... I want someone who looks at me the way Jude looks at you."

My knees buckled. "What do you mean?"

Ruby's eyes met mine. "He looks at you as if you're the most important person in the world. As if nothing else matters. As if he really loves you."

Joy bubbled through me. I felt the same way about Jude, and that feeling was intoxicating, addicting, and all-consuming. I was obsessed, drowning in nothing but thoughts of him day and night. I didn't want to be one of those girls who abandoned her friends for some boy, but Jude wasn't just some boy. He was the greatest love of my life, and I wanted to be with him constantly.

Reaching over, I squeezed Ruby's hand. "You'll find

someone like that. I know you will."

"What if I don't? What if I end up an old maid with a thousand cats?"

"Impossible," I insisted.

―――

AT THE HIGH school, Ruby and I found Jude behind the stage, dressed in a stylish black suit and tie. His hair was neatly combed, and he'd shined his shoes with a fresh coat of polish.

"Let me get a picture," Ruby said, holding up her camera.

Jude put his arm around me. "You look beautiful." Bending down, he brushed his lips across mine. Ruby snapped a photo, capturing the kiss.

I blinked hard from the flash and laughed. "Please don't show that picture to my father."

"Of course not." She wished us good luck, then left to find a seat in the audience.

"Are you nervous?" Jude asked when we were alone.

"A little."

He smiled and kissed me again. I ran a hand over his smooth jaw, but just as I began to relax in his presence, a hand clamped down on my shoulder.

"Nadine Greene," Sister Hildegard said, glaring down at me. "I'm ashamed of you. We'll have none of this

behavior! None of it!"

Jude stepped in front of me. "It was my fault. Nadine said something nice, and I got carried away in the moment."

The nun eyed him with disbelief. I often teased Jude about being the teacher's pet, insisting all of the nuns were secretly in love with him. He adamantly denied it, but he'd sweet-talked himself out of more than one situation.

This time, however, Sister dismissed Jude's confession and turned her attention to me. "You're a fine girl, Nadine, but you need to be more prudent with your suggestive comments toward young men."

"There was nothing suggestive about her comment," Jude said. "I just took liberties. Honestly, Sister, it was all my fault."

I didn't dare look at Jude and instead kept my eyes fixed on the black whisker just above Sister's lip. Were nuns allowed to use tweezers for facial hair removal, or was that considered too vain? My mother had an errant chin hair I was in charge of monitoring, lest she go out in public without plucking it. Would Sister appreciate the same courtesy, or would she consider it rude?

She held up tonight's program. "Ave Maria is one of my favorite hymns. I'm looking forward to your performance, so let's not taint it with sins of the flesh."

"Yes, Sister," Jude and I said together.

When she finally walked away, I let out a giggle and

nudged Jude. "Sorry I tempted you with sins of the flesh."

His face tightened into a serious knot. "We're forgetting about Jailhouse Rock and just performing Ave Maria."

"No."

"Yes. I refuse to ruin your reputation or get you in trouble."

I twirled a strand of hair around my finger, a flirtatious gesture I'd read about in one of the magazines at the hair salon. "Come on, Jude. It'll be fun."

He shook his head. "No. Your father would never forgive me if our performance got blown out of proportion and you got in trouble."

"I don't care."

"I do, Nadine."

I loved how he said my name. Loved the frown lines across his forehead when he was serious, and I loved how he was trying to protect me. "If Sister wasn't watching, I'd let you kiss me again."

That got a little smile out of him. He chuckled and shook his head. "If Sister wasn't watching, I'd do more than kiss you."

THE AUDIENCE CLAPPED politely as Jude and I took the stage. They clapped again when we finished Ave Maria, but they went absolutely crazy when I began playing

Jailhouse Rock *on the school's grand piano.*

Jude looked at me and raised his brow. "Come on," I mouthed, "You know you want to."

He hesitated a moment, but then his leg twitched to the beat. Turning back to the audience, he belted out the words and thrust his hips back and forth, causing every girl to scream as if he was actually Elvis.

I laughed and threw myself into the music, shaking my shoulders as my fingers flew across the keyboard. Jude sounded fantastic, and judging by the audience, I wasn't the only one to think so.

I was having the time of my life, and at that moment, I believed Jude and I could weather any storm. We were young, invincible, and in love.

Unfortunately, I hadn't counted on the irrational reaction of our parents and the school's administration. Their unfounded anger changed everything, altering the course of my relationship with Jude and threatening to destroy us.

Chapter 7

*A*S KYLE PACKED for his trip to Haiti, we continued fighting about his fellowship program. I understood his reasons for wanting to further his education, but it didn't change my mind. Besides my obvious objections, saying yes to the fellowship meant moving across Texas to a new town. I didn't want to give up my part-time job and take the boys out of their environment and away from my family. And what about starting my master's program? When was that supposed to happen?

"Maybe you could stay here with your mother while I commute back and forth," Kyle suggested, throwing a pair of swimming trunks into his suitcase.

"You want us to live apart ... for an entire year?"

"It might be easier on you."

I stared in disbelief at the man I thought I knew. The man I'd vowed to love, honor, and respect all the days of my life.

Shortly after Kyle and I were engaged, Eleanor had

vehemently advised me not to marry him. She'd compared him to the stray dog our brothers had rescued when they were in high school. All of us had loved and cared for that dog. He was blind in one eye and bore ragged scars from abuse, but he was part of our family.

We took him on walks, brushed him, and treated him with kindness. He slept on Michael's bed every night. Despite our efforts, though, he never learned to trust anyone outside our immediate family. One day he attacked a little boy riding his bike past our house. The boy wasn't hurt—just frightened. But we had to euthanize the dog. Both my brothers had sobbed, despite believing it was the right thing to do.

"Family and genetics matter," Eleanor had said, regarding Kyle's background. "Someone who grew up in the foster care system isn't going to be a good husband."

I hadn't believed her then, and I didn't believe her now. Although Kyle hadn't told me all the details of his past, I knew he'd survived a difficult childhood by clinging to academics and sports. He was a hard worker with a good heart, and he truly loved me. He was just distant sometimes and excluded me from parts of his life.

I took Kyle's swimming trunks out of the suitcase and rolled them into a tight ball so they would take up less space. "Families are supposed to stay together. We're not living apart for a year."

Sitting on the edge of the bed, he took my hand and hung his head. "I don't want to keep fighting. Can we please table this discussion until I get back?"

I agreed. We'd come to an impasse, and neither one of us wanted to part on angry terms. All I could do was pray that being away from me for a month would change his mind.

For dinner, we made mini pizzas with the boys and played a rousing game of Go Fish. Kyle and I acted so polite to each other, pretending everything was normal, that I fell into bed exhausted.

In the morning, my husband's excitement about working with the poor in Haiti reminded me of a little kid on Christmas morning. He kissed me good-bye at the airport and told me he'd miss me, but my heart was heavy as I piled the boys into the minivan and drove home.

———

NOTHING MUCH HAPPENED the rest of the week, but on Saturday, my sister hosted a family dinner at her house. Eleanor, a doctor herself, had a perfect life in a ritzy subdivision with her perfect husband and perfect daughter. My niece Aubrey was only a few months older than Logan but miles ahead in the obedience and intellectual departments. Not that I was one to compare my children, but still, Aubrey wrote beautiful thank you notes while Logan struggled with reversing his b's and d's.

I parked behind Eleanor's recently purchased BMW and surveyed the other cars. My mom and my brother Michael were here, but my other brother and his wife hadn't yet arrived, which instantly upgraded my status from late to on time.

Logan and Zane bolted from the car and raced up the walk, arguing over whose turn it was to ring the bell. Before they could work out a diplomatic solution, Eleanor's live-in help, the young and vivacious Vilda, answered the door wearing high heels and a miniskirt. I tried to keep my face neutral, but I was dying to ask if she'd swiped the skirt from Aubrey's closet since it seemed the perfect size for a small child.

Vilda slipped her ID and credit card into her bra and stepped onto the front porch. We exchanged pleasantries, then she said, "Gotta go."

"Where are you off to looking so ... nice?" I started to say trashy, but I didn't want to insult her.

She licked her bright red lips. "Drinks and dancing with the girls."

My brother-in-law came to the door. "Be careful, Vilda. And call if you find yourself in a situation where you need help."

"*Okay, Dad.* Don't wait up," she said sarcastically.

Vilda had worked for Eleanor and Jim since Aubrey was a newborn. She'd come over from Sweden on a temporary work visa, but now lived in the pool house, which was three times the size of my rental house. She earned an impressive salary taking care of my sister's family, and she drove Eleanor's slightly used Mercedes, which made my minivan look pitiful. Quitting my speech therapy job in favor of working for my sister and her husband had crossed my mind more than once.

Jim opened the door wide. "Did you bring your swim trunks, boys?"

"We sure did." Logan slipped off his boots and lined them neatly on the front porch, something he never did at home but always at my sister's house.

Zane imitated his older brother. "Do you really have a heater in your pool, Uncle Jim?"

"I sure do, and it's nice and warm. Grandma is already swimming with Aubrey and the boy cousins."

"I didn't see Dan and Darlene's car," I said, referring to the parents of the *boy* cousins.

"It finally died, so they're out buying a new one. Your mom brought the kids."

We followed Jim through the pristine house to the backyard where my mom and all the cousins splashed in the pool. Since Logan and Zane had worn their swimming trunks underneath their jeans, they quickly undressed and joined the others. Much to his consternation, I made Zane get back out and put on his life vest because even though he could swim, I didn't feel comfortable unless I was in the pool with him.

"I'll watch him," my mother offered.

I shook my head, not wanting to burden her with that responsibility when all the other grandchildren were vying for her attention. "He's fine."

With his life jacket on, Zane did a cannonball into the pool and swam to my mother. I wandered over to the outdoor kitchen where Jim was telling my brother Michael how to cook a steak to perfection.

"What's new with you?" Michael asked, interrupting our brother-in-law.

Um, my husband and I are in the middle of a horrible argument, and he's left for Haiti because he gets to do everything he wants and I get nothing. "Not much, what about you?"

"His divorce is final," Jim said, gesturing with a long-handled spatula.

I winced and kept my focus on Michael. "Are you okay?"

He shrugged. "She left me over a year ago. This was just the final step."

"Well, I'm sorry, Michael."

"Thanks." He took a long pull on his beer, and I made a mental note to be on the lookout for a single woman who might be interested in my brother. Michael wasn't bad looking, but he was going through a scraggly long-hair-long-beard phase. He basically looked like a terrorist, except for the Mickey Mouse tattoo on his forearm.

Clueless to the current conversation, Jim lifted the barbecue lid and launched into a detailed explanation of how the perfect steak started with the perfect cut of meat from the butcher. And not just any butcher, but the one in south Austin.

Michael rolled his eyes, and I smiled. Jim had a bad habit of being oblivious to anyone but himself.

My sister came out of the house looking gorgeous as ever in leggings and a long maternity sweater. Even at nine months pregnant, Eleanor could've been mistaken for a model with her high cheekbones and crystal blue eyes. Her hair was stylishly cut and colored, and what little weight she'd gained from the pregnancy showed only in her round belly.

If her looks weren't enough to make me feel inadequate, she was also somewhat of a celebrity in our small town as she'd co-authored several child-rearing books and frequently appeared on the local news. It was unfortunate she had such a harsh personality.

"It's too cold for swimming," Eleanor told her husband after giving me a brisk hello. "Mother has that cough, and I don't want Aubrey getting sick."

"They're fine," Jim said, dismissing her with a wave of a barbecue mitt.

Michael gestured toward the pool with his beer. "They're playing so hard; they're probably warmer than we are."

Eleanor gave Michael a look of exasperation and pulled her sweater tighter. The kids and my mother were now playing a game that resembled full contact Marco Polo. My oldest nephew lunged toward Aubrey, who screamed.

Eleanor jumped. "She's going to get hurt playing with those boys."

Aubrey splashed water in Bruce's face and swam away. Michael and I laughed.

"I'm pretty sure she can hold her own," I said.

Eleanor grimaced, not appreciating my comment. She worried too much, and I often marveled how she managed to go through life with so much stress. In some ways, she reminded me of Kyle. Maybe that was a side effect of being a doctor, although Jim had gone to medical school and didn't seem to worry about anything except his culinary skills.

When dinner was ready, we went inside and sat at the dining room table. I sliced into my steak and wondered what Kyle was having for dinner. Rice and beans? What did they eat in Haiti? I'd have to ask next time he called.

I was suddenly lonely for my husband. Kyle had missed a ton of family dinners in the past, but knowing he would be gone for an entire month left me with a huge hole. Did he feel the same? Or was leaving easy for him?

At least tonight, I was staying at my mom's and wouldn't have to go home to an empty house. But what about next year? If Kyle took the fellowship, would I be able to handle another year of this?

Since there was nothing I could do about it now, I turned my attention back to the table conversation. Dan and Darlene were still out car shopping, and Jim was telling everyone what kind of vehicle they should buy.

"I don't think they can afford a Mercedes," Michael said, giving me a wink.

No kidding. Dan and Darlene didn't have money. He worked as a maintenance man for several churches, and she ran an in-home daycare that Zane attended. Their four boys ranged from ages five to eleven, and although I loved my nephews, they weren't cheap as they played sports and had a habit of breaking everything.

And yet, there was a tenderness between Dan and Darlene that was downright inspiring. They truly loved each other, loved their children, and loved their life. If their relationship had a theme song, it would be "All You Need Is Love."

Couldn't Kyle and I have a life like that where time together was more important than work and money? Was this fellowship he so desperately wanted worth it? I didn't want to stand in the way of my husband's dreams and ambition, but where did I draw the line? How did I stand up for my own aspirations without thwarting his?

After dinner, the kids went swimming again while the men supervised, which basically meant lounging next to the pool and talking about sports or recent hunting trips. My brothers had turned Jim into a hunter, and in return, he'd taught Dan and Michael how to golf. Kyle had been too busy becoming a doctor to spend much time hunting and golfing, but he was more athletic than any man I knew.

I tackled the dishes with my mother and Eleanor, a sexist tradition, but a Kingsley family tradition nevertheless. Dan and Darlene were on their way over in their new car, a gently used Dodge Caravan.

My mother began rinsing the dishes but left when her cell phone rang. Without addressing us, she stepped onto the front porch, closing the door behind her.

"Who do you think she's talking to?" I asked.

"Probably her bridge partner. Tomorrow's bridge day, you know."

"I know," I said, but I didn't. I couldn't possibly memorize my mom's complicated social schedule. Maybe I was like Jim. Too focused on myself. Nevertheless, my mother was unbelievably active, golfing and playing tennis several days a week in addition to volunteering at the Boys and Girls Club of America.

For the next several minutes, Eleanor and I worked together in silence. As I unloaded the dishwasher, I did my best not to be envious of her custom cupboards, top grade granite, and state-of-the-art appliances. In contrast, the cupboards in our rental were falling apart, we had lime-green laminate countertops, and there was no dishwasher.

"Kyle's thinking about doing a fellowship in obstetrics," I said, casually.

"Why?"

"He wants to be able to deliver babies."

"That's ridiculous," my sister said, meticulously hand washing a kitchen knife. "He doesn't need to deliver babies to work at the clinic."

Even though I completely agreed, I found myself defending Kyle. "He said he could get a better job with an OB background."

She shook her head, disgusted. "If he was so desperate to deliver babies, he should've done an OB residency. Do you have any idea how hard fellowship is? It's worse than internship year. You will never see him."

"Well, that's encouraging," I said sarcastically.

She dried the knife and placed it in a neatly labeled knife block. "Jim wanted to do a fellowship, and I told him no."

"Really?"

She nodded. "You're not going to let Kyle do it, are you? What about finishing your education and buying a house?"

I cringed. Eleanor had trapped me between siding with her and supporting my husband. If Kyle ultimately took the fellowship, I didn't want Eleanor to know I'd been opposed to it. In the past, she'd twisted information I told her in confidence and used it against me.

I rinsed the plates and stacked them neatly on the counter. "We'll make a decision when he returns from Haiti."

Eleanor's brow lifted. She placed a hand on her belly and rubbed it in smooth circular motions, a sure sign she disagreed with me.

Ignoring her, I loaded the dishwasher. Kyle and I would somehow work this out. Maybe fellowship wouldn't be so bad. I shuddered at the thought and decided I'd better get busy praying he'd come home a changed man.

The sound of my mother laughing on the porch only made me lonelier. It seemed like she was flirting, not strategizing for tomorrow's bridge game.

"We need to talk about her," Eleanor announced, gesturing toward our mother.

"What do you mean?"

My sister placed the leftovers in the refrigerator and lowered her voice. "She needs to sell her house. It's too big for her, and the master bedroom is upstairs."

"No," I said, feeling a sense of panic. I'd grown up in that house and couldn't imagine my mom living anywhere else.

"You need to talk to her," Eleanor demanded.

"About what?"

"About moving."

"No, I'm not going to kick Mom out of her house."

Eleanor shook her head. "Michael already said he'd help clean out the attic, and Dan is going to paint the kitchen. You've always gotten your way with her, so just tell her she needs to sell."

As the baby of my family, I resented my sister's statement even though it was true. "Has Mom mentioned selling? Does she want to move?"

Eleanor removed the broom from the pantry and swept the floor. "It doesn't matter what she wants. Houses in her neighborhood are moving fast right now. We need to convince her selling is the right decision, even if she's reluctant."

"We need to convince *who* selling is the right decision?" my mother asked, entering the kitchen at that very moment. She coughed hard and narrowed her eyes at Eleanor. "Are you talking about forcing me to sell my home?"

"Of course not, Mother." Eleanor's gaze dropped. "We just want to make sure you're managing okay."

My mom scowled. "I'm managing just fine, thank you. I haven't gone completely senile yet. And I certainly don't need anyone making decisions for me behind my back."

"Of course not," Eleanor said. "But what about your cough? You need to see your doctor about it."

I expected my mom to complain Eleanor was interfering again, instead her whole face lit up at the question. "That was him on the phone. He called in a stronger prescription for me, so I'll stop by the pharmacy on my way home tonight."

I stared at her. Did she have a crush on her physician? Her giddiness gave me some insight to what she must have been like as a teenager when she fell in love with my father. It was kind of comical, and I couldn't wait to tell Kyle about it.

Eleanor glanced at the kitchen clock. "The pharmacy closes in half an hour. Why don't you send Autumn to get your medicine?"

I loved how my sister had no trouble volunteering me for errands. I'd do that for my mother, of course, but I didn't want to be bossed around by my bossy older sister. Eleanor had been telling me what to do, what to wear, and how to act my entire life. At some point, it had to end.

My mother declined the offer. "Thank you, but I've got some other things to pick up at the store." She collected her purse and slung it over her arm like a warrior going into battle. "Autumn, I'll see you and the boys at the house. And Eleanor—stay out of my business. I may be old, but I don't need you to take care of me."

"Yes, Ma'am," Eleanor said, sounding more like an obedient child than a successful physician.

Chapter 8

*O*NE THING I'VE *learned in my seventy years is that life is all about choices. Inevitably, those choices have consequences. Some good and some bad. When I was a little girl, my father chose to move our family from Texas to Seattle, thus changing my childhood. Ruby had chosen to befriend me on that first day of second grade, and I'd chosen to accept that friendship.*

At the high school talent show, I'd chosen to be immature and perform a song that led to Jude and me being suspended. My parents were beyond furious. They forbade me to date Jude, and my father insisted there must be something wrong with a boy who wore his hair long and imitated Elvis.

I cried and screamed in protest, but nothing changed my parents' decision. When my suspension ended and I returned to school, I learned Jude's situation was even worse. His father had sent him to a boys' boarding school on the east coast. We hadn't even been allowed to say good-bye to each other, and I had no idea how to contact him.

The pain of being separated from the love of my life nearly killed me. Would I ever see Jude again? Would he at least write and tell me he still loved me? Maybe because of what I'd done, he no longer cared about me. After all, he hadn't wanted to perform Jailhouse Rock. *I'd been the one to force the song on him.*

"Do you think he's forgotten about me?" I asked Ruby, sitting in the cafeteria during lunch.

Ruby's face grew serious as she attempted to peel an orange in one piece. "Jude cares for you deeply. I'm sure it's just a matter of time before you hear from him."

"I sure hope so."

Tim O'Connor, who was sitting at the end of our table, scooted down the bench. "I hate to tell you this, Nadine, but he's not coming back. Not after what your father told him."

My stomach lurched. "My father?"

Tim nodded and shoved the rest of his sandwich into his mouth. "Your dad threatened to press charges if Jude ever contacted you. I heard he even consulted a lawyer about issuing a restraining order."

"He wouldn't do something like that."

Tim shrugged. "Well, he did."

I was furious. How dare my father ruin my life like this! He couldn't keep me away from Jude. Wasn't that a violation of my constitutional right to happiness?

After school, Ruby and I rode the city bus to my father's

building downtown. She waited in the lobby while I marched into his office unannounced.

"Sweetheart, what a surprise," he said, rounding his desk to hug me.

Placing both hands on my hips, I glared at him. "Did you tell Jude you'd call the police if he ever contacted me again?"

My father flinched. I'd never spoken to him with such anger. I was an only child, and my parents and I shared a mutual level of respect. I'd never been spanked or grounded, and I'd certainly never glared at my father.

Straightening his tie, he gestured toward the chair in front of his desk. "Sit down, sweetheart."

"No, Daddy, I don't want to sit down. I want you to tell me the truth. Did you threaten to have Jude arrested?"

My father studied me carefully before responding. Leaning against his desk, he exhaled slowly and looked down at his shoes. "I did."

"Daddy!"

"Listen to me," he said, meeting my gaze. "That boy is no good. What he did at the talent show—"

"That was my fault. Jude didn't want to sing the Elvis song, but I insisted."

"No."

"It's true. I'm the one to blame, but it was one innocent song. It's not like we robbed a bank or committed some heinous crime. I don't see why everyone is so upset about *this."*

A tense silence filled the room. My father folded his arms and looked out the window. "You violated a school policy and were suspended. One of my clients asked me about it in front of my boss. I've never been more ashamed in my life." He shook his head with repulsion. "I'm disappointed in you, Nadine. Your mother and I raised you better than that."

Guilt filled me. He'd always been so proud of me. Always believed I could do no wrong, but that didn't justify his actions. "Daddy, I'm not your little girl anymore. Jude is important to me. I love him." My voice cracked, but I swallowed hard and repeated the last sentence. "I love him, and there's nothing you can do to keep us apart."

My father returned to his desk chair. "You're too young to understand now, but in time you'll see that he was not the right boy for you. Anyway, his father has been transferred, so the whole family is moving back to the east coast. Your relationship would've ended regardless of my involvement."

The hair on my arms stood. "You're wrong. It's not over." I fled from his office before he could see my tears. He hollered for me to come back, but I kept walking.

"What did he say?" Ruby asked as I stormed through the lobby.

I shook my head and waited to speak until we were outside. "It's true. He told Jude to stay away from me."

"What are you going to do?"

Tears pricked my eyes, and I held out my hands, palms up. "What can I do? Jude's gone, and I have no idea where he went." My throat burned with anger. I'd made such a mess of things. Why hadn't I been more responsible and anticipated this trouble? "My father also said Jude's family is moving, so our relationship would've ended anyway."

"Oh, Nadine."

Ruby and I rode the bus home in silence. I wondered if part of her was actually happy I'd lost Jude. After all, she'd liked him first, and spending time with Jude meant less time for her.

Out of the blue, she clapped her hands. "I have an idea."

"What?"

"Let's go to Jude's house and get his new address. Then at least you can write to him."

For a second, I dared to believe it could be that easy. Then rationality kicked in, leaving me more discouraged. "His parents aren't going to hand over his new address to me. Not after how my father treated Jude."

Ruby bumped me with her shoulder. "They're not going to give it to you, silly, but they'll give it to the president of the 'Young Republicans.'"

A smile tugged at my lips. "You?"

"Yes. Have you ever noticed the Nixon bumper sticker on the back of Jude's father's car?"

"No."

"Well, I have, and I bet you anything I can convince them to give me Jude's address. It's worth a try, anyway."

I bit my lip. "You'd do that for me?"

"Of course. You're my best friend."

I looked out the window, then back at Ruby. "I'm sorry I stole Jude from you, since you liked him first."

She stared down at her hands. "It doesn't matter. Jude fell in love with you, not me. And ..." She stifled a grin. "Well, I kind of like someone else."

"Who?"

Her face turned red.

"Come on, Ruby. You can't keep something like this from your best friend. Tell me."

She exhaled. "It's Tim."

"Tim O'Connor?"

She nodded. "Don't say anything because he doesn't know."

I said I wouldn't, but my mind began formulating a plan to get Tim and Ruby together. I could see them dating, and maybe if Jude came back, the four of us could go out together.

Hope filled me as Ruby and I got off the bus and walked six blocks to Jude's house. Maybe everything would work out after all.

My optimism crumbled, however, when I spotted the "For Sale" sign in the Kingsley's front yard. Ruby placed a hand on my shoulder. "It's going to be okay."

I wanted to believe her, but once Jude's family moved, what hope did I have of ever seeing him again?

I hid behind a bush while Ruby knocked on the front door. Mrs. Kingsley answered with a smile and listened to Ruby speak. I thought she was going to give Ruby the address, but in the end, she refused.

My heart twisted. I wasn't letting Jude go without a fight. Marching up the walk, I pushed past Ruby and demanded Mrs. Kingsley tell me how I could contact Jude.

His father came to the door, and recognizing me immediately, he scowled. "Haven't you done enough damage to our boy?"

"I—I'm sorry," I stammered, taken aback by the gruffness in his voice and the hatred in his eyes. "It was just a song—"

"You may think it was just a song, but do you know how many nasty phone calls we received from concerned parents? It was humiliating, so I'm telling you to stay away from my son. He's getting his life back on track, and the last thing he needs is someone like you derailing him."

I blinked hard. "I don't want to derail him, Mr. Kingsley. I just want to talk to him. I care about him very much."

"If that's true, then stay away from him. He doesn't want to see you." Jude's father pulled his wife back and closed the door in my face.

A cold wind swept across the porch and I shivered. Was it true? Did Jude not want to see me?

Ruby slipped an arm around my shoulders. "Come on, honey. Let's go."

In a trance, I allowed her to lead me back to the bus stop. I felt as if someone had stabbed me in the heart.

That night I lay in bed defeated. If only I could talk to Jude and find out how he felt. If he didn't want to see me, that was one thing, but if he still cared about me ...

A knock at my bedroom window startled me. Was it Jude? Had he come back for me? I bolted out of bed and flung open the curtain to find Ruby, smiling and waving.

Disappointment, followed by guilt, washed over me. Why couldn't I be happy to see my best friend? Why did I have to be so obsessed with a boy who probably hated me?

I opened the window, and Ruby thrust a piece of paper into my hands. "This is the address to Jude's school."

"What? How'd you get it?"

Her smile was full of pride. "When we were at Jude's house, I glanced at the mail on the entry table. I didn't put it together until tonight, but there was an envelope with a red and black shield. Tim and I found a library book that lists all the private boarding schools in America and ... we found it."

My eyes filled with tears. "This is his address?"

She nodded.

"But what if he doesn't want to talk to me? What if he

hates me?"

Ruby shook her head. "That's impossible. Write him a letter and tell him how you feel. I'm sure he'll respond."

Hope shot through me, and I gave Ruby a big hug. "Thank you. And tell Tim thank you. I don't deserve such a good friend like you."

She laughed. "You don't, but you've got me anyway."

We smiled at each other, and I knew regardless of what happened, Ruby was truly the best friend a girl could have.

That's why the excruciating pain of leaving her all those years ago continues. Knowing she's alive and just a phone call away breaks my heart every day.

If only I had the courage to tell her why I had to leave.

If only I had the courage to admit the truth.

Chapter 9

NADINE LEFT ELEANOR'S house and drove to the grocery store. Standing in the self-checkout line, she tried to figure out what to do. She hated getting old. Hated the way her mind lacked the patience and focus it once had to learn new things, especially when it came to technology.

Determined to stay young and keep Eleanor from running her life, Nadine scanned her own groceries, pleased it went well. When it came time to pay, however, things got a little tricky. Several options popped up on the screen, but since she couldn't see them without her reading glasses, she ended up pressing the wrong button.

"Please select method of payment," the machine chirped in an annoying, friendly voice.

Coughing, Nadine dug her reading glasses out of her purse.

"Please select method of payment," the voice repeated.

Nadine's patience cracked. "Give me a minute!"

"Everything okay, Mrs. Kingsley?" said a voice behind her.

Nadine spun around to find her Denzel Washington look-alike doctor smiling down at her. Her face flushed with embarrassment. "Dr. Henry. You didn't follow me to make sure I picked up my prescription, did you?"

He gave a charming smile. "You know me too well."

Without warning, she emitted a high-pitched, flirtatious laugh that she covered with a cough. Honestly, she had no idea why the man affected her so. He was young enough to be her grandson!

"I heard you coughing," Dr. Henry said. "If that medicine doesn't kick in by Monday, you come see me, okay? No appointment necessary."

"I'm sure I'll be fine. It's probably allergies. I haven't been sleeping well—"

"Anything bothering you?"

His question hit her hard. For a brief moment, she wondered if he'd been spying on her as she wrote her life story in the little journal. Did he know about Tim's letter? What about the letter she'd written to Ruby's daughter?

"Mrs. Kingsley?"

She shook her head to clear her thoughts. "Sorry.

I'm sure once I take this medicine and have a warm bath, I'll sleep like a baby."

The good doctor rocked back on his heels. In his dark arms he held diapers, a gallon of ice cream, and a bottle of wine. Melancholy filled Nadine as she remembered Jude running out for such items. Not diapers, of course, since they'd used cloth, but essentials such as milk, bread, eggs, and wine. Lord, she missed her husband.

"How's your son-in-law doing in Haiti?"

That's right. She'd told Dr. Henry all about Kyle going to Haiti for the month and her concerns about Autumn being on her own for so long. Sometimes Nadine had such a big mouth. It was a miracle she'd managed to keep her secret for so long.

"He's been gone a week, and Autumn seems to be doing okay. I visited her on Thursday and tried to clean the boys' room, but there were so many random pieces of Legos I gave up. Is there anything more painful than stepping on a Lego in your bare feet?"

Dr. Henry chuckled. "I know what you mean. I have two boys. My wife would like a daughter, but I can't imagine another child."

The checkout machine spit out her receipt. At least, she hoped it was her receipt and not some notification that she'd broken the machine. Tearing it off, she said, "You can never have too many children."

Dr. Henry raised his brow. "You think?"

She nodded. "I was in my forties when I had Autumn. At the time I considered myself much too old to be pregnant, let alone have a newborn. But ..." She paused, knowing she couldn't tell him everything. "I regret many things in my life, but having Autumn is *not* one of them. She's been such a blessing and has given me adorable grandsons I can brag about on the golf course."

Dr. Henry smiled and began scanning his groceries. Maybe because of Nadine's cold or allergies or simple loneliness, she felt compelled to keep talking. "I lost a daughter. Did I ever tell you that?"

He shook his head and gave that warm, nonthreatening expression that always made her tell him more than she should. He probably went home at night and complained to his wife about the old lady who wouldn't stop talking. If that was the case, then he needed to work on making his facial expressions more stern and unwelcoming.

"Angela was my oldest daughter," Nadine continued. "She'd just graduated from high school, and her death nearly broke me."

"I can only imagine. I'm so sorry."

"Thank you." Her chest clenched, and a moment of awkward silence followed as it usually did whenever someone found out about the horrible car accident that stole the lives of Angela and Jude. Nadine inhaled deeply, wondering how something that happened so long ago could still hurt.

"Of course one child can never replace another, but having my other children was a huge help in being able to move forward. I don't know what I would've done without them. They saved me."

"I can understand that."

"And my grandchildren are amazing."

"I imagine they are."

The checkout line grew, and Nadine felt guilty for taking up so much of the doctor's time. She placed a hand on his forearm and smiled. "You should give your wife another baby, Dr. Henry. You won't regret it."

He grinned and placed a hand on top of hers. "I think you're right. My wife will be grateful you talked some sense into me."

"Glad I could help. I'll send you my bill."

He laughed and Nadine sailed out the door with her groceries, feeling years younger. If only she could deal with her own issues so easily.

In his letter, Tim said he was certain Ruby's daughter would find her. Nadine suspected the unidentified number on her cell phone was Faith, even though the woman hadn't left a message. And for that reason, Nadine had written her own letter explaining what happened all those years ago. Oh, she hadn't mailed it, but maybe when she found the courage, she'd do that. Or maybe not.

Late this afternoon, she'd finished writing her life story in the journal. It had been cathartic to get it all down on paper. Then, she'd ripped out the last few pages and included them in Faith's letter. If she wanted to confront the truth, all she had to do was mail that letter.

Distracted, she walked to the end of the parking lot without seeing her car. Where was it? Had she completely lost her mind? One of Dan's boys had told her about a parking lot app, and even though Nadine had a smart phone, she wasn't going to depend on technology for something she was capable of remembering.

Lost in her own frustration, she spun around and headed in the opposite direction. A massive diesel-powered truck with enormous wheels backed out of a parking space toward her. She crinkled her nose at both the acrid smell and distasteful female silhouette decal on the rear bumper.

To Nadine's horror and confusion, the truck's red taillights bolted toward her. She sucked in a sharp breath. Didn't the driver see her?

She tried to move out of the way, but shock and fear paralyzed her, nailing her feet to the asphalt. "He's going to hit me!" Instinctively, she raised her hands as though she could stop such a substantial vehicle.

Seconds later, cold, hard metal rammed into Nadine, lifting her body in the air. Time slowed, then her head smashed into the windshield of another car. Shards of glass ripped through her skull and someone screamed. Indescribable pain overtook her. Her head spun, and she tasted blood.

Was this it? Was this how it was going to end? Would she never have the chance to explain and make things right?

Lord God, save me!

Chapter 10

*A*FTER DRAGGING LOGAN and Zane out of Eleanor's pool to admire Dan and Darlene's new car, I drove to my mom's house. Both boys were hyped up from playing with their cousins, and just as I managed to get them settled down for bed, Kyle called.

"It's Daddy!" Logan screamed, grabbing my phone. He talked animatedly to Kyle about swimming in the heated pool and how Grandma had cheated at Marco Polo, but it was okay because she let Zane win since he was the youngest.

Zane grumbled about always being the youngest and having to wear his life jacket even though Grandma said he swam like a fish.

When it was my turn to talk, I forced myself to sound cheerful. "How's everything going down there?"

Kyle hesitated, and I worried he was going to tell me he loved it and wanted to stay even longer. "It's wonderful, but I'm incredibly lonely."

The honest emotion in my husband's deep voice softened my heart, but my verbal response was mean and sarcastic. "Are you saying you miss us?"

He gave an exasperated sigh. "Of course I miss you, Autumn. I hate being away."

"Then why do you want to sign up for another year of living like this? Why is this fellowship so important to you?"

He groaned impatiently. "I thought we weren't going to fight about this until I got back."

"We're not fighting; I'm just trying to make a point. Eleanor said fellowship is harder than internship year. Is that true?"

"Some people say that."

I'd desperately missed Kyle all evening, but now that we were talking, I was suddenly mad. My hand tightened around the phone, and I said nothing, determined not to lose my temper.

Kyle yawned. "I love you. I really do, but I've been up for twenty-four hours, and I have an early morning meeting. Can we talk about this later? Please?"

Tears stung my eyes. I hated myself for being so emotional and needy. "Sure. I'll talk to you later. Love you. Bye."

He was silent and I wondered if he'd hung up, but then he spoke. "I love you, too, Autumn. More than you could ever imagine."

Then why are you constantly pushing me away? I closed my eyes and took a deep breath. "I know you do."

We said goodnight and ended the call, then I went to find Zane and Logan playing Hot Lava in the Grandkids' Bedroom. I scolded them for jumping on the furniture, even though I completely understood the temptation. Between the four twin beds and dresser stuffed with toys, the Grandkids' Bedroom was the perfect place to play Hot Lava.

Sitting first on Logan's bed, then on Zane's, I read several books before tucking the boys in and kissing them goodnight.

"Don't forget to set out the pennies," Zane said.

"I won't." I grabbed four pennies from the plastic baggie in the overnight duffle and set them on the dresser. In order to encourage the boys to stay in their bedroom at night, we had a system where they could earn two pennies. If they came out of the room one time, they lost a penny. If they came out a second time, they lost both pennies. But if they spent all night in their room, they were rewarded by two pennies in the morning.

Zane still couldn't make it through the night without crawling into our bed. Logan, on the other hand, was slowly becoming a rich kid.

"You're going to be in the bedroom next door, right, Mom?" Zane asked.

"That's right. Now go to sleep and I'll see you in the morning with your two pennies."

Logan chuckled, disbelieving his little brother could ever achieve such an amazing feat.

"Hey," Zane said, offended. "I'm going do it tonight. You'll see."

I stood at the door and turned off the light. "Of course you are. We believe in you, right, Logan?"

Logan giggled. "Yep, we sure do."

I walked down the hallway to my old room and got ready for bed. Realizing I'd left my book at home, I went to the bookshelf in my mom's bedroom.

I perused the titles, wishing she would get home so she could suggest something I might enjoy. Maybe a juicy romance or an intriguing biography? I was so grateful she'd passed on her love of reading to me because it was honestly one of my favorite things to do.

On the bottom shelf, I spotted Eleanor's book *Training Your Child to Sleep Through the Night*. How appropriate. I'd never actually read one of my sister's books, but I imagined Aubrey devoured all of them in utero, since she emerged from Eleanor's womb as the perfect child. In fact, the only time my niece defied her parents was when it came to sundresses. Even in the middle of winter, Aubrey insisted on wearing a sundress no matter how many times my sister said no.

Wondering what my mother was reading these days, I walked over to her nightstand and found the latest Steena Holmes book. Too bad I already read it because it was a fantastic story by a fantastic author. A piece of paper tucked between the pages caught my eye. I didn't consider myself a snoop, but the words "My Darling Nadine" leapt off the page, demanding my attention.

Whoa! Who in the world was writing to my mom and calling her "My Darling Nadine?" Did she have a secret admirer? A boyfriend, maybe?

My hand reached out and touched the paper, which had been crumpled and smoothed back out. I'd done that with an old boyfriend's letter in high school. Crumpled it into a ball, then dug it out of the trash hours later.

I was dying to read the letter, but I reminded myself I was almost thirty, not thirteen. Old enough to respect my mother's privacy. Despite my raging curiosity, I would act my age. I would exercise some self-control, grab Eleanor's parenting book, and crawl into my own bed where I wouldn't think about the letter.

I turned to leave, but just as I did, Zane startled me by appearing in the doorway and screaming, "Mommy!"

I jumped in surprise and knocked over the nightstand lamp. The sound of the light bulb shattering shook my nerves, and I pressed a hand to my temple. "You're supposed to be in bed."

"My dinosaur egg! I left it at Aunt Eleanor's house!"

I sighed. He'd been carrying around a smooth, round rock he'd found in our back yard that he swore was a *real* dinosaur egg. "We'll get it tomorrow, okay? Go back to bed."

His eyes filled, and he blinked several times. "Does this mean I lose one of my pennies? I was just trying to be responsible."

I refrained from rolling my eyes. "If you're back in bed by the time I count to three, you can have a do-over. But this is your only chance tonight."

He high tailed it down the hall, his bare feet making a thrumming sound on the wood floor. Squatting, I picked up the lamp. Part of the shade had been dented but thankfully, the base was still intact.

The book had also fallen, so now more of the letter was visible. It would be so easy to read it, but I wouldn't. I wouldn't. I'd be an adult and wouldn't let my curiosity violate my morals.

Averting my eyes, I picked up the letter and shoved it back into the book. Unfortunately, I accidentally read the last two lines. "All my love, Tim."

Quickly, I placed the book and lamp back on the nightstand. I picked up the broken light bulb and threw it away.

Tim.

Did I know anyone named Tim? Was my mother in love with this Tim? My resolve weakened, but before I could give into temptation, I ran out of the room.

"Mom," Zane called as I flew down the hall, past the Grandkids' room. "Come here. I have to tell you something."

Did Zane know about Grandma's boyfriend? I crossed the room and sat on the bed beside him. "What is it?"

He gave a deep sigh. "I'm just really worried about my dinosaur egg."

I brushed the hair off his face, loving how much he looked like his daddy. "It'll be okay. I'll call Aunt Eleanor in the morning. You go to sleep now."

I stood to leave, but he grabbed my arm with both hands and pulled me down beside him. "Now you're my prisoner, so you have to sleep with me," he said, victorious.

I laughed at my little manipulator who just wanted his mom to stay until he fell asleep. "Just for a few minutes, okay?"

"Okay."

We lay there in the dark, and soon his breathing grew slow and rhythmic. Just as he was drifting off to sleep, he jerked and slapped his palm to his head. "Oh, no!"

"What?" I asked, worried he'd wet the bed or something.

He placed both hands on my face. Even in the dim light, I could tell his eyes were bulging with fear. "What if my dinosaur egg hatches tonight?"

I shook my head and hugged my little guy tight. "Oh, Zane. I don't think that's going to happen. But as soon as you go to sleep, I'll send Aunt Eleanor a text to be on the lookout."

"Okay, Mommy. But if he does hatch tonight, Aunt Eleanor won't be pleased."

"No, probably not."

I FELL ASLEEP next to Zane and awoke several hours later to the sound of my phone ringing in the other room. My first dream-like thought was that Zane's egg had hatched, and Eleanor couldn't get the baby dinosaur out of the pool.

Half asleep, I stumbled down the hall, found my phone, and glanced at the caller ID.

Eleanor.

My blood ran cold because it was past midnight, and Eleanor never called after nine. Was something wrong? Was she having the baby? I hadn't heard my mom come in last night. Had she made it home?

"We're at the hospital," my sister said as soon as I answered. "You need to come immediately. Mother's been in an accident."

Chapter 11

*A*FTER WRITING TO *Jude, I tried not to think about his response but waiting was excruciating. Every time I checked the mail, I was disappointed he hadn't written.*

The Kingsley house sold quickly, and Jude's parents moved, giving him no reason to come back to Seattle.

With no choice but to live my life, I threw myself into studying and practicing the piano. I finished my junior year with straight A's and made the Honor Roll. It seemed that a broken heart was good for me, academically speaking.

In June, my parents sent me to summer camp with Ruby. We had a fabulous time swimming, canoeing, and hiking, but Jude was never far from my thoughts. What if he wrote while I was gone and my parents discovered the letter? Would they allow me to read it, or would they hide it, thinking it was for the best?

I returned home to no letter, but later that week, the phone rang while I was helping my mother prepare dinner. I went to the hallway to answer it and couldn't believe when a deep voice on the other end said, "I was beginning to think you weren't allowed to answer the phone."

My heart exploded. "Jude!"

"Shush. Pretend I'm a friend from camp. Pretend I'm Judy, your friend from Canada."

I stifled a giggle just as my mother poked her head out of the kitchen. "Who's on the phone, dear?"

For the first time in my entire life, I told a bold-faced lie. "It's a friend from camp."

She raised a questioning brow, but she returned to the kitchen without another word.

I cupped the phone with my hand. "Did you get my letter?"

"Yes, just yesterday. The school's mail delivery service is notorious for misplacing letters, but I've been assigned to the mail room now, so you can write me every day."

"Oh, okay," I said.

There was an awkward silence, and I didn't know what to say. Thankfully, Jude spoke. "So ... in your letter, you said you still care about me?" His voice faltered.

"I do," I answered, winding the cord around my arm. "For me, nothing's changed."

"Nothing's changed for me, either."

My soul soared. Jude loved me! "When will I see you again?"

"Soon. I'm sending you a postcard I made myself. Use a magnifying glass and read it carefully for a hidden message."

"What?"

"I've got to go." Someone in the background called Jude's name. "But I love you, Nadine. I do. I love you."

I started to say I loved him too, but my father appeared at the top of the stairs. He glared down at me, and my legs shook. The line went dead, leaving me empty. Hanging up the phone, I watched my father slowly descend the staircase.

"Who were you talking to?" he asked.

"Just a friend from camp." I looked away, afraid he'd be able to tell I was lying.

My mother called us to dinner, and we went into the dining room. As we sat at the table, both my parents grilled me endlessly about this "Judy from Canada."

My father swirled his meatloaf through a pool of ketchup. "Why didn't you mention her before?"

"I did. Her father's a doctor, remember?"

"Judy Jones," my father said, repeating the name of my fictitious friend.

The next few days passed slowly as I tried not to be too anxious or obvious about checking the mail. I must've failed miserably, because my mother asked if I was expecting something.

"Just a letter from my friend from camp."

"From Judy?" she asked, suspiciously.

"Of course."

On Friday afternoon, I came home late from my job at a small clothing boutique downtown to discover my father's car already in the driveway and the mailbox empty. A sickening feeling rolled through me.

Inside the house, I found my father sitting in his office, looking through the mail. "What are you doing home so early?" I asked, hoping I sounded pleased and not disappointed.

He folded his hands and set them on the desk. "I finished early and wanted to help Mr. Tanaka trim the roses."

By "help," he meant "tell our gardener what to do." Because of my father's poor health, he hired help for yard work, but he didn't trust anybody when it came to his prized roses.

I glanced at the mail. Was Jude's letter buried somewhere in there?

Mr. Tanaka's truck pulled up to the house, and my father stood. "He's here, sweetheart. I better go change."

I nodded and left the office with the intention of returning for the mail as soon as my father went outside. Before I reached the door, however, he called my name. "Your friend from camp sent you a postcard. I hope you don't mind that I read it, but I got a laugh out of the cartoon."

Fear wrapped around my throat, and my knees trembled. Bracing myself for the worst, I turned to see my father holding an ink drawn postcard. "She's a very good artist."

"She is," I said, hearing the wobble in my voice.

He glanced one last time at the postcard, chuckled, and

handed it to me. I looked at it and smiled, pretending it was from Judy Jones, and not Jude Kingsley. With all my restraint, I climbed the stairs to my bedroom and closed the door behind me. Once I was alone, I held the postcard to my nose, hoping it smelled like Jude. It didn't of course, but I imagined his scent. Imagined the pen in his strong hands, imagined the way he tilted his head to the side when deep in concentration.

Squeezing my eyes shut, I embraced this feeling of elation, never wanting it to end. Finally, I opened my eyes and stared down at the postcard. At first, I didn't understand. This was his surprise? This was what I'd waited for? A cartoon?

The picture was cute, showing Mickey Mouse carrying a large bouquet of roses, but I didn't understand. Then I remembered he'd told me to use a magnifying glass. I raced across the room and dug through the drawer of my bedroom desk until I found one. Even with the magnifying glass, I didn't get it.

Disappointment filled me, but suddenly everything shifted into place. Hidden in the border of the postcard was Jude's message to me. "I adore you, I adore you, I adore you, Nadine Rose. You're the love of my life, and we'll be together soon. Love, Jude."

Joy erupted inside me. I pressed the postcard to my heart and squealed. Jude Kingsley adored me. I was the love of his life! Soon we would be together again!

I read the postcard over and over. Now that I knew what the words said, I didn't need the magnifying glass. Jude loved me, and nothing was better than that.

———∽∽∽———

ALL THROUGH MY senior year of high school, Jude and I corresponded via letters and postcards. Every so often he would call, and while our conversations were brief, hearing his voice restored my belief that regardless of our distance, we were meant for each other.

Sometimes, when I hadn't heard from him in a long time, I'd wonder about our future. Was turning down dates from other boys and waiting for Jude the right thing to do? After all, I hadn't seen him since the spring of my junior year. Maybe I'd exaggerated his virtues. Maybe our love wasn't so special.

In my nightstand drawer, I kept a bottle of his shampoo I'd bought from the drug store. Each night, I'd unscrew the lid and breathe in its rich, woodsy scent, imagining Jude there beside me. But as my senior year came to an end, my faith slipped, and my feelings began to change.

Given what happened next, I'm ashamed to say if there'd been someone else who interested me, I might not have remained faithful. But faithful to Jude I remained.

In the fall, Ruby and I roomed together at the University of Washington. Several of our classmates, including

Tim O'Connor, ended up attending the same school. Jude talked about coming back to Seattle for college, but his parents would only pay for a school on the east coast, so our forced separation continued.

For me, college was a whole new world. Without the watchful eye of my parents, I experienced an incredible sense of freedom. I wrote Jude a long letter, saying we'd be able to communicate better now that we didn't have to hide things. I anxiously awaited his response, expecting a lengthy love letter, but all he sent was a catchy little postcard.

"What's wrong?" Ruby asked. "Don't you like the drawing?"

"I do." I leaned against the dormitory mailboxes, examining Jude's latest postcard for its hidden message of undying love. "I was just hoping for something more than a short message. I miss him so much, but it's been such a long time since we saw each other that—"

"That you worry nothing's there anymore?"

My heart gave a loud thud. It was the first time I'd voiced my fears out loud, but Ruby had read my mind. "I'm being a fool, right? Whenever he calls, I know he's worth waiting for—but am I ever going to see him again?"

Ruby's response was interrupted when Tim rounded the corner. "Hey, you two. How about letting me take my best girls out for a burger? What do you say?"

Ruby brightened and smoothed back her long, brown hair. "Sure, we'd love to."

I didn't respond, and Tim gave me a questioning look. Sometimes, I found it odd that many of his dates with Ruby included me. I wanted to believe he was simply being nice, but I feared he liked me more than he should.

I was fond of Tim, but Ruby was my best friend. I'd already stolen one boy from her; I wasn't going to steal another. Besides, I had Jude. Didn't I?

"What'd he say?" Tim asked, motioning to the postcard.

I held it up for him to see. "I won't be able to read the message until I look at it with my magnifying glass, but I recognize Elvis and the Space Needle."

Tim shook his head with disdain. "Elvis. You used to be crazy about that guy."

"I did," I agreed, regretting how much my obsession with Elvis had gotten me in trouble.

Ruby linked her arm through Tim's. "Did you talk to your cousin?"

Tim gave a self-satisfied grin. "Yes."

"And?"

All week, Ruby had talked excitedly about the possibility that Tim's cousin might be able to get us hired to play a part in the upcoming movie Elvis was filming here in Seattle next week.

"If we show up early, they'll pay us ten dollars to be in the movie," Tim said.

Ruby squealed. "Really? Wouldn't that be something, to be in an Elvis Presley movie?"

"You're going to come with us, Nadine, right?" Tim asked.

I shook my head. Initially, I'd shared Ruby's enthusiasm, but now I wasn't so sure. Jude's postcard had left me in a foul mood, and I needed to think about things. "I have a Humanities test to study for."

Ruby groaned. "That's not until later. You have to come see Elvis, right Tim?"

He rolled his eyes and spoke in a sarcastic tone. "Of course you do. It's the opportunity of a lifetime."

"I'll think about it," I conceded. "But I'm going to pass on dinner tonight. I'm tired and have a headache."

They left without much of a fuss, and I climbed the stairs to my dorm room. I no longer enjoyed listening to Elvis—not because I didn't like his music anymore, but because he reminded me of Jude, and I was tired of thinking about Jude all the time. We'd been together a year and a half, but instead of memories of dates and kisses, all I had was a shoebox full of postcards. What kind of relationship was that?

During the war, my parents had been separated for two years, but they'd been engaged. My father had written long, romantic letters to my mother, and she'd done the same. Things weren't like that with Jude and me. While we had professed our love to each other, I wasn't so sure we were still in love.

Flopping on the bed, I glanced at the postcard again.

Jude had drawn Elvis dancing in front of the Space Needle. "Meet me at the World's Fair" was written in bold letters across the top of the picture.

Using my magnifying glass, I found Jude's message written along the side of the Space Needle. "I would if I could, but I can't so I shan't. But one day, my precious Nadine Rose … one day, we'll meet again."

I heaved a deep sigh and turned onto my stomach. One day? Really? When would that be? Was I just supposed to continue waiting around for him? Maybe I was like an old sweater at the back of his closet. Something not worn in years but too sentimental to be thrown away. Maybe Jude already had someone else and was just stringing me along. I didn't think he'd do something like that, but why else did he find it so easy to stay away?

He'd talked about coming to see me for my birthday and then for high school graduation, but both of those dates had fallen through. I couldn't do this anymore. It wasn't fair to either of us to keep our lives on hold when we didn't have a future together.

Rising from the bed, I went to my desk, where I composed the most difficult letter of my life. With tears in my eyes, I ran downstairs and slid the envelope though the mail slot before I lost my nerve.

Back in my bedroom, I took the shampoo bottle from my nightstand, opened the top, and allowed myself one last deep inhale. The scent was incredible, but it was shampoo, *not a real person.*

I took the bottle to the bathroom, dumped its contents down the sink, and threw the container away. Then I returned to my dorm room, climbed into bed, and cried myself to sleep.

Chapter 12

*D*ESPITE THE ALARM of panic blaring in my head after Eleanor's phone call, I packed up the boys and drove to the hospital as calmly as possible. My mother had been struck by a car while walking through the grocery store parking lot!

As horrible as that sounded, I refused to freak out. My sister could be a little high strung, so maybe she was overreacting. Maybe I'd arrive at the hospital to see my mom striding up and down the hallway, insisting she was fine.

I wanted to call Kyle, but I didn't want to wake him, especially if everything turned out to be okay. Besides, how could he possibly help when he was in a foreign country?

"Is Grandma going to die?" Logan asked from the back seat.

My hands shook on the steering wheel. "No, of course not. She'll be fine."

"Then why are you driving so fast?"

I glanced down at the dash, shocked I was traveling several miles over the speed limit. "Sorry, Logan. I'll slow down."

"Thank you," he said politely.

At the hospital, I parked the car and unbuckled the boys. Logan took my purse while I carried Zane who was conked out and showed no signs of waking. I swore he weighed one hundred pounds more when he was sleeping, so by the time I found everyone in the waiting room, my arms were about to fall off. Michael took Zane from me and hoisted him over his shoulder.

"Thanks," I said. "How's Mom?"

My sister-in-law Darlene pulled me into a big hug. Her large body shook with quiet sobs. "Oh, Autumn, it's not good. Not good at all."

I felt a blow to my gut and pulled away. Michael shifted Zane to his other shoulder, avoiding eye contact with me. Zane stirred for a moment before weaving his hand through Michael's long beard and sinking back into a deep sleep.

"What's going on?" I asked my oldest brother Dan.

He gave me a strong pat on the back, which for him was a huge show of affection. I blinked away tears, dreading the answer to my question.

Jim stepped forward. "Your mother is unconscious,

but Eleanor's with her. I can take you back if you'd like, but the boys have to stay in the waiting room."

Darlene put her arm around Logan's shoulder. "I left my boys with the next-door neighbor, so I need to go home." Her bottom lip trembled, but she forced a brave smile. "Can I take Logan and Zane back to our house?"

I nodded. "Thank you, Darlene."

After hugging my kids good-bye, I followed Jim down the hallway of the ICU. The smell of antiseptic burned my nostrils, and acid settled in the pit of my stomach. Just a few hours ago, we'd all been at Eleanor's house complaining about the price of gas and never-ending construction on the highway. The kids had laughed and swam and played Marco Polo with my mother. How could things have changed so quickly?

Jim ushered me into the room, and I gasped at my mom's lifeless body. She was connected to several intimidating machines and her skin was incredibly pale. Her eyes were closed, and a large bandage covered the entire right side of her head.

My legs turned to rubber. "*Oh, Mom.*"

Eleanor spun around. "Autumn." Her voice was sharp, as if my outburst had been inappropriate. Against my better judgment, I crossed the room and tried to hug my sister, but unlike Darlene, Eleanor stiffened.

"Okay, you're fine," she said, patting my shoulder in a similar manner to Dan's.

I stepped back and crossed my arms, feeling vulnerable and afraid. "How is she doing?"

Eleanor smoothly transitioned into doctor mode, explaining everything with intricate details I didn't understand. "They had to intubate her since she stopped breathing, and right now the ventilator—"

"But she's going to be okay in the end, right?" I insisted. "She's going to pull through and be fine?"

My sister straightened. "She's a sixty-nine-year-old woman who's suffered a major accident, Autumn. There's not a lot of hope at this point."

I clenched my jaw. "I can't believe you just said that. There's always hope. Is that how you talk to your patients? That's awful."

She flinched, and I was glad because she shouldn't talk about our mother like that. Mom was a fighter. She was stronger than any woman, and she was going to survive this.

"Look," Eleanor continued, "I'm just trying to be realistic and keep things in perspective. We'll know more in the next twenty-four hours, but we need to prepare ourselves for the worst."

The lump in my throat throbbed. "No, we need to be optimistic and pray for a miracle. We need to expect

Mom will overcome this."

Eleanor said nothing. I turned away and stared down at my mom. Never in a million years would I describe her as frail, but lying in that bed, she looked as if she were a hundred years old and on the doorstep of death.

Rage shot through me. "Did they arrest the driver who hit her? He must've been drunk or on drugs or something."

It was Jim who responded. I'd been so focused on my mother and sister that I'd forgotten he was in the room. "No, they didn't arrest him, and according to the police, he was clean. I'm not sure what's going to happen. It's under investigation."

I shook my head, devastated. Nausea gripped my stomach. We couldn't lose our mother like this. We couldn't. I took her limp hand in mine and silently promised I would do everything possible to get her better.

FOR THE REST of the night, Eleanor, my brothers, and I stayed with our mother. I think it was the longest the four of us had been together without our kids or spouses, and it was a strange and awkward dynamic.

Around four in the morning, one of the doctors informed us that our mother was stable and we should go home to get some rest. Dan stood and reached for his jacket as if he were actually leaving.

"What about Tim?" I asked, feeling the need to do something, even if it was just tracking down my mother's boyfriend.

Michael tugged on his beard. "Who's Tim?"

"I don't know exactly, but there was a letter on Mom's nightstand from someone named Tim," I explained. "He addressed her as 'My Darling Nadine' and signed the letter, 'All my love, Tim.' He's probably important to Mom, and we need to find him."

Dan pulled on his leather jacket. "What'd the letter say?"

I shook my head. "I don't know. I only read the beginning and the ending. Nothing in between."

My brothers shared an amused smile, the first since coming to the hospital. They were two years apart and used to look a lot alike before Michael went all *Duck Dynasty*.

"We're supposed to believe that?" Dan said, a twinkle in his eye.

"It's true. I wanted to read the letter, but I didn't. I swear."

"Good, because it's none of your business," Eleanor said, her irritation palpable.

I studied my sister carefully. She knew every detail of our mother's life, from what day she played Mah Jongg to her cleaning lady's favorite tea. "Eleanor, what do you know about Tim?"

Her expression faltered, and she placed a protective hand on her stomach. "Nothing. I've never even heard of him."

Her jaw twitched and her hand made that circular motion over her belly. She was lying. But why? She'd been just a child when our father died, was the idea of our mother being with another man too difficult to take?

"Are you sure?" I asked. "In the letter—"

Anger lit Eleanor's eyes. "Why were you snooping through Mother's things?"

"I wasn't. I just found it when I was looking for a book to read."

She turned away to study the monitor on one of the machines. "We need to focus on Mother, not on some imaginary relationship she doesn't have. If she had a boyfriend, I'd know about it."

Dan nervously ran a hand through his thick black hair. My father had thick black hair like Dan and Michael's, and I wondered if he'd often done the same thing when worried. "It's hard to believe Mom has a boyfriend. Do you know his last name, or where he lives? Or was that not in the letter."

He winked at Michael, and I knew Dan was teasing, something else he did whenever anxious.

"I didn't read the letter," I repeated. "But maybe I should."

"No," Eleanor snapped. "Just let it go."

"What about Mom's phone?" Michael asked, ignoring our sister. "Maybe we could find Tim's contact information that way."

"The police are looking for it," Dan said. "It was probably tossed across the parking lot when the truck hit her."

I shuddered at the disturbing image and closed my eyes. I tried to pray, but the noisy rhythm of the machines distracted me. Taunted me with the idea that maybe this time, no amount of praying would help.

Dan zipped up his jacket. "I've got to get home to Darlene and the kids. I'm working tomorrow, but I'll come back in the evening."

"I'll walk out with you," Michael said, not bothering to give an excuse for why he couldn't stay.

Eleanor nodded, accustomed to our brothers leaving during uncomfortable situations. "I'll call if there's any change," she said, taking charge.

After they left, Eleanor and I sat in silence. I needed to do something to help, but of course there was nothing to be done. I wasn't a doctor, and I didn't have a supernatural way of making all this go away.

My mind drifted to Tim. Was he expecting my mother to call? I pictured a good-looking, older gentleman dressed in khakis and a polo shirt, waiting on the golf course tomorrow or at a restaurant. Maybe he was one of the other volunteers at the Boys and Girls Club.

I looked up at Eleanor and spoke in my kindest, softest voice. "He's probably worried about her."

"Who?"

"Tim. The man that wrote the letter."

She flicked an invisible piece of dust off her sweater. "You don't know that, and if he is, he'll contact us to find out what happened."

"He might not know where she lives. I never saw an envelope, so maybe he—"

"What? Passed the letter to her in study hall or during church? Maybe on his way up for communion, he handed Mother the note when the priest wasn't looking."

I blew out a frustrated breath. Eleanor was just upset, but I didn't deserve to be treated like this. "He should know. You may disagree, but I'm going to look around and see if I can find an envelope with his address."

"No. Don't read the letter. Don't look for an envelope. And don't go poking your nose into other people's business. Nothing good will come of it."

Her anger seemed over the top, even for Eleanor. "Why are you so agitated? What's going on, Ellie?"

"Nothing, and don't call me Ellie. I hate that name."

"Sorry ... *Eleanor*. But what is it?"

She shook her head, but her eyes filled with tears, stunning me. I'd never seen my sister cry or show any kind of weakness. She was the epitome of a tough and independent career woman. I wanted to reach over and embrace her, but I was afraid she might slap me. Wetting my lips, I chose my words carefully. "Did something happen?"

She looked away, and I expected her to dismiss my question, but she surprised me by confiding in me. "I found something on Jim's phone, unintentionally. I didn't have mine, and I needed to make a quick call and ..."

It took a minute for my mind to catch up with what she was saying. I pinched my bottom lip with my thumb and forefinger. "Eleanor—"

She tugged her sweater over her stomach. "That's why you shouldn't snoop through Mother's things. You might regret what you find. Everyone has secrets, and those secrets are best kept hidden."

My head spun. "What are you talking about? What did you find on Jim's phone?"

She paced the room, then stopped abruptly. "I'm done talking about this. It's late, and you should go home."

"Did you find a text from another woman?"

She stiffened. "I've got to go. I'm supposed to bake three dozen gluten-free cookies for Aubrey's dance recital, and I'm on call tomorrow night."

I stared at my sister. We'd been here for hours. How could she even think about normal life right now? I glanced at our mother's damaged body, unable to leave. "I'm going to stay longer. Darlene has the boys so ..."

"Fine." Eleanor gave me a curt nod and left the room without saying good-bye.

Chapter 13

*A*FTER BREAKING UP *with Jude, I fell into a deep depression. Even though I had to end our relationship, my heart ached, and I felt physically sick.*

The next week, Tim and Ruby dragged me to the fairgrounds where the movie production company hired us to be extras in Elvis's new movie. Our job involved riding one of the amusement rides over and over and over. It was fun at first, but after an hour, we all suffered nausea and feared we'd made a grave mistake.

Just as Tim suggested we quit, Ruby shrieked and pointed at something in the distance. "It's Elvis! It's Elvis!"

I twisted around to see Elvis himself walking with the adorable Vicky Tiu! Despite my insistence that I no longer cared about him, I squealed right along with Ruby.

Tim spoke with mock exaggeration. "Oh my gosh, I think I'm going to faint." He collapsed against Ruby, and we all cackled with laughter. The ride lifted, swooping us through the air and spinning us around. With our hands raised high, we screamed with joy.

Afterward, we ate at the Food Circus, which had about thirty different food vendors. Just as I was biting into my hot dog, I saw him.

Not Elvis, but Jude!

He strode toward me, a stern look on his face.

"Jude!" I stood and tried to walk toward him, but my legs wouldn't work. By the time he reached me, my heart was in my throat.

He held up my letter, and my stomach dropped. I opened my mouth to speak, but only managed to stammer his name again. "Jude—"

"Did you mean it?" he asked, shaking the letter.

"I—"

"I'm not losing you, Nadine. I've been on a bus for the past three days. I went to your dorm, and one of your friends said you were here. I've been looking for you all day."

My insides turned to mush. "You came all this way to see me?"

He nodded, his thick black hair swooshing forward.

I swallowed hard. "Can I see my letter?"

He handed it over, and I shredded it into pieces. One corner of his mouth tugged upward. "I should've come a long time ago. Sometimes, I'm an idiot and just need you to tell me what to do."

"Okay," I agreed.

Then, in front of everyone, he enfolded me into his

arms and squeezed me tight. I rested my head against his strong chest and listened to the solid beat of his heart. All my doubts vanished, and I knew Jude was the only man for me.

Leaning back, he cradled my face with his large hands. "So, you're still my girl?"

I nodded and he lowered his lips to mine, kissing me so hard my head spun. His mouth was soft and wet and urgent, causing a jolt of excitement to course through my body. Threading my arms around his neck, I hung on and forgot about everything but the two of us together.

LATER, WE STOOD in line with Ruby and Tim to ride the elevator to the top of the Space Needle. I would've preferred to have Jude all to myself, but I didn't want to appear desperate. As we waited, the four of us chatted easily about school, music, and Jude's bus ride from Boston to Seattle. Jude held my hand, giving me a warmth and strength I'd missed. Being with him was so easy; it was like he'd never left.

At one point, Ruby leaned toward me and whispered, "You should've broken up with him sooner."

"I know," I agreed, grateful my letter had inspired him to come see me instead of having the opposite effect.

At the top of the Space Needle, we took in the majestic

view of the World's Fair. Jude stood behind me, his hands around my waist and chin on my shoulder. I pressed my back into him, wanting nothing more than to slow time. I was afraid to ask when he had to leave, so I avoided the question.

On the elevator ride down, a young boy, his eyes wide with excitement, peered out the window. Jude grinned. "The view is impressive, isn't it?"

"Yes, sir. And tomorrow, I get to kick Elvis in the leg."

"What?" we all asked, confused.

"It's true," the boy insisted. "I'm one of the actors in the movie, and I get paid for kicking Elvis."

We laughed and discussed how acting seemed to be an easy profession unless you were prone to motion sickness. On the way back to the dorms, Ruby and Tim walked ahead while Jude and I lagged behind, holding hands.

At one point, Ruby linked arms with Tim and put her head on his shoulder.

"It looks like they're getting serious," Jude said.

I sighed and kicked the pebble in front of me farther down the sidewalk. "Ruby cares about him a lot. I just hope Tim feels the same way. He can be such a flirt."

Jude stopped, turned to face me, and narrowed his eyes. "He doesn't flirt with you, does he?"

I smiled. "Are you jealous?"

He put his hand on my waist. "Should I be?"

"No."

We exchanged a brief kiss, then resumed our walk, enjoying the presence of each other. When we reached the campus, Jude's voice grew serious. "I'm going to talk to your father, Nadine."

Panic shook me. "About what?"

"I want to ask his permission to date you."

"No, don't do that. Talking to my father is a bad, bad, bad idea. Besides, you're going to leave and—"

"I'm not going back."

My pulse jumped. "What?"

"I'm not going back. I dropped out of college, and I'm staying here for good. I know we're young, but ... I want to be with you."

My heart pounded. "Are you going to attend the university with me?"

"No." His shoulders sagged. "When I told my parents I was coming to see you, they cut me off. They refused to pay for any more of my school or living expenses."

"Jude—"

He held up a hand and lifted his chest. "It's okay. I'm on my own now, but I'll be fine."

"What are you going to do?"

"Get a job. Maybe go to school, eventually. Regardless, I'm going to make something of my life, you'll see. I promise I'll become a man you can be proud of."

My voice shook. "I'm already proud of you."

He pressed his forehead to mine. "That's all I need, ba-

by. Just keep believing in me, okay?"

———— ✦ ————

JUDE FOUND A *construction job and a small room to rent
in a boarding house just off campus. Ruby continued seeing
Tim, and the four of us often double-dated on the weekends. Sometimes we went to the movies or played cards,
while other times we just met at the library to study. Even
though Jude couldn't afford to go to college, he spent a
tremendous amount of time reading architecture books.*

*Every morning Jude and I met at the coffee shop for
breakfast. The waitress, realizing we were poor and in love,
took pity and often brought us a complimentary side of
pancakes or eggs.*

*As the Seattle rain beat against the diner's windows,
Jude and I talked about our hopes and dreams for the
future. We shared a common faith and the belief that there
was a reason for everything. Maybe we disagreed on movies
and fashion, but when it came to the important things in
life, we were a perfect match.*

*One morning, he told me about his goal to own a con-
struction company. "I've started saving a portion of every
paycheck for that purpose."*

*"I can imagine you doing that," I told him, taking a sip
of my coffee.*

He leaned back in the booth and placed his folded

hands on top of his head. "You have so much faith in me. Why is that?"

I studied the way his bicep tugged at his shirt. Working construction had made him strong. "I just do. I know you can accomplish anything you put your mind to."

He rocked forward and placed his arms on the table. "Then I want you to have faith in me and let me talk to your father. I hate this sneaking around and being dishonest. That's not the kind of man I want to be."

"Oh, Jude. I have faith in you. I'm just afraid of what my father will say. It's him I don't have faith in. He's conservative, old-fashioned, and extremely overprotective of his little girl."

Frustration encompassed Jude's face. "We're going to have to deal with this someday, honey. At least before we get married."

"Married?" My heart skipped.

"I'm going to marry you someday, Nadine. If you'll have me, that is."

Happiness filled me, but I feigned indifference with a little shrug. "I'll have to think about that."

Surprise, then humor filled his eyes. Laughing, he captured my hands and pulled me toward him. He kissed me hard right there in the diner, and I giggled against his mouth.

I had no problem imagining myself married to Jude and living happily ever after as Nadine Kingsley. But *telling my parents about us? I couldn't do that.*

Over the next few weeks, Jude continued to pester me about talking to my father. Finally, I relented and invited him to dinner. When I told my parents I was bringing "a guest," they asked me all sorts of questions. Afraid they might not allow Jude into their home, I refused to reveal his name.

"Is it Tim O'Connor?" my mother asked, a glimmer in her eye.

"No, of course not! Tim's dating Ruby, you know that."

We were trying on hats at Nordstrom's in the Northgate Mall. My mother studied herself in the mirror and adjusted the fabric on the ridiculous tulle cloud hat she proclaimed was the height of fashion. "Tim has always carried a torch for you."

"We're just friends," I insisted. Part of me had always wondered about Tim's feelings toward me. Then again, he had lots of friends, many of them girls. Still, I often worried he was going to break Ruby's heart since she was crazy about him, and he didn't seem to reciprocate the feeling. Hopefully, I was simply misreading the situation.

"So you're not even going to tell me this boy's name?" my mother asked.

"No, you'll learn all about him soon enough. Besides, if I give you any details now, Daddy won't be able to interrogate him in person."

My mother scoffed. "Honestly, Nadine. I wish you

wouldn't be so secretive. It's not as if we're going to hire a private investigator and look into his background. We're just curious and excited. You haven't brought home a boy since ..." Her voice trailed off, refusing to say Jude's name aloud, which wasn't a good sign.

She removed the hat and returned it to the rack. "Well, it's been a long time, and we're looking forward to meeting your gentleman friend, that's all."

Her voice sounded wounded, and I regretted hurting her feelings. The two of us had always been close. "It's Jude, Mother. Jude Kingsley. I'm sure you're disappointed, but please give him another chance."

Her expression was surprisingly reserved. "I thought his family moved to Boston."

"They did, but Jude came to Seattle to be with me. He has a good job and is supporting himself. We're in love, and if you forbid him from coming to dinner ... then you might as well forbid me."

She sucked in a sharp breath. "I see."

My heart pounded as I waited for her to say more. After what seemed like ages, she looked in the mirror and smoothed her hair. "Well, then ... we'll see the both of you at six o'clock, Monday night."

I breathed a sigh of relief. "Thank you."

She picked up the hat again, looked at the overinflated price, and strode toward the cash register as if the traumatic news of Jude justified the expense and fashion mistake.

"You should invite Ruby and Tim. They've always had a calming effect on your father, and I'm sure he'll need that. You can't go wrong with extra company to keep everyone civil."

I smiled, feeling I'd gained an ally. Maybe Jude was right. Maybe confronting my parents wasn't going to be so bad.

JUDE ARRIVED AT my parents' house with Ruby and Tim right on time. He greeted me with a quick kiss in the foyer before my mother joined us.

"Thank you for inviting me," Jude said, offering his hand.

My mother, who'd always liked Jude but worried too much about my father's opinion, timidly shook Jude's hand. "It's nice to see you again." She embraced Tim and Ruby warmly, then gestured toward the living room at the back of the house. "Mr. Greene is watching the news. I gave him a drink, but ... well, good luck to us all."

My father had never liked Jude. Even before the talent show performance, Daddy disapproved of how much time I spent with him. Perhaps, he just didn't like seeing me growing up and falling in love.

Jude straightened his tie and headed down the hall with a confident stride. I followed, praying all would go well. In the living room, my father sat in his usual leather chair, glued to the television. He barely glanced at us when we entered the room, and I suspected my mother had warned him about Jude, since he just seemed irritated and not surprised.

"Don't be mad," I said, stepping toward my father. "Jude and I are dating and—"

"Nobody is dating anybody," Daddy growled.

I lifted my chin. "I'm old enough to make my own decisions, and I've decided to—"

My father came to his feet and turned up the volume of the television. "None of that matters. We're about to go to war!"

We all turned our attention to the television where President John F. Kennedy was speaking from the oval office, informing us that Soviet nuclear weapons had been found in Cuba.

"Oh, Lord," my mother said, clutching the pearls around her neck.

I stared at the television, fear pressing down on me. Were the Russians going to start a nuclear war with us?

Jude took my hand and gave it a reassuring squeeze. I leaned against his arm, never more grateful for his presence than at that moment.

Chapter 14

*A*ROUND SIX IN the morning, Dan showed up to stay with our mother, insisting I go home and get some sleep. I stared at him, confused. "Don't you have to work?"

"My boss gave me the day off when he found out about Mom. Darlene told me I should come to the hospital to relieve you."

"So you don't want to be here? You're just following your wife's orders?"

He shrugged. "It's hard being here. I hate seeing Mom like this, and the hospital smell reminds me of when Dad and Angela died."

I'd never thought about how my father and Angela's accident affected Dan. He always seemed so stable; quiet and aloof, perhaps, but steady and confident in the role of husband and father.

"Did you go to the hospital after our dad's accident? Is that how you learned ... learned he died?" The phrase *our dad* sounded odd, but I never knew what to call my father since I'd never met him.

Dan nodded. "Just briefly, to help Mom. It was the hardest thing I've ever done."

Like our mother, Dan seldom spoke about the past or opened up about his feelings. I wanted to ask him more, but he escorted me out the door, insisting he'd be in trouble with his wife if I didn't leave immediately.

I gave him a hug. "You're a good brother."

"Your favorite brother?" His smile was weak, and his eyes didn't have their usual mischievous sparkle. Probably a combination of worry and lack of sleep, but I appreciated his effort to connect with me.

"Sometimes, you are my favorite brother, but if you ever hurt Darlene, I'd totally take her side."

He smiled. "Yeah, I know. Mom and Eleanor and Michael have all told me the same thing."

I walked out to my car, suddenly exhausted. A cold front had swept in, and I shivered, wishing I'd brought a warmer jacket. Wrapping my arms around my chest, I breathed in deeply, grateful for the fresh air, in spite of the chill.

I climbed into my car, started the engine, and turned on the heater. Still parked, I called Kyle. He didn't answer but immediately shot me a text. "Just starting rounds. Call you later?"

My fingers trembled as I returned his text. "A truck backed into my mom at the grocery store parking lot. She's in the hospital on a ventilator."

I stared at the phone, figuring he wouldn't receive my message until later since he never looked at his phone while seeing patients. To my astonishment, he called.

"Autumn. What happened?"

My breath hitched at the distress in his voice. As best I could, I caught him up to speed on everything. I couldn't relay all the medical terms accurately, but I did my best. "They're going to move her to a private room this afternoon."

"*Oh, honey.*"

The endearment made my eyes water. I grabbed a takeout napkin from the driver-side pocket and wiped my face. "I don't want her to die."

"I know you don't." He remained silent while I blew my nose, then he asked, "Do you want me to come home?"

Of course I wanted him to come home. I wanted him to be here and hold me and tell me everything was going to be okay. But I knew what this month meant to him. "No, thanks for asking. I don't know what's going to happen. Darlene's watching Logan and Zane, so I'm headed over there right now. I suppose we'll know more in the afternoon."

He hesitated. "Okay. But call me as soon as you know anything. I'm going to call Jim and try to get more information."

"Thanks. I'm sure he'll be able to give you all the medical details."

"I'll say a prayer for her, Autumn."

"Thanks."

"I love you."

Goosebumps prickled up my arms. "I love you, too."

I hung up the phone and drove to Dan and Darlene's house, feeling a little better. Kyle had the ability to improve even the most horrendous situation. Of course, he could do the opposite, too. But I was glad in this case, talking to him made me feel better.

Inside the house, Logan gave me a hug and asked about Grandma. Zane, however, offered me no affection and insisted I immediately take him to Eleanor's house to reclaim his egg.

"I'll make you an egg," Darlene said, helpful as always.

"I don't want an egg to eat. I want my dinosaur egg to love!" He broke into tears, like a kid half his age.

I held him on my lap, wanting to join in with my own tears. But right now, I was his mom, and whether I wanted to or not, I needed to be strong and save my tears for later.

———∼∼∼———

DARLENE, BEING THE wonderful sister-in-law she was, kept the boys all day so I could go home to sleep and shower. In the afternoon, I returned to the hospital and spent several hours sitting at my mom's bedside.

My thoughts kept returning to that letter I'd found on her nightstand. If Tim was her boyfriend, he must be sick with worry. Shouldn't we be trying to contact him? Maybe his presence would help her get better.

I held my mom's hand. "Who's Tim? Do you want me to find him and let him know what happened?"

She remained silent, of course, the only sound coming from the machines keeping her alive. I put my jacket back on to fight the chill in the room. Outside, the big Texas sky was gray and dreary, matching my depressed mood.

It'd been months since I spent any serious time praying, but lost and discouraged, I turned to God. Did He ever get tired of people like me who only talked to Him during their time of need?

Closing my eyes, I bowed my head and prayed for my mom's recovery. I prayed for Kyle, my children, and my sister's marriage. Eleanor hadn't told me what was going on, but she was obviously upset about something on her husband's phone. Had it been a suggestive text or a picture? Or something worse?

I also prayed that God would heal the emptiness in the pit of my stomach that only increased with age. Was it just loneliness? Did I need to stop expecting Kyle to fill that hole? Or was it something else? And what was I going to do if I lost my mother?

Faith, a voice whispered. I opened my eyes, certain someone must have entered the room, but nobody was there. Had my mom spoken? Had God?

I shuddered and chalked it up to lack of sleep and stress. *Faith. Okay, I'll have a little faith.*

IN THE LATE afternoon, I picked up the boys from my brother's house, thanked Darlene profusely, then drove home in the rain. The temperature had dropped to the low forties, which native Texans considered a national tragedy, even in the winter months. If the downpour continued and there was the slightest chance of ice, the whole state would shut down and school would be cancelled tomorrow.

I'd thought about staying at my mother's house to-night, craving the comfort of my childhood home, but our rental was closer to Logan's school and my work. I needed to go into work tomorrow, even if I didn't stay the whole day.

The rain increased as we turned onto our street. A bolt of lightning flashed across the sky, followed by thunder that shook the van. The boys screamed with delight, making me grateful that instead of being afraid, they found tremendous joy in the storm.

Seeing the road in front of me grew next to impossible, and I gripped the steering wheel tighter. When we finally pulled into the driveway, I breathed a sigh of relief.

"You left the lights on, Mom," Logan said.

I squinted through the rain at the house and noticed that not only were all the lights on, but smoke drifted from the chimney. Confusion and a yearning for home consumed me.

The front door opened, and Zane shouted, "Daddy!"

My heart soared as Kyle jogged through the rain holding a large umbrella. He was barefoot and wore faded blue jeans and a black hoodie. I'd never been so happy to see anyone in my entire life.

I pushed open the car door and flew into his arms. He pulled me tight under the umbrella as the rain pounded all around us. He was wearing the cologne I'd given him for Christmas, and he smelled amazing. Just like the slogan said, "Strong, sexy, and so incredibly masculine."

"You're home," I said, leaning into him.

"Yeah. I'm home, baby."

Chapter 15

*A*MERICA SURVIVED THE *Cuban missile crisis of 1962,
and somehow my father survived my relationship with
Jude Kingsley. Daddy wasn't happy about it, but he didn't
stop us from dating.*

*Four years of college flew by and right before gradua-
tion, Ruby entered our apartment looking forlorn. Sinking
onto the couch, she heaved a great sigh. "Tim asked me to
go to dinner with him on Saturday night. Just the two of
us. He said he has something important to discuss, and I'm
afraid he's going to break up with me!"*

*Deep down I shared her fear, but I didn't dare voice it.
"Why would he break up with you? You've been together
over five years."*

*She clutched one of the couch pillows to her chest. "He's
been withdrawn lately. All he does is work and study."*

*I didn't want to give Ruby false hope, but I couldn't
help asking if she and Tim had ever talked about a future
together.*

She shook her head. "Not really. Why? Do you think

he's going to propose? Do you think that's why he's so preoccupied?"

She looked at me with such hopeful eyes, I couldn't bring myself to disappoint her. "Maybe. What do you think?"

She tugged at a loose thread on the pillow. "I hope so. I really love him, you know?"

"I know you do."

She set the pillow aside and tucked her legs underneath her. "I just wish I knew what was going through his mind."

I laughed. "Is it possible to know what's going through a man's mind? Sometimes I ask Jude what he's thinking about, and with complete sincerity he says, 'nothing.' Other times he tells me something so random, I worry about his sanity."

"But you know he loves you," Ruby insisted.

I nodded because I definitely knew Jude loved me. We talked about our future all the time. We were planning on getting engaged next summer, after I'd taught school for a year and we'd saved enough money for a house.

I gave Ruby an encouraging squeeze. "Everything is going to be okay."

"I know. Remember when we were little girls and talked about marrying brothers and having a double wedding?"

I laughed. "We also fantasized about building a house with an indoor swimming pool for our pet dolphins."

Ruby clasped my hand. "Oh, Nadine, I don't know what I'd do without you. I'm so lucky to have you in my life."

I shook my head. "I'm the lucky one."

⚬⚬⚬

ON SATURDAY NIGHT, Jude told me to dress up because he was taking me someplace fancy. He arrived at the apartment, looking handsome in his black suit and tie. Clean-shaven, he smelled even better than the shampoo bottle I used to keep in my nightstand drawer.

In the car, I scooted next to him. "Now are you going to tell me where we're going?"

He placed his trembling hand over mine and fear shot through me. Why was he so nervous? He was never nervous around me.

"You know I love you, right?" he began, his voice shaky.

My heart clenched. "Are you breaking up with me?"

"No, of course not."

I exhaled with relief and placed a hand over my heart. "What's going on, Jude? You're scaring me. Why are you being so strange?"

"Sorry. I wanted this night to be special, but I'm too anxious to wait."

I bit my bottom lip. "Wait for what?"

He smiled. "I'm taking you to the restaurant on top of

the Space Needle."

I gasped. "But that's so expensive."

"I know. I've been saving for months. I had the whole romantic evening planned with champagne at your parents' house and—"

"Champagne? What are you talking about?"

He made an apprehensive groan. "I'm sorry. I'm ruining everything."

At this point, I had no idea what he was talking about. Looking back, it was so obvious, but I'd believed Jude when he told me he wanted to wait at least another year to get married.

To my amazement, he reached into his suit jacket and pulled out a small black velvet jewelry box. Slowly, he opened it to reveal a tiny diamond engagement ring.

"Nadine Rose, I know this is probably the smallest ring you've ever seen in your life, but … will you marry me?"

Tears blurred my vision. "Oh, Jude. Of course, I will. Of course."

"I don't have a lot to offer—"

I interrupted him with a kiss. "You're all I need. If you're offering yourself, then that's all I need."

"One day, I'm going to replace this ring with something much bigger."

I shook my head. "It's perfect. I love it. And I love you."

He slipped the ring on my finger and kissed me again.

I spread my fingers and stared down at my hand. "I

can't believe we're engaged! I can't believe we're getting married!"

After a romantic and extravagant dinner, Jude drove me to my parents' house for champagne and cake. Over the years, my father had learned to tolerate Jude, and the thought of them coming together to arrange this celebration touched me deeply.

"We asked Ruby and Tim to join us," my mother said, her face flushed from the alcohol. "Apparently, they had other plans, but Tim sent his regards. I hope everything is okay."

Jude's tone was distant. "It will be. In time."

"What's going on?" my mother demanded.

Jude forced a smile. "It's not my business to say, Mrs. Greene. I'm sure Tim will talk to you later."

I'd asked Jude the same thing at dinner, but he'd refused to talk about it. "Please trust me on this," he'd said. "You'll find out soon enough."

I'd agreed, but I was somewhat disappointed he felt the need to keep a secret from me. How were we supposed to have a strong marriage if we didn't tell each other everything?

Reaching across the table, he'd squeezed my hand. "I'll never be dishonest with you, Nadine, but I promised Tim I wouldn't say anything, and that's a promise I intend to keep."

I told him I understood, but in hindsight, I wished he

would've prepared me for what happened next.

———

LATER THAT NIGHT, *I entered the dark apartment nervous about Tim and Ruby. Turning on the lights, I jumped at the sight of my best friend curled up in a ball on the couch. My heart pounded with fear. "Ruby?"*

She looked up with red, puffy eyes. Streaks of black mascara ran down her face and crumpled tissues littered the floor.

"Oh Ruby, what happened?" I knelt to the ground beside her and placed a hand on her back.

She wiped her face and sat up. "Tim broke up with me."

Even though I feared it was coming, I hadn't wanted to believe it. I sat on the couch beside her and put my arm around her shoulders. "What did he say?"

Fresh tears pooled in her eyes, and she sniffed loudly. "He doesn't want to marry me. He said God is calling him to become a priest."

Confusion clouded my brain. "A priest? What are you talking about?"

"I know. It sounds like a joke, right? Tim O'Connor, a Catholic priest. But he's seriously going to do it. They've already accepted him into the program and everything. He's leaving the day after graduation. That's why he's been

working so hard. Not to raise money for a ring or to get married, but to pay off his debts so he can enter the seminary."

"I don't believe it. I thought—"

"You thought he was in love with me?"

I pursed my lips because that wasn't exactly the truth. "He treated you like a girlfriend. You've been together all through college. He took you on dates and kissed you goodnight. He never acted like someone preparing to take a vow of celibacy."

She launched into a fresh bout of weeping, and I regretted being so direct. "I'm sorry Ruby. I'm just so shocked."

"He said he loved me. And he claims he still loves me, but he can't ignore God's call."

I pressed a hand to my heart. "Oh, Ruby."

Her eyes bulged and her hand shot out to grab mine. "You're engaged?" she asked, staring at my ring. "Jude asked you to marry him?"

I nodded, feeling guilty for my happiness.

There was a moment's hesitation, then she burst into tears, collapsing against me. "That's wonderful, Nadine," she said, her voice desolate but not bitter. "I'm so happy for you."

OVER THE NEXT few months, I focused on finishing college

and planning my wedding. I tried to be sensitive to Ruby, but preparing for the wedding occupied so much of my time and energy our friendship suffered.

While I was busy choosing the dinner menu for the reception and selecting the band, Ruby began dating a much older man named Harold McCoy. He was decent looking, soft-spoken, and nice enough, but he was all wrong for Ruby.

Jude warned me not to say anything, but I ignored his advice and asked Ruby what she saw in Harold. She took offense, and despite my apology, things became strained between us.

Then, out of the blue, Ruby announced her engagement to Harold. I stared at the huge sapphire and diamond ring on her finger, easily worth ten times more than my ring. "Are you sure about this, Ruby?"

Her eyes flashed with anger. "You're not the only one who can be happy, you know."

"Of course not." I chastised myself for saying anything. Our relationship was at a crossroads, and I could either speak my mind or support my friend. "I'm happy if you're happy."

"Of course I'm happy," she said, perturbed. "I'm very happy. Harold is—well, he's perfect for me. We're very, very, very happy."

"Good. You wouldn't be marrying him if he wasn't wonderful, right?" I tried to keep my tone lighthearted, but

judging by the strained look on Ruby's face, I didn't succeed.

"We should double this Saturday," I suggested, taking a different approach. "Jude and I want to see the new Cary Grant movie. Why don't you and Harold join us?"

Ruby's face brightened, and I dared to hope everything would be okay. "Sure. I'll talk to him and see if he wants to go."

I tried to keep my expression neutral, but I wanted to ask Ruby why Harold got to decide what movie they watched. What about what she wanted?

***

ON OUR LAST night in the apartment together, Ruby and I shared a bottle of wine, ate takeout Chinese food, and talked late into the night about all the memories and good times we'd shared since second grade. I was incredibly grateful and relieved to have our friendship back.

"Thank you for taking care of me in second grade," I told her. "My life would've been so different without you."

"Mine, too," Ruby agreed.

I tried to imagine what it would be like living with Jude after my wedding instead of with Ruby. I loved Jude wholeheartedly, but I would miss sharing the apartment with my best friend.

"I don't want things to change," I said. "Please tell me

they don't have to change just because we're getting married."

She swirled the wine in her glass. "Change is the only thing you can be certain of."

"But you and I will always be friends, right?" My voice filled with panic. "No matter what happens, we won't let our friendship suffer?"

"Of course not."

I nodded and clung to the hope that the doubt in Ruby's voice was a result of the late night and not a hint of troubles to come.

If I'd known then what was going to happen, I might have done things differently—although what, I don't know. All I know is it's so easy to miss the beauty of our life when we're living it. So easy to forget that right now is a gift to be enjoyed to its full extent because who knows what tomorrow will bring.

MY WEDDING WAS everything I'd hoped for. Ruby was my maid of honor, of course, and we had so much fun together. Jude's parents traveled from Boston to attend the wedding in Seattle. They seemed truly happy for us. Mrs. Kingsley embraced me as though she'd always loved me, and Mr. Kingsley shared a cigar with my father after the rehearsal dinner.

A month later, Ruby married Harold in a small but expensive ceremony. Jude told me Harold was a good guy, and I was being too hard on him, so I did my best to be happy at Ruby's wedding. I even danced with Harold during the reception and laughed when he accidentally stomped on my foot. Twice.

After the wedding, Ruby and Harold honeymooned in Hawaii before moving to Spain, for Harold's work. Saying good-bye to my best friend was excruciating, and I wondered when I'd see her again.

"Are you going to be okay?" Jude asked as we drove home from the airport.

"I'm going to miss her so much. I can't imagine not being able to talk to her every day."

Jude reached across the seat and held my hand. "Harold is wealthy, so maybe Ruby will be able to make frequent phone calls."

"It's not the same as talking to her in person."

"I know, but what you have with Ruby is special. Time and distance aren't going to change that, Nadine. Just like it didn't change things between us."

I relaxed in my husband's love, grateful for his kindness and understanding. He'd never been jealous of Ruby. Never complained about all the time I spent with her.

Even with Jude's compassion, however, I'd never felt so alone and empty. I only hoped Ruby wasn't as miserable as I was.

FOR THE FIRST year of marriage, Jude and I lived in a small apartment complex where he handled basic mainte-nance duties for a reduction in our rent. He continued working for the construction company, and I taught first grade at the local elementary school. Several evenings a week I earned extra money by teaching piano lessons while Jude studied at the library, educating himself on how to run a business. His boss wanted to retire and had begun grooming Jude to take over the construction company.

Every penny we managed to save went into a special account for our future house. Jude wanted a big back yard where he could play baseball with his sons, while I wanted room for the grand piano my parents had given me when they moved back to Texas.

I loved Jude completely, but he couldn't replace my best friend. I desperately missed Ruby and loved talking to her on the phone when she called. Unfortunately, overseas phone calls were unbelievably expensive back then, even for Harold, so we mostly exchanged weekly letters.

Through our correspondence we shared recipes, house-keeping tips, and gossip from work. Ruby's life in Spain sounded so glamorous compared to mine. She often attend-ed extravagant parties with Harold and met dignitaries from exotic countries.

"Do you wish you lived in Spain?" Jude asked as I was

mopping the kitchen floor one Saturday morning.

"And give up this glamorous life?"

He laughed and took the mop from me. "Go change while I finish the floor. Then, Mrs. Kingsley, I'm taking you on a glamorous date to the grocery store."

I squealed with exaggeration and kissed him on the cheek. The truth was I loved going to the grocery store with Jude. I loved him, and I loved our life together—even if we spent more time engaged in mundane chores than attending international galas.

Since both Jude and I were working, our savings built up quickly. In December, however, I announced I was going to have to quit my job.

"What's wrong?" he asked, his brow furrowing. He sat at the kitchen table with his adding machine, going over our monthly budget.

I placed a hand on my stomach, hoping he wouldn't be too upset at my news. This was something we were hoping to delay until after we bought our house and he took over the company, but you couldn't always plan things like this. Taking a deep breath, I smiled. "I have to quit my job because I don't have anything to wear. Nothing fits."

Jude's face fell. "Oh honey, I know you've gained a little weight, and from what I hear, that's only natural when you get married—"

"You think I've gotten fat?" I didn't know whether to laugh or cry.

"No, no," he stammered, a stricken look on his face. "Of course not. You're perfect just the way you are. I always thought you were too thin, but now ..." He stopped talking, realizing he was only making things worse. "Honey, if I could afford to buy you a new wardrobe I would. I want to buy you the world, but—maybe we can rework the numbers." He hunched over his paperwork, scribbling down figures. Was there anything this man wouldn't do for me?

"I'm pregnant," I blurted out.

His head shot up. "What?"

"I know we wanted to wait, but ... "

"A baby?" His voice cracked and he squeezed his eyes tight. When he opened them, they were moist. He stood and stepped around the table. Tenderly, he brushed my face with the back of his rough hand. "I'm going to be a father?"

I nodded. "Yes. Are you okay with that?"

He placed his hands on my stomach and smiled. "I'm ecstatic. I can't believe you're having a baby."

Tears streamed down my face. Jude kissed me and pulled me close. "I'm so happy."

"Me, too."

What had I done to deserve this much happiness? My thoughts drifted to Ruby. Had she found the same joy with Harold? I hoped so. I really hoped so.

A FEW DAYS later, I received a letter from Ruby who had news of her own. She was pregnant, too! Calling Jude's name, I raced into the house and found him underneath the kitchen sink, fixing a leaky pipe.

"What's wrong?" he asked, sitting up too quickly and banging his head on the cupboard. He let out a painful yelp and rubbed his fingers across his forehead, smearing grease. "Is everything okay with the baby?"

"Yes." I squatted beside him and cupped his face with my hand. Ever since I'd announced my pregnancy, he'd treated me as though I were breakable. "Everything's fine. I'm sorry I startled you. Are you okay?"

He nodded and gestured toward Ruby's letter in my hand. "Let me guess. Ruby was invited to Buckingham Palace and can't decide what to wear."

"No," I said, swatting his arm with affection. "She's having a baby, too! Can you believe it? She's due a week after me!"

He rubbed his arm and laughed. "Are you kidding? This doesn't surprise me at all. The two of you are so close; it was inevitable you'd be pregnant at the same time."

I placed a hand over my belly. "Do you think she feels the same way I do? Excited and nervous at the same time?"

Jude reached into his toolbox. "I'm your husband, Nadine. Not your girlfriend. I have no idea what your best friend is feeling."

"Right, of course."

He chuckled then scooted back underneath the sink. I was quiet, lost in my own thoughts. Going through something so life changing as having a baby without my best friend saddened me.

"Why don't you call her," Jude said, reading my mind.

I scoffed at the idea. "I'd love to, but I know we can't afford it."

"It's a special occasion. You and Ruby are both pregnant. The world is never going to be the same. So call her."

"Seriously?" I bit the inside of my cheek, tempted by the suggestion but certain Jude didn't really mean it. "What about the money?"

He sat up, this time minding he didn't hit his head. "We'll be okay. I took a part-time job on Saturday night."

"You didn't tell me that."

He grinned. "Don't get too excited. It's just for one night, but they're going to pay me fifteen dollars."

"Fifteen dollars!" I was shocked. Our reduced rent was forty dollars. Fifteen dollars seemed like an absurd amount of money for one night. "What will you be doing? It's not illegal, is it?"

"Not exactly, but Sister Hildegard wouldn't approve."

"Jude Kingsley, what in the world are you talking about?"

He laughed. "I'm going to put on a little show for one of our clients. For his wife, actually."

I pinned him with my gaze. "What kind of show?"

He tossed his wrench in the toolbox and stood to wash his hands in the sink. "It turns out Mrs. Browning is a huge Elvis fan, and when she heard me singing—"

I thrust a hand to my hip. "When did she hear you sing?"

"When I was working on her kitchen addition. I didn't realize she was in the house, so I was singing along to the radio."

The idea of another woman listening to my husband sing bothered me, but I supposed that was a hazard in working residential construction. "How did that lead to a job?"

Jude smiled. "I told her all about you and our disastrous high school talent show. She must've mentioned it to her husband because next thing I knew, he called and asked if I could do an Elvis impersonation at her birthday party."

"Are you telling me the truth? It seems a little farfetched."

He laughed, then feigned insult. "You don't think I can do it?"

"I know you can do it, I just can't believe you're going to get paid for it."

He shrugged. "Mr. Browning said I was a lot cheaper than hiring four guys to imitate the Beatles."

"I bet," I said, laughing.

Jude turned off the faucet and dried his hands on a towel. Then he entwined his fingers with mine and gave a sheepish smile. "Will you play the piano for me? Like old times?"

I smirked. "That sounds like fun—as long as Sister Hildegard doesn't catch wind of it."

Jude grinned. "We're married now, so even if she finds out, there's nothing she can do to separate us. You're stuck with me forever."

"I like the sound of that."

He wrapped his arms around me and kissed my neck. Then he reached over my head and grabbed the phone. "Call her. It's been almost a month since you heard her voice, and I know you miss her. You, me, and the baby … we're going to be just fine."

"Okay." Holding the receiver, I dialed Ruby's phone number. She answered on the first ring, and we talked as if only a few feet separated us instead of an entire ocean. I told her about some of the kids in my classroom, and she told me about the cooking lessons she was taking from a world-famous chef. We fantasized about our babies and motherhood and all our dreams from childhood.

"Maybe I'll have a little boy, and you'll have a girl, and they can grow up and get married," I suggested, twirling the phone cord around my arm, like I used to do as a teenager.

Ruby liked the idea, and I held on to the possibility that she and Harold would eventually move back to the states. I wasn't crazy about the man, but if she was happy, so was I.

Chapter 16

*O*N SATURDAY, JUDE and I performed our Elvis tribute at Mrs. Browning's birthday party. We had a lot of fun and appreciated earning a little extra money, which we planned on using for date night the following weekend.

As luck would have it, however, the car broke down, so all the money from the Browning's—plus some from our house savings account—went toward paying the mechanic. Instead of going out, we stayed home, cooking chicken bought on sale, rice, and green peas. For dessert, we took dishes of vanilla ice cream onto our small balcony overlooking the parking lot.

Jude swirled his spoon around the rim of his ice cream bowl. "It's no view from the Space Needle."

I placed a hand on his thigh. "It's perfect."

He gave a skeptical smile and squeezed my hand.

"It is," I insisted. "I couldn't think of a better way to spend an evening ... or my life."

He leaned down and kissed my ever-expanding belly. "That's why you have the best mother in the world, little one. She always manages to find the good in every situation."

I ran my hands through Jude's thick hair. "Your father's not so bad either."

He set his ice cream aside and pulled me onto his lap. I laughed and struggled to get away. "Let me go. I'm going to crush you!"

"No, you're not." He placed his hand on the back of my head and pulled me close for a kiss.

———

OVER THE FOLLOWING months, Ruby and I continued exchanging letters, commiserating about weight gain, lethargy, and swollen ankles. We talked about setting up the nursery and putting together the layette.

Then, in the last trimester, Ruby's letters suddenly stopped. Jude surmised there must be some kind of delay in the overseas post office. "One day soon, you'll receive a huge package, full of her letters, and you'll spend the entire day curled up on the couch with a coke, getting caught up on your best friend's life."

I ignored the queasiness in my stomach and prayed Jude was right, but when I called Ruby on the phone, nobody answered.

"They probably went on vacation," Jude insisted, trying to put my mind at ease.

Hoping he was right, I continued writing letters to Ruby, discussing possible baby names and the various houses Jude and I wanted to buy but couldn't quite afford.

I lived my life and pretended everything was fine, but deep down, I was worried.

THROUGHOUT THE WINTER *and spring of 1967, Jude and I worked hard, lived frugally, and saved every penny we could. We watched the Vietnam demonstrations on television and prayed for our country as the baby inside me grew.*

The school year ended in May, and in June, we bought a little white house in the Laurelhurst neighborhood. It was small and needed updating, but Jude and I had never been so excited. Everything was sliding into place for us.

The only dark cloud was my concern for Ruby. I tried calling again, but the overseas operator said her number was no longer in service. Her parents had moved away, and I didn't know how to contact them. When Jude called the embassy, nobody would give him any information.

In late June, I gave birth to a healthy baby girl we named Angela after one of my favorite students. Jude cried the first time he held his baby girl. "She's so tiny," he said, his voice breaking. "I can't believe she's ours."

We brought Angela home, and while I sat on the back

porch nursing, Jude planted a cherry blossom tree to commemorate our daughter's birth. Gazing down at our beautiful baby, I couldn't stop smiling. Her hair was red, and her eyes were a faint green I hoped would turn a shade darker like her father's.

As she nursed, her mouth eventually slowed, and her eyes grew heavy until at last she surrendered to sleep. I pulled down my blouse and shifted the baby to my shoulder so she could burp. Without inhibition, she let out a loud belch that frightened the goldfinch bathing in the birdbath just outside the kitchen window.

Jude chuckled and shook his head. "Such a lady."

"She takes after her father," I replied.

He threw his head back and laughed so hard Angela jerked. I patted her back, and she immediately fell back asleep.

Coming to my feet, I winced at the pain the simple movement of standing caused. My mother had warned me giving birth was "uncomfortable." but nobody had prepared me for the pain afterward. Would my breasts ever stop hurting? And when would I be able to sit or use the restroom without pain?

I smiled at Jude, knowing it was all worth it. "I'm going to lay Angela down in the bassinet, then I'll make us some lunch."

"I'll make it as soon as I finish," he said, placing the tree in the hole and shoveling dirt on top of it.

"The doctor said as long as I didn't push myself too hard, light household chores were fine. I'm pretty sure making a turkey sandwich isn't too taxing."

Jude rested his hands on top of the shovel and met my gaze. "I just want to take care of you, Nadine. Of both of you."

I smiled. "I know you do, but I'm fine. Honest."

He nodded reluctantly, and I walked into the house where I heard soft knocking at the front door. Expecting it to be a neighbor or someone from church bringing us a meal, I peeked out the window, shocked to see Ruby.

My heart did a little dance, and I flung open the door. "Oh, Ruby. I've been so worried about you." I wrapped my free arm around her and hugged her tight. "What are you doing here, and where have you been? Are you okay?"

She broke away and gave a sad smile. "I'm fine. It's good to see you. And your baby ..." She placed a hand on Angela's back. "She's amazing."

I tilted the baby so Ruby could see her face. My friend blinked several times, and her eyes filled with tears.

"What is it?" I asked.

She shook her head, refusing to meet my gaze. "I'm just so happy to see you and meet little Angela. I've missed you so much."

"I've been worried. You stopped writing, and I didn't know how to find you. We called, but—"

"I'm sorry." Self-consciously, she placed a hand on her

flat belly ... a belly as flat as the day she married.

"Oh, Ruby." My chest filled with sorrow.

"The baby didn't make it," she said. "I lost her."

Tears stung my eyes, and I pulled Angela a little closer. Breathing in the sweet smell of my baby, I shuddered at the thought of life without this miracle. "What happened?"

Ruby shook her head. "I don't know. She just stopped kicking, and we lost her."

Chapter 17

THE FIRST YEAR of Angela's life was tough. Motherhood exhausted me—something I hadn't expected, given the fact I loved kids. But Angela was colicky and often cried for hours on end. There were times when neither Jude nor I could soothe her, regardless of what we did.

When she slept, which was rare, she was so beautiful. She had fat, rosy cheeks and a perfect cupid's bow across her upper lip. Unfortunately, I didn't always appreciate her beauty because I was so tired.

My mother flew up from Texas and stayed for almost two months. Full of patience and energy, she walked the hallway with Angela for hours on end. The day my mother left, I sank into a deep depression.

Then in February 1968—right after Peggy Fleming won the Olympic gold medal for women's figure skating— Harold took a job in Seattle. Best of all, he and Ruby bought the house directly behind ours, causing me to retract every bad thing I'd ever said or thought about the man.

Jude offered a smug, "I told you so," but I was so happy,

I didn't care.

Once again, Ruby and I were able to see each other any time we wanted. We joked that being backyard neighbors was like being college roommates again, except we were a little older and married.

Ruby's house was substantially larger than ours but in need of serious repair. Because Harold believed restoring the house would be a wise investment, he allowed Ruby to make all the renovations she wanted.

Without a job or a baby to distract her, Ruby threw herself into transforming the run-down house into a magnificent home. She handled all of the subcontracting and much of the labor herself, including the sanding and painting.

On the rare occasions when Angela allowed me to lay her down for a nap, I helped Ruby hang wallpaper and sort through flooring samples. I welcomed the break from washing diapers and keeping my clingy baby happy, but mostly, I held Angela and watched Ruby work.

I imagined it was cathartic to have such a huge project after losing a child, although I worried about my friend's health. She worked long hours, often foregoing sleep and food. Upon the completion of each project, she immediately dove into a new one.

Because of the close proximity of our houses, we could wave at each other while cooking dinner or cleaning the kitchen. One evening, I was feeding Angela strained carrots in the high chair. My baby girl loved carrots and giggled each time she tasted the sweet vegetable. When she fell asleep in her high chair, food smeared across her face, I laughed and snapped a picture.

With a warm washcloth, I wiped her face and hands before lifting her into my arms, inhaling her delicious baby scent. She'd been such a difficult infant, but things were getting better as she neared her first birthday. While she still demanded to constantly be at my side, she now slept through the night as long as she was in our bed, something neither Jude nor I minded.

Tossing the washcloth in the sink, I glanced up and caught Ruby watching me from her own kitchen window. A clenched fist was pressed to her heart, and although I couldn't see her tears, I imagined they were there. "Oh, Ruby." My heart split wide open for her, knowing how desperately she wanted a baby.

Over the next several years, Ruby suffered numerous miscarriages. Meanwhile, I had no problems with infertility. Dan followed three years after Angela, then came Michael, and finally Eleanor. Having four children under the age of ten wasn't easy, but I never complained in front of Ruby.

In the summer of 1977, I discovered I was pregnant again. At the time, Angela was ten, Dan seven, Michael five, and Eleanor had just passed her first birthday. The pregnancy came as a complete shock, and I'm ashamed to say I didn't welcome it. Even though I was only thirty-three, I didn't want any more children. My life was busy enough with the four I had.

Jude insisted the pregnancy was a blessing, and he was thrilled by the news. Of course he was thrilled, I thought with disdain. He wasn't the one who was pregnant. He wasn't the one who was going to gain weight, endure childbirth, and stay up all night nursing a newborn.

I loved my children. Loved my family. But another baby?

Jude held my hand as we sat the children in the living room and announced the news. Eleanor was too young to understand, but the older three surprised me with their excitement. Dan and Michael raced around the living room, shouting at the top of their lungs, "It's a boy! It's a boy!"

Angela disagreed and insisted the baby would be a girl this time. She offered to help set up the nursery, which was a sweet gesture but did bring up another problem. Where were we going to put this baby? We'd long since outgrown our three-bedroom house, and we couldn't afford to buy a new one.

"We should switch houses with the McCoy's," Dan suggested, oblivious to how much his words would hurt Ruby.

I gave Jude a look of sadness, and he placed a firm hand on Dan's shoulder to stop our son from saying more. "How about you boys help me convert part of the garage *into a bedroom?"*

The boys enthusiastically agreed and couldn't wait to get started. Jude gave me a proud wink, and I didn't have the heart to ask where he was planning on storing the yard equipment and camping gear.

Five kids! Such an outrageous number. How in the world would we manage? Jude owned his own construction company, but we weren't exactly on easy street.

To celebrate our good fortune, Jude insisted we find a sitter for Eleanor and take the older kids to see the matinee showing of Star Wars. *I reluctantly agreed, and as Luke Skywalker battled to save the empire, I sat in the darkened theater lamenting my pregnancy.*

Why did God continue to bless me with baby after baby while Ruby's arms remained empty? Where was the justice in that? Why couldn't The Almighty give Ruby a baby?

When the movie theater lights came on, I stood and felt a sudden gush of blood between my legs. Panic enveloped me.

"What is it?" Jude asked, concerned.

"I ... I need to use the restroom."

The worry line between his brows deepened. "Is every-thing okay?"

"No." I raced to the bathroom, and in the stall, I discovered what I already knew: I was losing the baby. Hot tears burned my eyes. I hadn't wanted this child, yet now that I was miscarrying, I'd do anything to keep it.

"Oh, God, please save my baby. Please." I knew it was too late, but I couldn't stop praying. Couldn't stop making promises that I'd never complain again if He'd just let my baby live.

At the hospital, tests confirmed my greatest fear. The baby had died. I held back my tears until I was alone in the car with Jude. Then I sobbed, heartbroken over our loss.

Jude brushed back my hair and held me close. "Don't cry, honey. We'll try again."

"That's not the point. I didn't even want this baby, I just ..." I couldn't finish my sentence. How could I possibly explain my feelings of guilt and sadness?

Jude drove home in silence where he made me a cup of hot ginger tea. I took it onto the back porch and sat in the rocking chair while the rain fell and my children fought over who ate the last piece of Jude's Father's Day cake.

Closing my eyes, I longed to take the umbrella and go for a long walk, but the doctor told me I needed to stay off my feet for the next few days.

The distant sound of a screen door slamming shut echoed across the wet grass. I glanced up to see Ruby jogging toward me, a rain jacket held over her head. She leapt onto my porch, laughing. Brushing the water off her clothes, she whistled. "That's quite the storm."

I nodded but said nothing. Her face grew serious, and she sat in the other rocker next to me. "Jude told me about the baby. I'm so sorry."

I bit the inside of my cheek and looked away, afraid speaking would bring fresh tears. The door behind us opened, and Jude brought Ruby a cup of tea. His face relaxed with relief now that my best friend was here. He placed a tender hand on my shoulder. "Can I get you anything else, sweetheart?"

I shook my head, and he went back into the house. I felt guilty for speaking so harshly to him in the car. He was only trying to help, and I shouldn't have taken my frustration out on him.

For a long time, Ruby and I sat in silence, sipping our tea and listening to the rain. I was grateful she didn't try to placate me with empty promises that everything was going to be okay. She could've even pointed out I was lucky enough to have other children, but she didn't.

Up until I lost the baby, my other children had been enough. More than enough. It didn't make sense to mourn the loss of a child I'd never even held, never even named, never even wanted. But I was so unbelievably devastated.

After awhile, the sun came out and the neighborhood children rang the doorbell, asking if the Kingsley kids could play kick the can at the park. I listened to the sound of my children racing around the house searching for their shoes. Angela yelled at the boys to hurry up, and Eleanor cried, probably desperate to join her older siblings.

The front door slammed shut, and I could hear Jude trying to calm Eleanor. He must've bribed her with a cookie, because she stopped crying, and the house fell silent. The older children laughed outside, but their voices faded as they moved down the street.

"I want a baby so bad," Ruby said, breaking the silence.

The lump in my throat ached. "I know you do."

"I was jealous and mad when I found out you were pregnant again. It just seemed so unfair. You can't imagine how empty I feel."

"I'm sorry."

She nodded. "Hearing you lost the baby—" Her voice broke, and she pressed a hand to her mouth. "I'm so sorry. I never should've been jealous. I'd never wish something like this on anybody. Especially not you. Please forgive me?"

I nodded and we embraced in an awkward hug over the armrests of the rocking chairs. Despite the fact nothing had changed, I felt comforted. Ruby stood and crossed the porch to a pot of geraniums where she deadheaded a few brown blossoms before throwing them in the trash. She turned back to face me. "I don't think I'll ever have a baby, and I want one more than anything in the world."

My heart tightened, and I formed my words carefully, wanting to be helpful and not aggravate the problem. "What about adoption?"

She flinched. "Harold doesn't want to raise another man's baby."

I swallowed back my anger. I'd heard his pathetic excuse before. "The child wouldn't be another man's baby. He'd belong to the two of you. He'd be your baby."

"Don't you think I told him that?" Ruby struck a defensive pose, her stance wide and her arms folded across her chest. "I can't adopt a baby without my husband, and Harold doesn't want to adopt."

I softened my voice. "What about what you want?"

She returned to the rocker, pulled up her legs, and placed her head on her knees. "I don't think I'm ever going to get what I want."

My heart shattered. If only there was something I could do. If only I could give Ruby a child. I'd read about the recent experiments with test tube babies and the possibility of infertile couples using a surrogate mother, but Jude wouldn't want me to do something like that. Harold would definitely forbid such an "unnatural" method of conceiving, not to mention my own hesitation.

I'd once believed there was a reason for everything, but watching my dear friend suffer with infertility made me doubt that belief. It wasn't like she wanted something selfish; she simply wanted a child to love.

Feeling helpless, I reached out and took her hand. "I'd do anything to help you. You know that, right?"

She squeezed my hand. "I know, but there's nothing you can do."

I pressed my lips together tight, determined that somehow I would find a way to help her.

Two months after my miscarriage, I was washing the dinner dishes with Angela while Eleanor sat in her high chair, meticulously eating one Cheerio at a time. Instead of sweeping the kitchen floor like they were supposed to do, Dan and Michael were sword fighting with the broom and dustpan.

"Nadine!" Jude shouted from the living room. "Come here!"

My first thought was one of the cats had died. Shadow hadn't been looking so good lately, and he often brawled with the other cats in the neighborhood.

I scooped Eleanor out of the high chair and went into the living room where Jude was standing in front of the television. His furrowed brow reminded me of my father during the Cuban Missile Crisis and immediately, my heart stopped.

"What is it?" I asked.

He pointed to the TV where David Brinkley was delivering the evening news in front of a picture of Elvis and the words, "Elvis Presley 1935-1977."

"No!" My legs wobbled. "It must be a hoax. Elvis can't be dead. He's only forty-two."

Jude shook his head. "He died of a heart attack."

"A heart attack?" Eleanor wiggled to get out of my arms, so I set her on the floor and walked over to Jude. He *placed an arm around my shoulders, and together we watched a clip of Elvis performing* You Ain't Nothing but a Hound Dog. *As impossible as it seemed, the news was true. Elvis was dead.*

Later that night, Ruby and Harold came over to watch the NBC late night documentary on the life of Elvis. It all seemed so sad. Such a waste. Elvis had been a huge part of my life, and now he was gone.

Despite my grief, I couldn't imagine abandoning my life to join the numerous mourners standing outside Graceland, wailing as though they'd lost their spouse. Sure, I'd loved Elvis, but the love I had for my husband and children was so much greater. Didn't these people have jobs or housework to do?

When the show ended, Jude reminisced about our performance of Jailhouse Rock *during the high school talent show. We all laughed over Sister Hildegard's outrage as she marched onto the stage to stop us.*

"But what happened after that wasn't funny," I said, a palpable sadness in my voice. "I thought I'd lost you forever."

My husband shook his head. "Not possible."

Had Ruby and Harold not been there, I know Jude would've kissed me. Instead, we exchanged a smile and talked about other memories. Harold had attended high school in California, and he told us about the senior prank that involved putting the principal's car on top of the cafeteria roof. We all laughed at that, and I found myself grateful Ruby had married a man who loved her enough to buy the house behind her best friend. Not a lot of husbands would do something like that. Now, if only I could change his mind on adoption.

After that night, hopelessness settled over Ruby. "What is it?" I asked, worried.

She insisted she was fine, but her growing depression worried me.

And then in an unexpected turn of events, Ruby's old boyfriend, Tim O'Connor—Father Tim as he was now called—transferred to our parish church. I worried seeing him might be difficult for Ruby. After all, he'd broken up with her to become a priest. To my relief, however, his presence had the opposite effect.

The priesthood hadn't changed Tim at all. He still joked and was friendly with everybody. In addition to spending time with Jude, he struck up a close friendship with Harold. The two would sit in Ruby's living room, playing chess and discussing politics for hours on end.

"Is it strange to see your ex-boyfriend having a beer with your husband?" I asked one evening as Ruby and I washed the dishes while Tim, Jude, and Harold sat on the back porch after dinner. We'd fallen into the nice tradition of getting together every Sunday night for dinner and cards.

"It's a little awkward," Ruby conceded, "but it's been good. Tim has encouraged me to appreciate Harold more, *and it's actually working."*

Harold still wasn't my favorite person, even though I was trying to be less judgmental toward him. Jude continued to claim I was too protective of Ruby and needed to be more accepting. After all, Ruby had vowed to love and honor Harold all the days of her life. Who was I to stand in the way of a sacred vow?

Ruby hung the dishtowel on the side of the sink and smiled at me. "I have news. Really good news."

"What is it?" Earlier this year, she'd opened an interior design company, so I expected her news to be about a particular client she'd been pursuing.

"I don't want to jinx myself, but I think Tim has convinced Harold to look into adoption."

"Seriously?"

Ruby nodded. "They talked about it last Sunday and ... remember Tim's older brother, Ray?"

"The lawyer?"

"Yes. He specializes in adoption, and we have an appointment with him tomorrow."

I squealed and threw my arms around Ruby. She laughed and hugged me back but spoke in a somber tone. "It's just an appointment. We have to fill out all the paperwork and be approved—"

"Are you kidding me? Any baby would be lucky to have you as his parents."

"Just say a prayer everything goes okay tomorrow."

The next day, things went better than okay. Ray insisted there wouldn't be any problems, and he already had a baby in mind. A young secretary had accidentally gotten pregnant and wasn't keeping her baby. She hoped to find a local family that didn't have other kids, so her child would be sure to get enough attention.

Harold smiled at Ruby. "If my wife has her way, the baby's feet will never touch the floor."

A few months later, Ruby and Harold became parents to a beautiful baby boy with olive skin and brown eyes. They named him Eric, and he was the most delightful baby. He had a calm disposition, sleeping and smiling all the time.

Since all of my children except Eleanor were in school, she and I spent a lot of time with Ruby and Eric. Eleanor adored Eric and treated him like her own live baby doll.

Jude constantly teased me about spoiling the little boy, but I didn't care. Having Eric in my life was like being a mother without the responsibility. I could spoil him rotten, then return him to Ruby whenever he became difficult. But Eric was never difficult as a baby. Toddlerhood, however, was a completely different story.

Eric entered toddlerhood like a tornado. He screamed and ran away from his mother in public. If Ruby told him not to do something, he did it anyway. He broke a display window at an expensive children's clothing boutique and chipped his tooth while running up the altar steps at church to say "hi" to Father Tim during mass.

At Nordstrom, Ruby told Eric to hold her hand, but he shouted a defiant "no" and raced ahead only to get his foot caught in the escalator. Fortunately, he wasn't hurt, but the fire department had to cut Eric's favorite pair of cowboy boots in order to free him.

Although Ruby loved her wild boy, his challenging behavior exhausted her. Harold frequently traveled or worked long hours, leaving Ruby with most of the parenting responsibilities. She needed a break but felt guilty taking one, given she'd waited so long to become a mother.

When I saw the advertisement for a painting class offered at the community center, I encouraged Ruby to attend. After all, she'd once loved drawing and painting. Over the years, most of her creative energy had gone into renovating her house and later working as an interior designer. Now that she was a full time mother, her only creative activity involved keeping Eric out of trouble.

Ruby was interested in the class, but she didn't like the idea of leaving her high-spirited toddler with a babysitter.

"What about Angela?" I suggested. "She's a fabulous sitter and adores Eric. I'm sure he'd behave for her."

Ruby laughed. "Have you met my son? The little boy who's obsessed with throwing my makeup in the commode? The little boy who's on a first name basis with the police and fire departments?"

I laughed. "He's a good boy. Just a little spirited. I'm

sure Angela can handle him, and I'll be right across the yard if she has any problems."

"I don't know."

I could see the wariness in Ruby's eyes, and I didn't want her to miss this opportunity. As a mother myself, I knew the importance of having a little something for yourself. I didn't make a lot of money teaching piano lessons, but it was something I enjoyed that was separate from being a wife and a mother.

"You'd actually be doing me a huge favor," I said, taking a different approach.

Ruby raised her brow. "How?"

"Angela is so boy crazy it scares me. I think watching Eric for a few hours might make her think twice about wanting a boyfriend."

"She's twelve."

"Yes, and if I can convince her at this age that having children is a huge responsibility, then I'll be ahead of the game."

Ruby frowned. "So you want to use my son as a form of birth control? The poster child for why you shouldn't have children?"

I smiled. "When you put it like that, it doesn't sound very good."

"No," she said, laughing, "but it's true."

Eventually, Ruby agreed to try the class on a temporary basis. It took only one lesson for her to fall in love with *painting. As much as she enjoyed home renovation projects, painting on canvas was an entirely different experience.*

Her eyes lit up when she talked about the class. "Painting reminds me of being young, when I believed life was full of possibilities. I love Eric, and I adore being a mother, but painting inspires me. It makes me feel whole. Is that bad to say?"

I shook my head. The two of us were sitting in our usual spots on my back porch, sipping raspberry tea and watching Eric play hide and seek with Dan. The endless Seattle rain had persisted all week, but today the sun fought its way through the clouds, warming the weather.

"Being a mother is the most wonderful thing in the world," I said, "but it's okay to have something of your own."

Ruby set her tea on the table and added more sugar. "Then I shouldn't feel guilty about enjoying the class so much?"

"Not at all."

Eric jumped out from behind the cherry blossom tree Jude had planted in honor of Angela's birth. Dan screamed as though scared to death. He fell to the ground and Eric jumped on him, cackling like it was the funniest thing in the world.

"Be careful, honey," Ruby called. "Don't hurt Dan."

"It's okay, Mrs. McCoy. He's not hurting me." Dan gently tackled Eric and threw a few fake punches at him,

which only caused the little boy to laugh harder.

Ruby picked up her mug and held it against her chest. "I really am happy to be a mother. I can't imagine life without him."

I took a sip of my tea and smiled at my own son. "I know what you mean."

Chapter 18

*H*AVING KYLE COME home from Haiti when I hadn't even asked him was wonderful. He'd explained the situation to his adviser, who'd been able to make arrangements for him to finish the rotation here at a hospital in Austin, just an hour away.

"But you were looking forward to working in Haiti," I said.

We were in the kitchen, making chicken and corn quesadillas for dinner as the rain continued. He placed an arm over my shoulders, and I leaned into him. "I was looking forward to the rotation, but this is where I need to be right now."

And what about next year?

I pushed the angry thought away because all that mattered was my husband had come home when I needed him the most.

After dinner, Kyle studied while I cleaned the kitchen and bathed the boys. When they were in their pajamas, Kyle declared it was Wrestling Mania in the living room. For the next half hour, I took pictures of Logan and Zane attempting to pin their father to the ground. I vowed to print out the photos and frame them so I could remember this moment the next time Kyle and I argued.

Eventually, Kyle let the boys win, then he tossed them over his shoulders like sacks of potatoes and carried them to bed. I followed and watched all three of my guys kneel beside Zane's bed to pray for my mom.

"Hey, when is Grandma getting out of the hospital anyway?" Zane asked, clenching his dinosaur egg in his fist. Vilda had brought the egg over to Darlene's house, assuring us it'd been well cared for by her and Aubrey.

"I bet Grandma is better tomorrow," Logan said.

I cringed at his optimism. His only experience with hospitals had been when I'd given birth to Zane, which had been a happy experience. He'd brought me balloons and a notebook full of pictures he'd drawn showing him playing war with the new baby.

Kyle placed a hand on Logan's shoulder. "It might be awhile, so we'll just have to be patient and hope for the best."

Satisfied with the answer, Logan crawled into bed.

"Don't forget the two pennies," Zane said.

Kyle placed two pennies on the dresser for Zane and

two for Logan. Then he took me by the hand and led me down the hall to our bedroom.

Once in bed, I asked Kyle if he'd talked to Jim about my mom. "Yes," he said, spooning me and kissing my shoulder. "That's when I decided I needed to come home."

My throat clogged. "Because you think she might not make it?"

He hugged me tighter. "Because I wanted to be with you."

"Thanks." I swallowed the lump in my throat.

He let out a huge yawn, patted my hip, then rolled away from me. "Sorry, babe. I'm just so tired. Can we talk in the morning?"

"Sure," I said, turning over and rubbing his back.

He moaned appreciatively, then promptly fell asleep. I'd always been envious of his ability to sleep so easily. Both my mother and I suffered bouts of insomnia, and already, I could tell it was going to be one of those nights.

Instead of fighting the inevitable, I got out of bed and opened the hall closet where I'd left the box of photos I'd found in my mom's attic. I carried the box to the kitchen table and sifted through random pictures of my family's life.

There were endless photographs of my siblings, including Angela, the sister I'd never known. Dan once told me I looked like her, but other than our red hair, I couldn't see the resemblance. Maybe in the eyes since they were the same color as our father's.

One picture showed Angela building a sandcastle on the beach with my brothers while Eleanor sat on a towel, reading a book. I chuckled, imagining Eleanor probably hated going to the beach because of the messy sand.

I continued digging through the box of photos until I found a white photo album engraved with the words, *Jude and Nadine.* Opening the album, I read the inscription written on the inside cover.

> *June 1981*
>
> *Dear Mom and Dad,*
>
> *Happy Fifteenth Wedding Anniversary! We're so lucky to have you as our parents. Please enjoy this walk down memory lane and know that we love you.*
>
> *Love,*
>
> *Angela, Dan, Michael, and Eleanor*
>
> *P.S. We couldn't have made this album without the help of Ruby. So thank you, Ruby!*

I knew from Eleanor that Ruby had once been my

mother's best friend, but something had happened, and they no longer spoke.

Was Ruby still alive? Should I try contacting her about my mom's accident? I imagined she'd want to make amends—especially if the worst happened, and Mom didn't make it.

I leafed through the album, looking at pictures of my family and their friends. There was a photograph of my parents, Ruby, and a goofy-looking kid with red hair brighter than mine standing in front of the Space Needle. Below the picture was a newspaper clipping announcing that Elvis Presley would be filming his next movie, *It Happened at the World's Fair*, in Seattle.

I continued turning pages, growing more broken-hearted over the early photos of my parents skiing, dancing, and holding babies. They had no idea my father's life would be cut short. No idea that despite my mother's incredible health, she too might meet an untimely death.

Stop, I told myself. *She's going to be okay.*

I pressed a hand to my chest, grief-stricken for my family. I thought about Eleanor, who'd only been nine when my dad and sister died. No wonder she had control issues. I shouldn't be so hard on her. If I'd suffered such a horrible tragedy when I was nine, I'd probably be just as neurotic.

Yawning, I glanced at the clock. Three a.m.! I would never be able to get up by seven unless I went to bed right now. I closed the album and started to return it to the box, but as I did, a manila folder, marked *Angela's Medical Records*, caught my attention.

Curious, I opened the folder and leafed through my deceased sister's documents. There was nothing too exciting, but then—wedged between Angela's shot record and the bill from her broken arm when she was eight—was something I couldn't believe. Something nobody had ever told me about.

My hand trembled as I read the information over and over and over.

Angela had been pregnant!

Pregnant!

And more shocking than the pregnancy was her due date.

September 15, 1985.

The exact day I was born.

Chapter 19

*I*N THE SPRING *of 1985, Angela wanted money to go shopping for a prom dress. Jude stipulated she earn the money by cleaning out the garage, but our strong-willed daughter wasn't interested in manual labor.*

When Jude refused to give her the money, she responded by stomping out of the living room and slamming her bedroom door. "I can't wait to graduate and move out!"

"Neither can we," Jude said under his breath.

I threw one of the couch pillows at him. "The two of you are so stubborn. Go talk to her, please. She's your daughter."

Our old, worn-out couch creaked as he scooted closer to me. After eighteen years of marriage, four kids, several dogs, and cats, everything in our house needed replacing. Jude groaned. "She's just been so grumpy lately. All she wears these days are those baggy jeans and oversized sweatshirts. Why does she even want a prom dress?"

I patted his strong arm. "Every girl wants to feel like a princess and wear a prom dress. It's our job to help her find one that flatters her figure, regardless of her weight. Before long, she'll be graduating and going off to college. Let's make these last few months special, okay?"

Jude sighed. "I'm not relenting about making her pay for part of the dress. She doesn't have to clean out the garage, but she has to do something in exchange for our help."

"I agree. I don't want her to think we have an endless supply of money."

He snorted. "Yeah, I doubt anyone would ever make that mistake."

In the end, Angela helped me reorganize and paint the kitchen. Well, she helped me pick out the paint color. When it came to the actual painting, she insisted the smell made her sick. I thought she was faking until she threw up in the bathroom.

Nevertheless, I agreed to take her shopping to find the dress of her dreams. I realized I was basically buying my daughter's love, but I refused to feel guilty. Angela's last year of high school had been rough with her on-again off-again boyfriend. She'd put on a lot of weight from emotional eating.

A new boy had asked her to prom, so if an expensive dress could put a smile on my moody teenager's face and allow me to be the hero for once, I didn't mind the slightly unethical practice of bribery. Besides, what was motherhood without a little bribery now and then?

ON A RAINY Saturday morning, I woke Angela, who would've slept all day if given the chance. Lately, sleeping, eating, and watching television were her only activities.

That morning, however, I didn't criticize. Ruby had lectured me on keeping my mouth shut if I wanted the shopping trip to be successful. "Unless she asks for your opinion, don't make any comment on the dresses she likes or doesn't like."

I grimaced. "What if she chooses one that's hideous and accentuates all the weight she's gained this spring?"

"Just bite your tongue."

"I don't know if I can."

"You have to."

At the store, I stood outside the dressing room as Angela tried on several dresses with no success. She wouldn't let me see any of them on her, so I couldn't help in finding one that fit.

"How are you doing in there, honey? Can I see what the blue one looks like?"

"No," she said on the verge of tears. "I just want to go home. All of these dresses are stupid."

"Let me see." Without waiting for permission, I slid open the dressing room curtain and peeked inside.

"Mom!" she shouted, covering herself and turning her back to me. But it was too late. I'd already seen what she *was trying to hide.*

Angela hadn't gotten fat. She was pregnant!

"Everything okay?" the sales lady asked, passing by. "Do we need any more sizes?"

"We're fine." I spoke politely and tried to keep my emotions hidden despite the shock surging through me.

The bell above the boutique jingled, and the sales lady headed to the front of the store, greeting her new customer.

"Angela," I whispered, peeking through the crack in the curtain. "Why didn't you tell me?"

She hastily threw on her clothes and sank onto the little stool in the corner. Her body collapsed in on itself, and she sobbed. "Dad's going to kill me."

I slipped inside the dressing room and took a deep breath. Then I put my arms around my daughter and held her tight. "We'll figure this out, okay?"

※

W̲HEN̲ J̲UDE̲ L̲EARNED̲ about Angela's pregnancy, his anger shot through the roof. "Who's the father?" he demanded.

"Rodney Smith. That boy who took her to the winter dance."

"Rodney ... I'm going to kill him! I'll make him marry her first, but then I'm going to kill him."

I sighed heavily, grateful I'd had the foresight to make Jude go for a drive with me instead of telling him at home.

"Father Tim said—"

"You've already discussed this with O'Connor?" A vein in Jude's forehead pulsed.

"I needed a third party's perspective. Someone who wasn't so closely involved."

Jude swore and pounded his fist on the steering wheel. I exhaled slowly. Despite the fact I'd never dated Tim, Jude was often jealous of my friendship with the priest.

Resentment thickened my husband's voice. "What'd he say?"

I wrung my hands together. "We have lots of options. And as he pointed out, there are worse things in life than an unplanned pregnancy."

"I can't believe this. Is that boy going to marry her?"

"I don't think so."

"He better."

"No," I said firmly. "The last thing either one of them needs is to be forced into a loveless marriage."

Jude shook his head. "She slept with him, and she doesn't even love him?"

I stared down at my hands. "No, honey, she doesn't."

Jude swore again. "Unbelievable."

That had been the hardest part for me to digest. Angela had slept with a boy she didn't even love. If love had been part of the equation, I would've understood. After all, Jude and I were no strangers to passion. I'd been young once, and I still felt a thrill when he reached for me in the middle of the night.

But passion without love felt cheap to me. Maybe I was old-fashioned, but I wanted true love for Angela, not just some romp in the back of a dirty car with a boy who didn't care enough to prevent a pregnancy.

Jude was silent for a long time, but when he finally spoke, his voice was full of determination. "We'll have Father Tim's brother, that adoption lawyer, take care of it. I'll give him a call when we get home."

I clenched my fists. "Who said anything about adoption?"

"Well, if she's not getting married, she's not keeping it."

"I think that's exactly what she wants to do."

Jude exploded, punching the roof of the car. "She lost the privilege of deciding what she wanted when she got herself into this mess."

I flinched, not used to seeing my husband's temper. Placing a gentle hand on his leg, I held it there for a long time. "We'll figure this out, honey. We'll think about it and help Angela make the best decision for herself and the baby."

"Will we?" he asked, a little softer now. "What was she thinking?"

"I don't think she was."

He shook his head. "No, I suppose she wasn't. But she can't keep this baby, Nadine. The lawyer will find a good home for it. A loving couple who's older and married and can actually afford it."

My stomach churned at Jude's use of the word "it." This was a baby, not an "it."

This was our grandchild, for heaven's sake. How could he dismiss this baby so easily? How could he expect Angela to give up her own flesh and blood without serious consideration?

Jude and I drove home in silence, a heavy tension filling the car. Angela was already several months pregnant, so we couldn't wait too long before making a decision regarding the baby. How were we going to figure this out?

My mind drifted to thoughts of Ruby and how much she wanted a little brother or sister for Eric. The idea came to me so clearly, I believed it had to be an answer to prayer. I glanced at Jude, his jaw tight as he drove through traffic. I wouldn't tell him my idea right now. Maybe after things calmed down ... maybe after he had a chance to talk with Tim ...

Maybe then we could find a way to turn this disappointing situation into something positive. Something that would keep me in touch with my grandchild and allow Ruby to expand her family.

Chapter 20

*I*T DIDN'T TAKE a genius to make the connection between Angela's due date and my birthday. She'd been my biological mother. I should've figured it out years ago. Angela giving birth to me at age eighteen made so much more sense than my mom having me at forty-one.

But why had everyone kept the secret? Why had my mother—or rather my grandmother—decided to raise me as her own without ever telling me the truth? And why hadn't Eleanor or my brothers said anything?

An inconsistency gnawed at me, and I scanned Angela's medical records for more information. I don't know what I expected to find—a picture, maybe? A letter? Adoption papers?

I had a copy of my birth certificate, of course. It listed Nadine Rose Kingsley as my mother and Jude Francis Kingsley as my father, but maybe there was another document. An original birth certificate that listed Angela as my mother.

Instead of going to bed like I needed to, I continued digging through the contents of the box, hoping to find something that would answer my questions. Had Angela delivered me before the accident?

Maybe she hadn't died on impact and had lived long enough to give birth to me. Or maybe an emergency team had saved me moments after her death. Was it possible for a baby to survive in the womb after a deadly car accident?

The idea of being torn from my dead mother's belly deeply disturbed me. If I confronted Eleanor and my brothers, would they tell me the truth?

And then it hit me.

Ruby.

If anyone would know about the circumstances surrounding my birth, it would be my mom's best friend. Would I be able to find her, and if I did, would she tell me the truth?

"Autumn?"

I screamed in reaction to Kyle saying my name as he came into the kitchen, wearing only his pajama bottoms.

He rolled his eyes with amusement, and I buried my face in my hands. "You freaked me out!"

"So I noticed. What are you doing up so late? Don't

you have to work tomorrow?"

Standing, I shoved everything back in the box before changing my mind and retrieving Angela's medical records. "I found something, and you're not going to believe it."

He gave a lighthearted sigh. "Okay, Nancy Drew. Let's have a look."

My HUSBAND WOKE me in the morning with a kiss and a strong cup of coffee. "I've got to go, but I made eggs for breakfast and woke up Logan for school."

"Thanks," I said, sitting up in bed and taking the coffee from him.

"Are you going to talk to Eleanor and your brothers about Angela?"

I took a sip of my coffee, noting that coffee made by someone else always tasted so much better. "I don't know. It will depend on how my mom's doing today. I'll call Eleanor, but if everything is the same, I'll go to work and stop by the hospital in the afternoon."

Kyle frowned. "She's the same. Stable but critical. I called this morning."

"Thanks."

He nodded and kissed me good-bye. After he left, I dragged myself out of bed and stumbled through the morning routine of getting everyone ready. I dropped Zane off at Darlene's, then took Logan to school, and drove across the street to Sunshine Speech Therapy.

Suzanne, my boss and dear friend from college, gave me a huge hug. She was a short, stocky woman with shoulder-length curly blonde hair, and she reminded me of one of Aubrey's American Girl dolls. Sturdy and loving.

"Honey, are you sure you want to be here today?" she asked. "We can manage if you need to take a few days off." We'd spoken earlier on the phone, and she'd told me the same thing.

"Thank you, but I want to be here. I need to be here. It's Owen's last day."

Suzanne brightened. Owen was a five-year-old who barely spoke when I first started working with him. Now his parents said they couldn't get him to stop talking. Next fall, he would enter a normal kindergarten class and continue therapy through the school district.

Suzanne closed a client's file. "Last year, when my mother was going through chemo, work was an escape for me. I'd get lost in the kids and their progress, and for at least a few moments, I'd forget about my own problems. So I understand your need to be here today, but don't try to do it all. If you need time off, just ask."

"Thank you. I will."

After work, I took the boys to the hospital. Zane held onto my hand tightly as we entered my mom's room, but Logan walked right up to the bed and studied my mother carefully. He examined all the machines and tubes, and he even squatted to look under her bed as if expecting to find something important.

Standing back up, he clapped his hands, making a solid boom that echoed across the cold tile floor. "Okay, Grandma, it's time to wake up. Come on, get up!"

I didn't know whether to be amused or stunned by the forcefulness in his voice. I'd tried explaining the word coma to him last night, but it was beyond his comprehension.

"Grandma can't wake up," I said, giving Zane's hand an I-love-you squeeze. I noticed his other hand had turned white from clenching his dinosaur egg so tightly.

Logan narrowed his eyes. "Why can't she wake up?"

"Because she's in a coma. Remember, we talked about this?"

"What about a bucket of ice water?" he asked, completely serious. "Has anyone tried dumping a bucket of ice water on her?"

Trying not to smile, I launched into another explanation of my mother's medical condition, but Logan shook his head as if this were no excuse. I tried to reassure him—and myself—that even though Grandma was sleeping, she could still hear us. We needed to tell her we loved her and couldn't wait for her to get better.

"So she can hear us talking to her, but she can't feel a bucket of ice water?" Zane asked.

"Exactly."

Logan blew out a big breath that lifted his bangs. "Well, how long is this going to take? When is she going to wake up?"

"I'm not sure." I stared at the woman who'd raised me. The woman I'd always believed was my mother. *Why didn't you tell me Angela gave birth to me?*

Zane placed a hand on my leg. "Mom, can we go now?"

I gave him a weary smile. I'd wanted to spend at least an hour here, but neither boy was interested in staying, and honestly, I was restless, too. We stayed a few more minutes, then left.

In the hall, we ran into Eleanor, who looked quite the professional with her starched white lab coat and stethoscope. I wanted to ask her about Angela but knew this wasn't the right time. "How is Mom? Medically speaking?"

"The same. She's stable but not improving." Eleanor glanced at the boys who were tiptoeing across the tiles, trying not to step on any cracks. "The doctor wants to talk to us. We need to make some decisions."

Nausea swished through my stomach. "What kind of decisions?"

Eleanor's expression was compassionate, and for the first time, she looked tired. Leaning forward, she lowered her voice. "Decisions about Mother's health care and how long to keep her on life support if her situation doesn't change."

I squeezed my eyes tight, just wanting to curl up in a little ball on my mother's bed and be a child again.

KYLE WORKED LATE that night, so I was sound asleep by the time he crawled into bed and scooted next to me. He'd taken a shower and smelled like soap and shampoo. "Hey."

I placed my hand on his arm and pressed it against my chest. "Hey, yourself."

We fell asleep in each other's arms without another word. That night, I had wild dreams about my sister Angela being pregnant with me. Would I ever think of her as anything else but my sister? In my dream, she flew through the air on an electric guitar with Elvis, my father, and an olive-skinned little boy I didn't recognize.

The next day, I drove to Dan and Darlene's house. Zane gave me a quick hug good-bye, then ran across the living room and joined the other kids in the kitchen where they were rolling clay snakes.

"Did you sleep okay last night?" Darlene asked. "You look tired."

I shrugged. Despite my crazy dream, I'd slept hard last night, but honestly, I was exhausted and in the middle of a pity party.

My mother was in the hospital, and I'd just found out my entire life was a lie. My marriage was the only thing going well, but that was just because Kyle hadn't brought up the issue of his fellowship.

Pulling my jacket tighter, I stared at my sister-in-law. "Did you know Angela was pregnant?"

Darlene's face went blank. "Angela? Angela who?"

"My sister ... my ..." I stopped, unable to say *birth mother*.

"Oh. Yes. Dan told me."

I shook my head, feeling sorry for myself. Being deceived by so many people—by my family—stung.

"What's going on?" Darlene asked. "Why are you so upset about this?"

I started to speak, but we were interrupted when one of her daycare kids chucked a plastic cookie cutter at another child, hitting him in the face. Darlene raced across the living room as both the victim and perpetrator burst into tears.

"I better get going," I said, knowing she'd be occupied for awhile.

"All right. Sorry. We'll talk tonight?"

"Sure."

As Logan and I drove to school, he studied one of his favorite books on the solar system. His space phase had come after his dinosaur obsession but before his current interest in mechanics. I was surprised he'd chosen this old book instead of a new one.

"Everything okay?" I asked, watching him in the backseat through the rearview mirror.

He closed the book and gazed out the window. "Did you know most people think Mercury is the hottest planet in the solar system since it's closest to the sun?"

Even though I'd read the solar system book aloud about fifty times and could probably get my PhD in astronomy without even trying, I pretended to be fascinated by this piece of information. "Really?"

"Yep." He traced a figure eight on the window with his finger. "Do you know why it's not Mercury?"

I pulled into the carpool line at school and followed the other cars. "Because Mercury doesn't have an atmosphere?"

"Yep, you got it!" he trilled, using the exact intonation my mother used whenever one of her grandchildren did something extraordinary.

He climbed out of the car, and I told him to have a nice day. Before driving off, I reached into the back seat and grabbed his book. Opening the cover, I read the inscription. *"For Logan, a very smart boy on his fourth birthday, Love Grandma."*

Some uptight mother behind me honked her horn. I tossed the book on the back seat and gave a wave of apology I didn't really mean. Then, blinking back tears, I drove to work.

Parking next to the Sunshine Speech Therapy sign, I kept the engine running and stared across the street at the elementary school. Yesterday, working had been helpful, but my heart wasn't in it today. I was worried about my mother and confused whether or not to talk to Eleanor and my brothers about Angela.

A knock at the passenger side window startled me. Without waiting for an invitation, Suzanne opened the door and slipped inside. "You okay?"

I sighed and turned off the engine. "Well, I can't exactly afford the luxury of falling apart, so yes. Despite everything, I'm keeping it together."

"Why don't you take the day off," she suggested.

As tempting as it sounded, I didn't want to leave her in a bind. "I'll be okay."

She was quiet for a moment then spoke softly. "I never regretted the time I spent with my mom. Even at the end when she was out of it and didn't know who I was."

Her words knocked the wind out of me. Perhaps I was avoiding taking time off to spend at the hospital because I didn't want to face the devastating fact that my mother's future didn't look good.

"Don't take that as an omen," Suzanne said, squeezing my arm. "I honestly believe your mother is going to pull through. Let's face it, she's in better shape than both of us."

"Thanks. It's just ... things are bad. Eleanor said we need to discuss some issues ... and I don't want to do that." My voice cracked on the last word.

Tears filled her eyes. "Those decisions are tough, especially when all of a sudden you're the parent."

I nodded, afraid I'd break down if I spoke.

"Look, I have a light client load today, and I can easily reschedule some of the others. Take the day off. Go to the hospital and see your mother. Take Kyle out to lunch—"

"He's working in Austin this month."

"Okay ... catch up on your laundry or get a massage. Do something for yourself."

"I wish I could, but—"

"You can. I'm the boss. Now, do as I say before I fire you."

I smiled sadly. "What if I need to take more time off … later?"

"Then we'll figure it out. But go." Suzanne opened the door, signaling the issue was settled. "I'll see you next week."

"What about tomorrow?"

"I'm giving you that day off as well."

"Okay. Thank you."

As I drove away, I turned on the radio, pleased to hear an old Taylor Swift song that immediately put me in a better mood. Kyle often made fun of the blonde superstar, but I'd caught him singing along to her songs on more than one occasion.

The farther down the road I traveled, the better I felt. When I reached the exit for the hospital, however, I couldn't do it. Not yet, so I continued down the highway to the shopping center.

In Target, I wheeled my cart up and down each aisle, tossing in random items—pull-ups for Zane, dish soap, paper plates, new pajamas for Logan, and toilet paper. Instead of feeling elated by my shopping trip, a sense of futility settled over me. What was I going to do next? Go to the hospital for the rest of the day and watch my mom lay in her comatose state?

Suzanne had suggested having lunch with Kyle. He was probably too busy to meet me, but what if I just dropped something off for him with no expectations? It would take me about two hours round trip to drive into Austin, but I could use the time to think.

For the first time since my mother's accident, I was inspired. And in the cosmetic section, I found even more inspiration: nail polish. Giving manicures was one thing I'd always been good at, and my mom could use one right now. I gathered a couple different colors and a nail file then headed to check out.

Along the way, I passed a display showcasing old movies, including several starring Elvis Presley. I dug through the movies until I found *It Happened at the World's Fair*. I could hardly believe my luck, and I actually laughed right there in the middle of the store. I could watch this movie while I did my mother's nails. Maybe it would be just the thing to bring her out of her coma. I threw the movie in the cart, grateful the hospital had DVD players hooked to the TVs.

After I paid for my purchases, I drove south where I stopped at Whole Foods to buy two salads with chicken, pico, corn, and guacamole. If Kyle wasn't available to eat now, he could stick it in the refrigerator for later.

Somewhere along the way in our marriage, I'd stopped taking care of Kyle's meals for him. The feminist side of me argued that I shouldn't have to. After all, he often ate at the hospital and came home full. Still, having me think about his meals was one way Kyle knew I loved him, which made sense, given his childhood.

At the hospital in Austin, I texted my husband from the parking lot and told him I'd brought lunch. When he didn't answer, I left his salad at the reception desk. Hopefully, he'd retrieve it before it spoiled, but if he didn't, at least he'd know I was thinking about him.

Back at the hospital in Turtle Lake, I entered my mom's room, shocked all over again to see her pale and lifeless body lying in bed. Did I feel any different now that I knew she was my grandmother instead of my mother? Not really. She'd raised me as her own, and while I didn't appreciate her secrecy, I couldn't have asked for a better mother.

"Hi, Mom," I said, trying not to feel self-conscious about talking to someone in a coma. "I brought nail polish to give you a manicure while we watch an Elvis movie: *It Happened at the World's Fair*. I found—" My throat went dry. Would she be mad to learn I'd looked through the anniversary album? Mad I'd found out about Angela's pregnancy?

Maybe. But maybe anger would bring her out of the coma. Maybe Logan had been right in demanding she just wake up.

I sat beside her and began filing her nails. "I found

the album Angela made for your fifteenth wedding anniversary. There was a picture of you and Dad with another couple at the World's Fair. Were you in the movie?"

She said nothing, of course, and I continued my monologue. "What about Ruby and her husband? Well, I assume that redheaded kid was her husband. Did they meet Elvis?"

I examined her cuticles, wishing I'd brought a cuticle pusher. "Mom ... I found Angela's medical records ... and I know the truth. I know she was my mother."

Tears filled my eyes, and I blinked them away. "I'm sure it wasn't easy for you to raise me after Dad and Angela died, but thank you for being my mom. I love you, and while I don't understand why you kept the secret, I'm not upset. I just want you to wake up."

Chapter 21

$\mathcal{H}$APPINESS FILLED ME as Elvis flew his red airplane across the sky, singing about the green grass beyond the bend. I painted my mom's nails and realized I'd seen this movie before. I must've watched it with her when I was a kid.

Eleanor appeared in the doorway, demanding to know what I was doing.

I tightened the cap on the nail polish and set it aside. "I'm just giving Mom a manicure while we watch an old Elvis movie. Doesn't she look fabulous?"

Pressing a hand to her stomach, Eleanor glanced at our mother's hands and then at the movie. I braced myself for disapproval, but my sister's voice turned wistful. "This is the part where Kurt Russell kicks Elvis."

Sure enough, Elvis walked up to a kid and offered him a quarter if the kid kicked him in the shin. The kid did, and Elvis feigned great trauma.

"Wow, I can't believe that's Kurt Russell," I said,

remembering him from the movie *Touchback*.

To my surprise, Eleanor smiled and her entire face changed. "Mother loved Elvis. If anything will bring her back, it will be his music. Good call on the movie."

I tried not to pass out from Eleanor's approval. "Thanks. How are you doing?"

Instead of answering, she emitted a slow, strange groan. At first, I thought she was crying, but when I looked at her, I realized she was in pain.

"Eleanor, what is it?"

Shaking her head, she hunched over slightly and took several shallow breaths. She pressed her hands to her stomach and closed her eyes.

"Eleanor! You're scaring me. What's wrong?"

Opening her eyes, she straightened and spoke in a calm voice as if nothing had happened. "It's just a contraction. I've been having them all morning."

"What?" I jumped to my feet and circled the bed to her side. "Are you serious?"

She bristled as though worried I might touch her or overreact to the fact she was in labor. "I'm fine. I'm on my way up to obstetrics to get checked, but—"

She couldn't finish her sentence because another contraction grabbed her. Her face tightened and perspiration broke out across her brow and face. I held my breath, waiting for it to end. When it finally did, she grimaced. "Ouch. I forgot how much that hurts."

"Those last two were close together. We better go."

She hesitated and shot a glance at our mother. "I wanted to see her before I had the baby, in case ..."

"Mom's going to make it, and you'll be fine, too," I said, willing it to be true.

Eleanor avoided my gaze and looked at our mother without speaking.

Fear gripped me. What if my sister knew something I didn't? What if she'd already spoken to the doctors, and there was no hope for recovery?

"I'll wait outside," I said, thinking it might be easier for Eleanor to talk if I wasn't there.

"No, it's fine." She turned and walked toward the door, stopping as another contraction hit. She breathed through it before asking me to call Jim. "Tell him to pick up Aubrey from school, okay? I've left several messages, but—"

"Don't you want him here with you? I'll get Aubrey. Let me help you to labor and delivery and—"

"No, I can go on my own."

I stared at my sister as though she'd grown two heads. "I'm coming with you. You can't have a baby by yourself."

Her response was interrupted by a huge contraction that caused her to bend over and release a very un-

Eleanor-like moan. She tightened her fists, and her face turned red. She wasn't going to have the baby here, was she?

I moved beside her and took her by the elbow. "That looked like a tough one. I'm walking with you, and I'm not taking no for an answer. I'll call Jim on the way upstairs, but I'm staying until he gets here."

She relented and said nothing more as we climbed the stairs to labor and delivery. I'd suggested the elevator, but Eleanor insisted that was tempting fate, and she refused to make headline news by delivering her own baby in a broken elevator.

"Good point," I agreed.

When her phone rang, she answered it immediately. I assumed it was her husband saying he was almost here, but it became obvious it was someone she worked with. Between catching her breath from contractions and climbing the stairs, my amazing, overly ambitious sister rattled off various test results and medical terms I didn't understand. Sometimes it was easy to forget her uptight personality contributed to a successful career.

Once on the third floor, I opened the stairwell door, where an older nurse greeted us. Her eyes widened when she saw my sister. "Dr. Fairchild?"

Eleanor scrunched up her face and folded her arms into her chest as another contraction hit. "I might be in labor."

I stepped aside and held the door open so Eleanor could pass through. "Ignore her. She's definitely in labor."

The nurse moved behind the counter. "Okay, we're busy, but we'll put you in a room as—"

"I need to push," Eleanor said.

Those four magical words stopped everything. The older nurse tore around the counter to my sister's side. She called for a younger nurse to "Get Dr. Gilbert now!"

I hung back, not sure what to do, but Eleanor yelled my name. "Autumn, don't leave me."

"I'm right here."

As another contraction hit, she grasped my hand, squeezing so hard my arm turned white, but I was happy to be there for her. Happy she wasn't trying to get rid of me.

We moved down the hall, and as soon as we reached the exam room, Eleanor leaned forward, clinging to the bed. "The baby's right there. He's right there!"

"Hold on, Dr. Fairchild. Don't push," the nurse said.

Eleanor ignored the command and bore down hard, her face turning purple. Even though I'd experienced that primal need to push, I was shocked to see my sister so out of control and defiant.

When the contraction ended, she took a deep cleansing breath, just like the one they showed on the birthing video. Her voice returned to its normal calm and authoritative state. "He's not going to wait much longer."

"Okay," the nurse said. "Let's get you settled and see where we are."

All modesty was tossed aside as I helped Eleanor remove her clothes, put on a gown, and climb into the bed. The nurse checked her, confirming that yes, not only was Eleanor in labor, but she was completely dilated and fully effaced.

"Just get him out," Eleanor said as the next contraction hit.

"Okay," the nurse said, moving into position.

Panic struck me but to my relief, the door opened and the younger nurse, followed by a familiar looking doctor, entered.

"I told you to get Dr. G.," the older nurse spat.

The younger nurse gestured behind her. "This was the best I could do. Dr. G. is delivering a C-section."

Kyle grinned. "I'll try not to take that personally."

"Kyle?" I said, confused. "What are you doing here? Aren't you supposed to be working in Austin?"

He turned on the faucet, washed his hands, and

slipped on his gloves. "They transferred me here this morning. I guess they knew Dr. Fairchild might need me."

Eleanor held out a hand to stop him from coming any closer. "I'm not having a medical student deliver me!"

Kyle gave his easy, confident smile. "At this point, I'm all you've got. And for the record, I'm a third-year resident, not a med student."

"Dr. Anderson is very capable," the older nurse said. "I only requested Dr. Gilbert because I assumed you'd be more comfortable with him, but I don't think it matters at this point."

Eleanor gave a sigh of exasperation. "Fine."

Kyle examined her and confirmed what the older nurse had determined. Ready or not, the baby was on his way.

Without warning, an animalistic scream shot out of my sister's mouth. Fear gripped me almost as hard as her hand around mine. She raised her head and pushed as if her life depended on it.

And then a tiny, blue creature slipped into my husband's arms. "Here he is," Kyle said, reverently. "A little boy."

He suctioned the baby before placing him on Eleanor's stomach. The older nurse rubbed the infant with a blanket until he let out a loud cry. My heart exploded, and I laughed at the excitement of it all.

Eleanor placed a hand on her son's head and grinned. "Oh, baby! Look at you. You're here! You're here, and you're so beautiful."

The nurse patted Kyle's back. "Well done, Dr. Anderson."

My husband shrugged. "Dr. Fairchild did all the work."

"But you caught him," I said, gazing at my husband in amazement. "If you hadn't been here ..."

Kyle winked at me, and my heart did a little flip flop. He'd just delivered Eleanor's baby! My husband— the doctor!

I'd known he was a doctor, of course. I'd even known he felt comfortable delivering babies, but I'd never seen him in action. Usually, I only saw Kyle in the I-have-to-go-back-to-the-hospital and leave-his-dirty-dishes-in-the-kitchen-sink way. Seeing him in his profession overwhelmed and impressed me. How many marriages could be saved by encouraging spouses to take field trips to each other's place of employment?

The younger nurse motioned to the baby. "What are you going to name him?"

Eleanor smiled. "I was thinking about Kyle."

Kyle's head snapped up. "Seriously?"

"No. I'm joking," Eleanor said for perhaps the first time in her life. She looked down at her baby, and her expression softened. "I'm going to name him Jude ... after Dad."

My heart squeezed tight, and I felt an overwhelming need to protect this newest member of our family. It was amazing the bond I had with a baby I'd just met.

Is that what happened when I was born? Had my mom been present when they pulled me from Angela? Had her love for me been so great she decided to raise me as her own, hiding the painful truth in order to spare my feelings?

I understood that, but why hadn't Eleanor, Dan, or Michael ever said anything? And what compelled them to keep the secret as I got older?

The door opened, and Jim rushed to Eleanor's side, embracing her. "I'm so sorry, honey. I got caught in traffic and—"

Eleanor stiffened and shot her husband a resentful look. She placed her hands protectively over the baby. Jim didn't seem to notice his wife's bitterness. He stared down at his son and his breath hitched. "Oh, wow. He's incredible. Can I hold him?"

Without waiting for permission, Jim scooped up the baby. Immediately, Eleanor criticized him, saying, "You've got to support his head better. He's only a few minutes old."

Trying to please his wife, Jim shifted the baby in his arms. "How's this?"

She responded with a huff that her husband either didn't hear or simply ignored. I glanced at Kyle to see if he felt the tension as well, but he was focused on taking care of my sister.

Later, when Kyle finished and was leaving, Eleanor called after him. "Dr. Anderson?"

Kyle turned around. "Yes?"

"You did a great job. Sorry I overreacted when you walked in the room. I just wasn't expecting you."

Kyle grinned. "No problem."

"And I wasn't expecting you to do such a good job, either. But you did."

He chuckled, the sound rumbling in his chest, making me love him even more. "I'm glad I exceeded your expectations. Congratulations on the baby."

I stared as he walked out the door, my soul full of tenderness for him. "I'll be right back."

I left the room and strode down the hallway until I found Kyle standing at the nurses' station, logging onto a computer. My heart skipped like a silly schoolgirl with a crush on the quarterback.

"Hey," he said as I approached. "Does Eleanor need something?"

"No, it's just ..." I tried to find the right words. "Well, I just wanted to say that was pretty amazing back there. You did a really good job. I didn't know you could do that, and I'm so impressed."

He tried to hide the smile tugging at his lips. "It was a pretty easy delivery."

"*For you*. I couldn't have done something like that. I'm amazed. I mean, I know you're smart and a doctor and have done this before, but I've never seen you do anything so incredible. I—"

Kyle frowned. "What did you think I was doing at the hospital all this time? Sitting around drinking beer and playing video games?"

I flinched at his words until he laughed, and I realized he was joking. Returning his laugh, I said, "Well, those are two activities you're fairly good at."

He chuckled. "Touché."

"Dr. Anderson," a medical assistant called. "Can you check on the patient in room twelve?"

"On my way." Kyle smiled at me. "Gotta go, but I'll see you tonight."

I needed to hug him before he left, so I threw my arms around his slim waist and squeezed tight. "I love you."

I could tell I'd embarrassed him, but I didn't care. He was my husband, and despite the fact he could make me so mad, we were together for better or worse.

He put a limp hand around me. "I love you, too, Autumn."

The attending physician came out of a patient room and shouted, "Way to go, Dr. Anderson! Now, get back to work."

Kyle laughed, then kissed me hard on the lips, leaving me breathless. "We'll continue this tonight."

Chapter 22

*A*FTER LEAVING THE labor and delivery ward, I returned to my mother's room. Someone had restarted the movie, or maybe it was on a continuous roll, because Elvis and the other man were on their way to the fair in the back of Mr. Ling's truck with Sue Lin.

I placed a hand on my mother's forehead and brushed back her hair. "You have another grandson, Mom. Eleanor named him Jude after Dad. He's beautiful."

I waited for a response. Imagined my mother's eyes opening as if waking from a long nap on the couch. During Christmas break, we'd watched a lot of movies together, both of us napping on our separate couches while the boys colored at the kitchen table.

In the movie, Elvis began playing the ukulele and singing, "Take Me to the Fair." My mom used to play that song on the piano, and I remembered it well. I sang along, rocking my shoulders back and forth to the happy music.

Then, in perfect synchronization with the beat, my mom's finger twitched.

Everything inside me froze. "Mom?"

I waited, holding my breath for what seemed like an eternity. "Mom? Can you hear me? Can you hear the music?"

She didn't respond, and no matter how long I waited or how many times I called her name, her body remained still and lifeless. Had her movement been just a mere coincidence? I wanted to believe it was more than that.

Discouraged, I glanced up at the TV, and that's when I saw her. "Mom! Is that you in the movie?"

I jumped to my feet and hit rewind until I found her again. Pressing pause, I moved closer to the TV. My mom was walking next to the geeky redhead from the photo album. They weren't holding hands, but their arms were touching.

On the other side of him walked Ruby. I forwarded the scene slowly and watched Ruby point to the bank building. My mom laughed and followed her friend's gaze.

The geeky redhead's gaze, however, remained completely focused on my mother. He said something, and she leaned into him, swatting him on the arm in a flirtatious manner. They both laughed, and he slung an arm around her shoulders, squeezing her tight.

A sickening feeling of awareness skittered across my chest. I shuddered and pushed the idea away.

***

LATER IN THE week, Darlene met me at my car when I picked up Zane from daycare. She handed me an aluminum wrapped casserole dish, a pre-made salad, and a loaf of French bread. "I'll feed your boys dinner if you take this to Eleanor."

"Don't you want to deliver it yourself?" I asked, placing the meal on the passenger seat.

Ignoring my question, she addressed Logan. "Why don't you go inside, honey? The kids are eating pizza at the kitchen table, and I even have your favorite: plain cheese."

"Yum!" Logan leapt out of the van and ran into Darlene's house without asking my permission or saying good-bye.

I eyed my sister-in-law cautiously. "What's going on? Why don't you want to take the meal to Eleanor yourself?"

"I just spoke to her on the phone, and she's in a prickly mood."

"Great. So you're sending me?"

Darlene laughed. "Hey, you were there when she gave birth. You're probably best friends now."

"Hardly!" Although, if I was honest, I secretly hoped childbirth had brought me closer to my sister. At least close enough that we could have an honest discussion about our family history.

Agreeing to Darlene's arrangement, I drove over to Eleanor's house and parked behind the lawn service trailer. Vilda answered the door and lifted Darlene's dinner from my arms.

"How was girl's night out?" I asked.

"Fabulous."

"Did you dance with any cute boys?"

"You know it!"

I followed her into the living room where Aubrey, wearing a bright yellow sundress with a white sweater and white leggings, practiced the piano. My sister sat on the couch nursing the baby. She looked so disheveled I barely recognized her.

"Darlene sent you dinner, and I brought cookies." I held up the white bakery box tied with a blue ribbon in honor of my new nephew.

Aubrey twirled around on the piano bench. "May I have one, please?"

"Not until after dinner," Eleanor said.

My niece, the wonder child, simply nodded.

"Come on, Eleanor," I said, untying the ribbon and opening the box. "One little cookie isn't going to kill her. It's a special occasion."

Aubrey looked at Eleanor with hopeful eyes. "Please, Mom."

My sister gave an exasperated sigh and reached for a chocolate chip cookie. "We never eat cookies before dinner or during the week. You're the worst aunt ever. You know that, right?"

I grinned. "You should give me a coffee mug with that slogan."

Eleanor shook her head with disgust. "Okay, Aubrey. You can have one cookie, but you have to eat it at the kitchen table."

"Can I take one for Vilda?"

"Of course," I said, eager to fatten the young nanny.

Aubrey chose her cookies and skipped away. I closed the box and set it on the coffee table before sitting across from Eleanor on the brown leather swivel chair. "How's little Jude doing?" I asked, rocking side to side.

"Stop rocking," she snapped. "You're giving me a headache."

"Sorry." I brought the chair to a standstill and pressed my lips together tightly.

Eleanor stifled a yawn. She hadn't looked so ragged after Aubrey was born. Maybe Jude was keeping her up at night.

"I want to show you something," I said, reaching into my purse for the anniversary album.

Recognition filled her eyes. "Where did you find that?"

"In a box in the attic. Do you remember it?"

She nodded. "Angela made it for Mom and Dad's anniversary."

I moved to the couch and set the album on the cushion between us. Eleanor leafed through the pages with a sad smile. When she came to the clipping about Elvis's movie, I asked her about the boy with the red hair. "Was this Ruby's husband? I saw him, Mom, and Ruby in the movie."

A strange look crossed her face. Cradling Jude, she lifted her shirt so he could latch onto the other side. "I don't know who that is."

I studied her carefully. "Why are you lying to me?"

"I'm …"

Jude fussed and kicked his legs. Eleanor put him on her shoulder and yanked down her shirt. "He won't nurse on the left side. I'm so engorged, I'm about to explode."

Why was she avoiding my question? "A friend of mine had that problem. She had to pump on one side until the baby decided it wasn't so bad."

"How long did that take?"

I shrugged. "A few months or so."

Eleanor grumbled, insisting she'd never tolerate that kind of behavior from an infant. She tried nursing the baby again, but Jude wasn't having any of it. Finally, she gave up and pushed herself off the couch. Pacing the living room, she patted the baby's back, bouncing him up and down.

Jude let out a huge burp that echoed across the living room. Eleanor crunched her face and returned to the couch. Without all that air in his belly, Jude nursed from the offending side. My sister relaxed and even smiled.

Instead of pursuing my questions about the boy from the movie, I changed topics. "Did you know Angela was pregnant?"

Her eyes widened, and she looked down at her baby, placing a hand on his head. "Of course I knew she was pregnant."

"Why didn't you ever tell me?"

She shrugged. "It never came up."

"No?"

She shook her head and looked up with a sad smile. "Dad was so mad when he found out."

I swallowed hard. "What did he say?"

"He wanted Angela to give the baby up for adoption, but neither she nor Mother would do that. In the end ..." Eleanor paused. "Well, in the end, he relented and agreed to let Angela and the baby live at home."

"Who was the baby's father?" I blurted out, suddenly struck by the need to know where my biological father was in all of this. Was he still alive? Did he know about me?

Eleanor's expression darkened. "He was a real jerk. He pretty much raped Angela, although our parents didn't know that part."

My stomach contracted. "She told you that?"

"We shared a room. She came home crying the night it happened. She wouldn't tell me at first, but when she did, she begged me not to say anything."

"That's horrible."

She nodded and ran a tender hand over Jude's head. "Despite all that, Angela really wanted the baby."

My heart lifted. "She did?"

"Yes."

We both looked down at Jude. His eyes closed and his head lolled to one side, milk trickling over his fat cheek.

Eleanor pulled down her shirt and held her son close. "Angela said the baby would give her healing, would give her a purpose in life. She was about to graduate from high school and go to college, but I think she was lost."

I knew that feeling. I was almost thirty, and I still felt lost. Still felt as though something was missing.

"When the baby died in the accident, Dan tried to comfort me by insisting it happened so fast, she didn't suffer. Still, losing everyone, including her ..."

I blinked several times. "But you didn't lose the baby. I didn't die."

Confusion marred Eleanor's eyes.

"It's all right. At first I was angry everyone hid it from me, but I'm okay now. Honestly, after Jude was born, I understood why you didn't tell me. You wanted to protect me and give me a normal life."

Eleanor frowned. "What are you talking about?"

I thumped my chest. "Me. I know Angela was my biological mother. I found her medical records, and it's okay. I get it now."

Eleanor stared at me. "Is that what you seriously believe?"

"Of course."

She shook her head. "Oh, Autumn. That's not it at all."

"It's not?"

"No, you've got it all wrong."

Chapter 23

RUBY FOUND OUT about Harold's affair on the day the library chose her design for the new mural in the children's wing. Although devastated, she was determined to stay in the marriage and work things out.

"I'd like to work things out by beating Harold over the head with a frying pan," I told Jude, setting his usual breakfast of eggs, blueberry pancakes, and bacon on the kitchen table.

My husband folded the Seattle Times and set it aside. He pulled me onto his lap and rubbed my thigh. "Please don't resort to physical violence against that man, my dear. You'll be sent to jail and ruin your frying pan. Then where will we be?"

"Men are pigs," I said with a false pout.

He snorted against my neck. "You've always been fond of pigs."

I giggled and squirmed to get away, but he held me tight. Surrendering to his strength, I relaxed against him. After eighteen years of marriage, he was still the love of my *life. Still my soul mate.*

A noticeably pregnant Angela waddled into the kitchen and winced. "Are you sure you want to be doing that? You understand what that leads to, don't you?"

Jude, calmer but not quite at peace with his oldest daughter's pregnancy, growled. "We're married. I take care of your mother, and she takes care of me. See the difference?"

Jude had tried to convince Angela to put her baby up for adoption, but she'd refused. I'd talked to her about an open adoption with Ruby and Harold, thinking that would be the perfect solution, but Angela wanted no part of that.

I climbed off Jude's lap and ran a hand through his hair, which was still thick but now contained several strands of gray I found downright appealing. I smiled. Now would be a great time to hit him with my unexpected news.

He looked up at me and grimaced. "Are you okay, honey? You look a little pale."

Pale? I'm pregnant, I almost said, but the words clung to my throat, refusing to be released into the world and made real. I was forty-one and almost a grandmother. How could I be pregnant?

And yet, when I'd voiced those same words eight years ago, I'd been devastated to suffer a miscarriage. Since then, I'd spent a lot of time talking to Father Tim about feelings of guilt. For a man who'd never been married, he definitely understood women. He assured me my negative feelings toward the pregnancy hadn't caused me to lose the baby.

But now I was pregnant again, and those same apprehensive feelings were back. Why in the world had God granted me another baby? Wasn't my fertility supposed to be winding down about now? Weren't my eggs supposed to be all dried up? Apparently not.

"Nadine?" Jude asked, interrupting my thoughts. "Are you all right?"

"I'm fine. I just haven't had my coffee this morning."

Satisfied with my answer, he returned to his breakfast and morning paper. I walked to the stove where Angela was dishing up the remaining eggs and bacon. "Leave some for your brothers and sister, please."

"But I'm so hungry," she whined. "And the baby wants food."

"Then you can cook more. These are for your siblings."

Angela started to huff but stopped herself. Jude and I had warned her about following our rules if she wished to stay and raise her baby under our roof.

Jude had also talked to the baby's father about child support. Rodney agreed to take responsibility, but he only earned minimum wage working at his father's garage.

"There was a time when you only earned minimum wage," I'd reminded Jude.

"But I had you, and you inspired me to work hard so we could carve out a good life. These two aren't even in love. They're just having a baby together."

"It will work out in the end," I insisted, despite my doubts.

Opening the refrigerator for the orange juice, I tried to imagine myself at the park, pushing my baby and grand-daughter on the swings next to all the young mothers half my age. My own daughter would be receiving hand-me-downs from her niece. Angela, who was convinced she knew everything about pregnancy and babies, would probably give me advice on breastfeeding and changing diapers. I laughed at the absurdity of it all.

Angela eyed me suspiciously. "What's so funny?"

"Nothing," I answered.

LATER THAT DAY, I met Ruby downtown for lunch at Juliet's. Usually I ordered a glass of Chardonnay with my salmon, but since I was pregnant, I feigned a headache and stuck with water.

Ruby frowned. "Why aren't you drinking wine?"

"I told you, I have a headache."

"Wine is good for headaches."

I straightened the silverware and avoided her gaze. I didn't want to admit I was pregnant again, although I suspected Ruby already knew. Anybody who looked closely at me could see the signs. I was already beginning to show, especially in my breasts, which resembled gigantic head-

lights heralding my arrival.

I imagined the only reason Jude hadn't noticed was because he was so distraught over Angela's pregnancy. Plus, he was smart enough not to comment on my recent weight gain.

"How far along are you?" Ruby asked.

"Just a few weeks." I covered my face and shook my head. "I'm so embarrassed. I don't know how it happened."

"Really?"

"You know what I mean. I'm too old to start over again."

"No, you're not." Ruby's voice held a note of longing. "I don't think you're too old at all. In fact ... well, it's a moot point now."

"What?"

She shook her head and stared out the window where a mother with two little boys strolled past, each of them licking an ice cream cone. "Before I found out about stupid Harold's stupid affair, we were talking to the lawyer about adopting another baby."

"Really?"

Ruby nodded and the skin around her eyes tightened. "When Harold agreed to adopt another child, I thought life was pretty perfect. I had a beautiful son, the prospect of another baby, and what I thought was a good marriage. Then I found out about the affair, and everything changed."

I smoothed the cloth napkin in my lap. "Ruby, what exactly happened? You said Harold's former secretary contacted you to confess she'd slept with Harold eight years ago. Why after all this time did she feel the need to tell you?"

Ruby tugged at a loose thread on the tablecloth. "She wants to see Eric."

"Eric? What do you mean?"

Tears pooled in Ruby's eyes, and she shook her head. "She's Eric's mother. She's the secretary who accidentally got pregnant and gave her baby up for adoption."

It took a minute for my brain to comprehend what she was saying. "Does that mean Harold is Eric's biological father?"

She nodded. "I feel so betrayed. Not only did my husband sleep with another woman, but he had a baby with her. He had Eric, and he never told me."

I took a sip of my water, wishing it was wine. No wonder Harold finally agreed to adopt. He was adopting his own kid!

"He swears it was just one night," Ruby continued, "and it never happened again, but how can I trust him after something like that?"

"Oh, Ruby, I'm so sorry."

She took a large swig of her wine. "I went a little crazy and barged into Father Tim's office this morning, demanding to know how he could be so dishonest."

"What'd he say?"

Ruby gave a derisive chuckle that caused me to question her rationality, although what woman wouldn't be half-crazy after discovering her husband's deception. "Tim claims he didn't know, but I'm sure his brother—the adoption lawyer—did."

All I could do was shake my head. "That's incredible."

"Incredible is one word for it." Her voice was sarcastic and irritated. The waiter came to the table and asked if everything was all right. "Not really," Ruby replied.

"We're fine," I said. "Perhaps some more bread?"

"Certainly."

After he left, Ruby apologized. "I'm just so angry, but Father Tim thinks attending Retrouvaille will help."

"What's that?"

"A marriage retreat for couples on the brink of divorce."

I started to tell her she didn't have to go, but Ruby held up a hand to stop me. "I know you don't like Harold. I know you never approved of our marriage, and I'm sure this whole mess only makes you detest him more. Believe me, I understand. I've never been more furious in my entire life. But ... he's my husband. He's Eric's father, and I can't ignore that."

My disdain for Harold had waned over time, but this stunt reignited my contempt. Regardless, Ruby needed my support right now. Not my judgment. Still, how in the world was she going to overcome something like this?

"Ruby, are you sure you don't want to just end things with Harold?" You can do better, I thought but didn't say.

She stared at me for a long time, and I worried I'd overstepped. I started to apologize, but she didn't let me finish.

"I'm afraid if I can't work things out with Harold, he'll take away my son. So, for that reason, I have to find a way to make my marriage work. At least until Eric is older. I can't lose him. I can't!"

I simply nodded, my own eyes burning with tears. Ruby was trapped in a difficult situation, and as a mother, I completely understood her choice.

Blotting her face with her napkin, Ruby forced a brave smile. "I need you to do a favor for me."

"Of course. Anything."

"I need you to watch Eric while Harold and I attend the retreat."

I told her I would, wanting to help, but years later, I would regret this moment. I would regret nodding my head and insisting Eric would be fine while Ruby went away with Harold to save her marriage.

But mostly, I would regret that this was the last time Ruby and I had our friendship intact.

This was the last time we were together before the police officers knocked on my front door, informing me that my husband and daughter had been killed.

Chapter 24

*I*SAT ON the living room couch at Eleanor's house holding Jude. "Are you sure Angela couldn't possibly be my mother? I've heard stories of babies surviving horrible accidents because they were protected in their mother's womb."

"That can happen," Eleanor agreed. "But not in this case. I know because I kept asking Dan the same question until he finally showed me the newspaper article. There was a picture of the car, and trust me, *nobody* could've survived that accident. Not even a baby."

I mulled this over, exploring every possibility. "So Mom and Angela were pregnant together? Mom really had me when she was forty-one?"

Eleanor groaned. "Forty-one isn't that old. Just three years older than me. And yes, Angela and Mother were pregnant together."

To prove her point, she stood and walked into her

home office. Moments later, she returned with a small photo box. Sitting across from me, she dug through the photos until she found what she was looking for.

"Here," she said, handing me the photo.

I took the picture and laughed. The image showed my mom and Angela, both of them wearing floral maternity dresses and proudly holding their bulging bellies.

I held up the picture. "Can I keep this?"

"I'll make you a copy."

"Thanks."

Jude grew heavy in my arms and gave a huge yawn. I smiled as he closed his eyes and fell asleep.

"I should put him in his crib," Eleanor said. "I don't want him getting used to being held all the time."

I tightened my grip around my nephew. "He's a baby. He's supposed to be held all the time."

She didn't argue but sat back on the couch defeated and changed the subject. "I was nine that summer and so excited to have both my mother and sister pregnant. I offered to let the babies sleep in my room."

"Didn't you share a room with Angela?"

"I did, but Dad and the boys converted the garage into a bedroom for Angela and her baby."

The idea of my father doing something like that warmed me. "I wish I could've met him."

Eleanor gave a sad smile. "He was wonderful. Even though he grumbled about Angela's pregnancy, he built that room for her and found a slightly used crib. In fact, that's where they went the night of the accident—to pick up the crib. Dad wanted to make sure Angela liked it."

My heart fell, devastated that such a joyful outing had turned sour.

"Before that, though, I was happy," Eleanor continued. "We all were, except when Mother used Angela's unplanned pregnancy as an excuse to lecture us about pre-marital sex."

Aubrey came into the living room at that moment. "What's sex?"

I looked at Eleanor and smiled. My sister returned my smile and shook her head.

"What's so funny?" Aubrey asked.

Eleanor, who never shied from telling her daughter the truth, took a deep breath. "Sex is how you make a baby."

Aubrey gently kissed her brother's head. "Oh, can I have sex?"

I burst out laughing, but Eleanor shouted a defiant, "No. Not until you're married. And have your degree."

"Can I hold Jude then?"

"Sure." I scooted over to make room for her on the

couch.

She sat beside me, and I carefully transferred the baby to her arms.

"Don't you just love him so much, Aunt Autumn?" she asked, smiling up at me.

I returned her smile. "I do."

THAT NIGHT, KYLE stayed at the hospital since he was on call and had two women in labor. Over the phone, I told him all about my conversation with Eleanor.

"Do you feel better, knowing your mom didn't lie to you?" he asked.

"I do," I said, even though it wasn't entirely true. Seeing that redheaded kid in the movie with my mom had made me tense. I'd wanted to talk to Kyle about it, but he was called into a delivery.

"Sorry, babe. We'll talk later?"

"Sure."

We didn't get a chance to talk later because I fell asleep in Zane's bed. Around two in the morning, I awoke with my son's foot jammed in my face. I got out of bed, turned Zane around, and kissed him goodnight. In the kitchen, I checked my phone and saw Kyle had called at ten. I hated to call him now if he was sleeping, but I was wide awake, so I made myself a cup of chamomile tea and looked through my parents' anniversary album again.

It was interesting that almost every page contained a picture of Ruby. If she was such great friends with my mother, what in the world happened to end their friendship? And where was she now?

I turned to the picture of my parents with Ruby and the redheaded boy in front of the Space Needle. As carefully as I could, I peeled the picture from the scrapbook so I could read the inscription on the back. *Nadine, Jude, Ruby, and Tim. Hollywood's next biggest stars.*

Tim?

Was this my mother's Tim? The "My Darling Nadine" Tim? All my instincts told me yes.

Collecting my laptop from the bedroom, I brought it back to the kitchen. Eleanor said she'd seen a photo in the newspaper of our dad's car after the accident. Was that something I could find in the online archives?

It took a little effort, but I accessed the *Seattle Times* for 1985. Because I didn't know the exact date of the accident, I started with the first of August and worked forward until I came to the headline "Fatal Car Crash Kills Three."

My hands trembled as I clicked the link to the article. The picture from the newspaper showed a squished pile of metal and a random sandal. Shuddering, I closed my eyes, wanting to erase the image from my mind. Eleanor had been right. Nobody could have survived that accident. Especially not a little baby.

Taking a deep breath, I opened my eyes. Then I scrolled past the devastating picture and read the article.

On Saturday evening, a station wagon driven by local resident, Jude Kingsley, ran a stop sign and crashed into a semi-truck, killing all three occupants in Mr. Kingsley's car. The driver of the truck sustained only minor injuries.

Victims included Jude Kingsley, age forty-one, his daughter Angela Kingsley, and Eric McCoy, age eight, son of Ruby and Harold McCoy.

Oh, no! My stomach lurched and bile burned my throat. Ruby's son had been killed in the accident. Was this what destroyed my mother's relationship with her best friend?

Returning my attention to the article, I continued reading. The police didn't suspect drugs, alcohol, or even excessive speed were an issue. My father had simply run the stop sign. According to the article, there had been three recent accidents at this intersection, and officials were discussing actions to install a traffic light or at least make the stop sign more visible.

The article went on to talk about my father's success and involvement in the community. It also mentioned the fact he had no criminal record or prior driving violations.

> *Jude Kingsley leaves behind a wife and three children. Eric McCoy is survived by his parents, Ruby and Harold McCoy.*
>
> *Father Tim O'Connor, the family's priest and longtime friend, stated, "All three victims will be deeply missed. It will take a long time for our community to heal from such a great loss." Father Tim also stressed the need to address the dangerous intersection.*

I wiped my hands on my jeans. *Father Tim O'Connor?*

My pulse raced as I opened a new window on my internet browser. A search for Father Tim O'Connor took me to a website for a church in Ireland. I clicked on the link to the parish priests, and there he was!

He was several years older than he'd been in the pictures from Angela's photo album, but it was him all right. Even though his hair was now silver, he had the same thick brow and ruddy complexion. Father Tim O'Connor.

He hadn't been Ruby's husband. He was a priest!

So why had he addressed my mother as "My Darling Nadine" and signed his note "all my love, Tim?"

Sitting back in my chair, I allowed my mind to sift through everything. A sick feeling tore at my gut. Was my mother romantically involved with a priest? I couldn't imagine her doing something so unethical. Maybe the Tim who'd written the letter was an entirely different Tim. It was a common name after all.

I suppose I wouldn't know until I read the letter myself.

IN THE MORNING, I drove to my mother's house, determined to get the letter, but I couldn't find it. I turned the book on her nightstand upside down and shook out the pages. I looked under and all around the bed.

How in the world could it have disappeared? Had someone taken it? Had the cleaning lady accidentally thrown it away?

I began searching through my mother's desk, but stopped since it felt too much like violating her privacy. Too much like accepting the fact she might not recover.

Discouraged, I took the boys to visit my mom in the hospital. She'd been there a week and looked awful. Her skin had turned a sickening yellow, and blue veins raced across her hands, making the bright and shiny nail polish look out of place.

I'd been so hopeful the day her finger twitched to the music of Elvis. I'd believed she was going to wake up. Today, however, doubt curled up in my stomach, refusing to budge.

A nurse about my age with blonde hair, blue eyes, and lots of curves checked my mom's vitals. She wrote something down in her chart and gave me a kind smile. "You just missed your brother. He's such a good son. He comes every morning and every evening."

"That sounds like Dan."

"No, not Dan," the nurse said. "The other one. The one who likes ice cream? Michael?"

The tenderness in her voice caught me off guard. "Michael? The one with the long hair and beard? And the tattoo of Mickey on his forearm?"

She blushed and quickly turned away to straighten my mom's bed sheets. "He eats his breakfast at her bedside while watching *Wheel of Fortune*."

I stared at the nurse, shocked. Michael hadn't mentioned any of this to me. Even though there was a huge age gap between us, we were pretty close. After his wife left, Michael and I spent a lot of time talking on the phone. And I'd been the first to learn he was thinking about quitting his job to go back to school.

Logan leaned over to help the nurse straighten my mom's bed sheets. "Grandma *loves Wheel of Fortune*."

The nurse beamed. "I think your uncle does, too. He's brilliant at guessing the words. I keep telling him he should try out for the show."

Thoughts of Michael eating breakfast while watching TV with our comatose mother tore me up. Unlike Dan, Eleanor, and me, Michael was no longer married. He didn't have kids or a serious girlfriend or even a dog. How would he handle it if our mother actually passed? For that matter, how would I?

"Can we go home now?" Zane asked. "This room smells bad." Although he was dressed identical to his big brother in an oversized sweatshirt, shorts, and black rubber boots, at that moment, he looked incredibly young.

Wrapping my arms around him, I kissed the top of his head. "We'll go in a little bit, okay?"

"But I'm hungry," he whined.

"Hey, I'm hungry, too," Logan said.

I exhaled, understanding their desire to leave this depressing room. Some of the flowers my mom's friends had sent were starting to wilt, and all the cheerful "Get Well" cards mocked her hopeless condition.

"We'll stay with Grandma a little longer, then we'll go downstairs and get a snack at the cafeteria," I said.

The nurse adjusted her stethoscope as she moved toward the door to leave. "Oh, the cafeteria serves fabulous strawberry ice cream."

Both boys brightened, but I shook my head. "I think it's a little too early for ice cream. We just finished breakfast."

She shrugged and held the door open with her hip. "It's five o'clock somewhere."

The door closed behind her, and Logan swished his mouth to the side. "How long are we going to stay?"

I glanced at my phone. "Ten more minutes."

He set his digital watch, lest I forget, something I tended to do quite often. "Okay. Ten minutes. I mean nine minutes and fifty-nine seconds. Nine minutes and fifty-eight seconds ..."

He continued counting down the seconds until he reached eight minutes fifty-three seconds. "This is so boring. What are we supposed to be doing?"

I nodded at Zane who was standing on one leg in modified tree pose. "What about yoga?"

Logan stomped his foot. "I'm not in the mood for yoga."

Zane placed both feet on the ground. "Yeah, me neither. Want to play coma?"

Coma was their latest game, which basically involved one of them lying still while the other person talked about their day and the weather. I'd caught them playing it while I was making dinner the other night.

Logan glanced at his watch, then looked out the window without informing us of the time. "I don't want to play coma. I'm tired of that game."

"Yeah, me too," Zane said.

Me, three, I thought.

I beckoned them over with my hand. "Come talk to Grandma. Tell her what you've been doing in school."

Both boys reluctantly came over and rambled off a few interesting tidbits. Logan was excited about his upcoming field trip to the turtle refuge, but Zane complained it wasn't fair he couldn't go on the field trip, too.

Then the room grew silent, and I just wanted to leave. I hated the stale stench of my mom's room. Hated the fluorescent lighting and pale color of the walls. Hated the fact that every day my mother was slipping further and further away from us and the life she'd once enjoyed.

Grasping for something to say, I talked about Eleanor's baby Jude and his cute little face. I told my mom about Aubrey, and how she was such a good big sister. Then I, too, grew silent.

I wanted to ask about so many things; the letter, Tim, Ruby. But what would be the point? She couldn't answer me and may never be able to do so again.

Feeling discouraged, I gathered my things and left with the boys. In the elevator, we ran into an enthusiastic Kyle who told us he'd been up all night, delivering his first breech.

Even though his eyes were bloodshot from lack of sleep, I'd never seen him so excited about work. Maybe delivering babies was his calling in life. Maybe I should stop fighting and let him do the fellowship. It was only one more year.

I winced at the thought and vowed not to think about it until Kyle mentioned it. Maybe on his own, he'd conclude the fellowship wasn't good for our family.

"Dad," Logan said, taking Kyle by the hand. "You should come with us to the cafeteria for ice cream, so we can celebrate the *beach* baby."

Kyle chuckled. "Isn't it a little early for ice cream?"

"It's five o'clock somewhere," Zane said.

That made Kyle laugh, and he gave me a *don't-we-have-the-cutest-kids-in-the-world* smile. He scooped up Zane and ruffled his hair. "Okay, buddy, since you put it that way, how can I refuse? Ice cream it is."

In the cafeteria, we sat by the window overlooking the hospital's courtyard playground. When the boys finished eating, they ran outside to play while Kyle and I stayed at the table.

My husband was quiet, passing his coffee cup back and forth between his hands. "I know this isn't good timing because of your mom and everything ... but they want to know my final decision about the fellowship."

My heart sank. "When do they need to know?"

"Two weeks. But if I can tell them sooner ..."

I swallowed hard. "So, you still want to do it?"

He looked at the boys, then back at me. "I do."

Before his trip to Haiti, we'd discussed all the details that extra year would entail. Knowing how hard it would be just made me want to throw a fit and tell him no. Was it wrong for me to feel this way?

I ran my finger over a crack in the table. "Can we think about it a little longer?"

"Yeah." He leaned back in his chair and folded his arms across his chest. I stared at the muscles in his biceps and forearms, thinking how much I loved those arms around me. I didn't want to hold Kyle back, but I was tired of missing him all the time. Tired of living so much of my life without him.

Avoiding further discussion of the fellowship, I told him about the newspaper article, Father Tim O'Connor, Eric McCoy, and not being able to find the letter at my mom's house.

"Wow," he said. "You've been busy. That's a lot to digest."

"I know. Do you think the Tim who wrote the letter and Father Tim are one in the same?"

My husband looked out the window and waved at the boys who were on top of the play structure. They waved back before throwing themselves down the slide headfirst.

Kyle turned back to me with a serious expression on his face. "I can't imagine your mother doing anything as unethical as having an affair with a priest, can you?"

I exhaled and shook my head. "No, I can't. But I was thinking about calling him and letting him know she's in the hospital. I'm just afraid of what he'll tell me."

Kyle slid his hand across the table and clasped mine. "I never knew your father, but judging by what little your mom has ever said about him, they were in love. Your mother loves the church, too. I can't imagine her ever violating her beliefs and having an affair with a priest."

Unexpected tears stung my eyes. "Thanks for saying that."

Chapter 25

*A*S THE BOYS and I left the hospital, dark angry thunderclouds rumbled overhead. We drove across town for story time at the library where we ran into Darlene and her four boys.

Technically, some of my nephews were too old for story time, but the town's beloved librarian, Mrs. Foss, often invited speakers that appealed to readers of all ages. Today's guest was a local falconer and his falcon Horus.

After Logan and Zane settled on the floor next to their cousins, I asked my sister-in-law if she minded watching the boys while I bought a cup of coffee.

"Go for it," she said.

"What can I bring you?"

"Small vanilla latte." She reached for her wallet, but I stopped her. "Don't worry about it. It's my treat."

Walking toward the library's coffee shop, I took out my phone and opened the web page for Father Tim's church in Ireland. I took a deep breath and punched the phone number under his picture. My pulse pounded as the phone rang. Should I just hang up? Ireland was six hours ahead of us, maybe I'd be interrupting his dinner hour.

"Father Tim," a man with a slight Irish accent answered.

My mind froze. I hadn't expected to reach him directly. I thought I'd reach his voice mail or a secretary or someone else. "Hello?" Both my voice and my nerve wavered.

"Yes, dear?"

"Father Tim … I'm Autumn Anderson. Jude Kingsley was my father. I …" My throat constricted. What exactly was I supposed to say?

"Autumn," he said slowly. "I knew your father quite well. We went to high school together, and he was a good friend of mine."

I hadn't expected him to talk about my father. I dug my water bottle out of my purse and took a huge gulp. "My mother was in an accident. She's in a coma, and we're not sure if she's going to make it."

He inhaled sharply. "Oh, goodness. What happened?"

I told him everything, except my suspicion about his relationship with my mother and the missing letter.

"Give me the name of the hospital," he demanded.

"Cedar Bridge General. It's in Turtle Lake, Texas."

"Okay, I'll be there as soon as I can. I'll text you my flight information, but if you can't pick me up at the airport, I'll take a cab to the hospital. Hopefully, I won't be too late."

AFTER STORY TIME, I drove to Eleanor's house without calling first. It may sound strange, but my sister and I didn't have the kind of relationship where we just showed up at each other's houses unannounced. Being with her for the birth of Jude had improved things, but I was taking a risk by coming over without calling.

At the front door, Zane rang the bell several times before Eleanor finally answered, looking dreadful. She was dressed in a ratty T-shirt and yoga pants, and her hair was pulled into a messy ponytail. Unless you counted what looked like yesterday's smudged mascara beneath her eyes, she wore no makeup. Somewhere in the background, Jude was screaming.

Logan kicked off his boots and stepped inside. "Aunt Eleanor, did you know your baby was crying?"

Aubrey came to the door wearing a pink sundress and purple fuzzy earmuffs. "The whole neighborhood knows he's crying. He's supposed to take a nap, but he doesn't want to."

Eleanor gave me an exasperated look. "I don't know what's wrong with him. He barely slept last night, and he won't stop crying. I just need him to be quiet before I lose my mind."

"Did you check his ears?" I asked, trying to be helpful.

Eleanor glared at me.

"What? A lot of babies get ear infections."

Her glare intensified. "Even though my baby's screaming is destroying my brain cells, I still have my medical degree. I still know a thing or two about children."

She spun around and strode down the hall. The boys and I followed her into the living room, which was uncharacteristically messy. Magazines, dishes, and library books littered the coffee table, and there was a burp towel on the couch. I would've made a sarcastic comment if Jude's howling hadn't distracted me.

Logan approached the bassinet and examined the baby carefully just like he'd done in the hospital with my mother. "Hmm ... no scorpions or obvious flesh wounds ... maybe he just wants to be held. When Zane was a baby, he cried all the time unless we held him. Remember, Mom?"

I nodded and waited for Eleanor's backlash. She'd

chastised me severely for constantly holding Zane, insisting I was creating a monster by catering to him. If I would just read her book ... if I would just let him cry it out ... if I would just put him on a schedule.

But I couldn't do it. I hated hearing him cry. Everything inside me said to hold him because as long as he was in my arms, he was happy. So he'd spent the first year of his life against my chest in a sling. To my relief, he'd learned to sit up, crawl, and walk at a normal age. And given the fact he was turning out to be a pretty cute kid, I obviously hadn't completely destroyed him.

"You could put him in the swing," Zane said, pointing across the room.

Eleanor exhaled. "He likes the swing and stops crying whenever I put him in it, but—"

Jude let out a blood-curdling shriek and my body tensed. "For all that is holy, Eleanor, put him in there!"

My sister bit her lip. "What if he develops poor sleep habits?"

"His crying is going to damage our hearing," I insisted. "Besides, Zane took the majority of his naps in the swing and he's fine."

As if to prove my point, Zane squatted and pushed up to a headstand. "I'm better than fine. I can stand on my head for thirty-two seconds."

"Not if I push you down," Logan said, doing exactly

that.

Zane toppled over. "I'm going to kill you," he yelled.

Logan laughed. "Not if I kill you first."

Eleanor pressed a hand to her temple as the boys chased each other through the living room. Aubrey shook her head with disapproval until I intervened and put both boys in time out on the couch.

Meanwhile, Eleanor scooped up her baby and marched toward the swing, giving me a warning glance. "Don't you dare say anything."

"I wouldn't dream of it."

Jude did the gasping-for-breath thing that babies do when they've been crying for a long time. Eleanor jiggled him until he settled down and fell asleep in her arms.

"Ah, he just wanted his Mama," Zane said, imitating my mom's voice perfectly.

Although I couldn't be certain since Eleanor's back was turned toward me, I was pretty sure Zane's comment caused her to smile.

WE SENT THE kids upstairs to the playroom, and I made a pot of coffee. "He's beautiful," I said, joining Eleanor on the couch where she was gazing at her sleeping son.

"He is," she agreed, fingering his earlobe. "But how am I supposed to get anything done if I'm holding him all day?"

I looked around the messy living room. Even the couch cushions were askew, something I imagined was driving Eleanor crazy. "Maybe you aren't supposed to get anything done right now. You go back to work in six weeks, right? Maybe until then you're just supposed to be Jude and Aubrey's mom."

She sighed and looked toward the laundry room door, which was slightly ajar. I followed her gaze, and when I caught sight of the mess inside, I gasped.

I jumped to my feet and strode across the room. "What on earth happened?" I pushed open the door, shocked to see dirty clothes, wet towels, baby blankets, and socks covering every surface. "Wow! I had no idea your family was capable of producing such a mess. It's extraordinary." I pulled out my phone and snapped a picture.

"If you put that on Facebook, I'll smash your phone," Eleanor said, standing outside the door. "It's disgusting. What kind of a person lives like this?"

I gave a grunt of disbelief. "Every mother with little kids lives like this. Trust me, your immaculate house is the exception."

"Well, it's not immaculate today, and we certainly

didn't live like this when Aubrey was a baby."

"Aubrey was a *different* baby. She was a textbook perfect baby who didn't require a lot of attention. Most babies aren't like that, Eleanor. You got lucky with Aubrey. Honestly, for a leading expert on childhood behavior, you can be a little dense."

I meant my last sentence as a joke, but I could tell I went too far. My sister bristled, shoved open the door, and stepped into the mess. Still holding Jude, she removed a load of clothes from the dryer and chucked them on the counter. A clean T-shirt tumbled to the floor.

"Unbelievable," she muttered, picking up the T-shirt and pounding it on the counter.

I nudged her aside. "I'm sorry. Here, let me help."

"Just hold Jude." She thrust the baby into my arms and returned to the laundry.

I felt guilty for teasing her. She probably did see herself as a leading expert in childhood behavior, and I'd just belittled her. It wasn't her fault she only had one perfect child and didn't understand how the rest of us lived. "I'm sorry, Eleanor. I didn't mean to give you a bad time."

She shrugged and opened the washing machine to transfer the wet clothes to the dryer. "It's fine."

Jude puckered his lips as though preparing to cry. I

rocked him from side to side, and thankfully, he sank deeper into my arms and fell back asleep. Shifting him in the crook of my elbow, I began folding the laundry, but Eleanor stopped me. "Just go check on your boys and make sure they're not destroying the playroom. It's the one room that's actually clean."

I pushed down my frustration, refusing to be offended. Even on her best day, my sister could be abrasive. I'd obviously pushed her to the limit, and she needed a break. Deciding to be generous, I left.

With Jude in my arms, I climbed the stairs and found the boys quietly playing with pink Legos while Aubrey sat on the couch reading to them. Eleanor had been right about the playroom—it was extremely clean. The toys were neatly arranged on clearly labeled shelves, and the dress-up clothes were hung on hooks according to color.

"Everything okay up here?" I asked, feeling inspired and ashamed that at our house, the boys simply threw all their toys into one large plastic toy box I'd bought at a garage sale.

Logan placed a finger over his mouth and shushed me. "Aubrey's reading us a story about a dinosaur that went to space."

"Perfect," I said.

Zane placed a hand on his hip. "Mom, you should

teach Logan how to read."

"I know how to read," Logan said, making a fist.

"Yeah, but not as good as Aubrey. She even makes the voices of the different people like Mom does."

Logan raised his fist and looked at me as if expecting me to say *Sure, go ahead and slug your brother. You have my blessing.*

I shook my head in warning. "Logan is a great reader, and soon you'll know how to read, too."

Satisfied with my answer, Logan lowered his fist. Aubrey returned to reading the book, and both boys resumed playing with the Legos. I crept down the stairs, regretting my intrusion. You would think with all of Eleanor's money, she'd install a video camera in the playroom accessible from the kitchen.

Returning to the living room, I placed Jude in the swing. His eyes widened at first. "Don't you dare," I said in a singsong voice. I turned the switch on high, and moments later he fell back asleep.

In the laundry room, I told Eleanor I was going to help her take care of the mess. "Then I'll make us both a nice cup of coffee."

"You and Mother drink too much coffee," she told me, not for the first time.

I gritted my teeth. "Okay, we'll have a lovely glass of tap water. Doesn't that sound delicious and heartwarming on a cold winter's day?"

"Just go take care of your kids. Don't worry about me, I'm fine."

"You're not fine," I said, folding one of Aubrey's sundresses and setting it on top of the pile with the others. "Whether you want to admit it or not, you need my help. Or someone's help. Where is Vilda, by the way? Did she run to the grocery store?"

Tears welled up in Eleanor's eyes, and she shook her head. Before I could feel sorry for her, she yanked Aubrey's neatly folded dress from my pile and shook it out. "Like this," she said, folding it into a perfect rectangle before slamming it on the pile. "They all need to be folded the same, or they won't stack correctly in the dresser drawer."

I gritted my teeth. "I'm trying to be nice, but I really want to slap you right now."

She pressed her lips together tightly but said nothing. I turned away and focused my attention on sorting the dirty laundry. Surely I couldn't mess up *that* simple task, but apparently I could. Eleanor complained I needed to keep the dish towels separate from the bath towels.

She pointed at the offending pile of wet and disgusting towels. "You can't just wash everything together."

"Says who?"

"Says everybody. If you want to help me, you have to do it my way, otherwise, just go watch TV or something."

"Where's Vilda, and why are you being so rude?"

Fire raged in her eyes, and she pounded her fist on the counter. I waited for her to yell. Instead, her shoulders slumped forward, and she hung her head.

"Eleanor, what's going on?"

She straightened and picked up a pair of Jim's boxers. Methodically, she folded them into a neat little bundle and placed them on the counter. "It's the oldest cliché in the book. Jim slept with her."

"With who? Vilda?"

She nodded. "He says it was a mistake and only happened once, but—"

"Oh, Eleanor …"

She started folding another pair of boxers, and something inside me snapped. I ripped the boxers out of her hands and threw them on the floor.

"What are you doing?" she asked, horrified.

"What are *you* doing folding your cheating husband's underwear?"

She looked at me, then at Jim's boxers, then back at me. "You're right," she said, astonished as if she never imagined I could be right about anything.

"Of course I'm right. He can do his own laundry."

Eleanor frowned. "I don't think he knows how."

"Well, too bad for him."

For the next twenty minutes, my sister and I worked together in silence until the laundry room reached some semblance of order. Eleanor put away her clean and correctly folded clothes while I helped the kids put on their jackets so they could go outside to play. It'd stopped raining, and the sun was peeking through the clouds.

In the kitchen, I poured a tiny bit of wine into two coffee mugs and carried them outside where I found Eleanor sitting on the back porch under a heat lamp. I handed her one of the mugs, and she scowled. "This isn't coffee."

"No, it's better than coffee. It's wine."

She hesitated, then took a sip and shook her head. "Jude is sleeping in the swing, and I'm drinking wine out of a coffee mug in the middle of the day. What's wrong with this picture?"

"Nothing." I raised my mug and clinked it against hers. "This is motherhood at its finest. Not something I'd recommend every day, but in moments like this, I think it's okay."

She stared into her mug. "Why didn't you use a wine glass? A mug makes it seem like we're doing something illegal."

"I was afraid the wine glass might break around the kids. A mug just seems safer. More sturdy."

"That makes sense. Maybe I'll put that tip in my next book." She smiled weakly, then without warning, she began to weep.

I hesitated a moment, not sure what to do. Eleanor never cried. Ever. Reluctantly, I placed a hand on her shoulder. "Hey, it's okay."

She wiped her tears with the back of her hand. "I don't know what's wrong with me. Ever since Jude was born, I can't stop falling apart."

"Oh, Eleanor." I gave her a tight squeeze. "Let's see … your mother is in a coma, your husband is a slimeball, and you just gave birth to a colicky baby. Am I missing anything?"

She pushed out a breath. "No."

"Oh!" I said, clapping my hands. "I know what I'm missing. You're probably feeling fat because you can't fit into your pre-pregnancy clothes yet, and you have nothing to wear."

She blinked, her brow wrinkling. "No, I can fit into my pre-pregnancy clothes. They're a little tight, but they fit. I only gained about fifteen pounds during the pregnancy."

"Of course you did." I swirled my mug of wine. "Now, I really hate you."

Chapter 26

*I*N AN UNPRECEDENTED move, Eleanor spontaneous-ly invited me to stay for lunch. Together, we made pimento cheese sandwiches and cut apple slices. After eating, I convinced her to take a nap while I looked after the kids.

She awoke two hours later in a much better mood. We bundled everyone up and walked down to the lake.

The lake was beautiful during the summer, but I loved how it looked during the winter. Loved the way the big gray sky met the rippling water. Loved how even though the live oaks remained green and strong, the landscape was desolate due to the barren deciduous trees. Somehow, I found the bleakness oddly comforting, and today was no exception.

"Thanks for letting me sleep," Eleanor said, as we stood on the shore, watching the kids chuck rocks into the water.

"You're welcome."

Jude started to fuss, so Eleanor sat on the bench and nursed him. I sat beside her and told her about reading the newspaper article online last night.

Gathering my courage, I asked the difficult question, most on my mind. "So, is Father Tim the same Tim who sent Mom the letter? Is that why you acted so strange when I mentioned him?"

She started to deny it but changed her mind and simply nodded.

"Is Mom having an affair with him?" Given Jim's indiscretion with Vilda, I regretted the question as soon as it was out, but I had to ask.

"What?" Eleanor's eyes widened. "No."

"No? Then why would a priest write to Mom addressing her as *My Darling Nadine*? And why would you lie about not knowing him?"

She tightened the scarf around her neck. "It's a long story."

"I have time."

She glanced at the kids, who had moved on to throwing sticks into the water. "Remember what I said about people having secrets? I think this secret is best left untold."

"It might be too late for that," I said. "I called Father Tim. I told him about Mom, and he's flying from Ireland to see her."

All the color drained from Eleanor's face. "Oh, Autumn. You shouldn't have done that." Her voice sounded small. Vulnerable. Frightened.

"Why not? What are you hiding from me?"

She closed her eyes for a long time. When she opened them and spoke, her voice was shaky. "I always thought Father Tim was the reason Mother and Ruby lost their friendship."

I kept my mouth closed as she looked at the ground and slowly exhaled. "After the accident, Mother was depressed. We all were, but she couldn't get out of bed. I know that's impossible to believe, given how active she is, but the depression crippled her. Seeing her like that was incredibly disturbing, and I was afraid the doctors would send her away."

"Oh, Eleanor." My heart ached for that terrified child my sister had been. How horrible to endure the loss of your father and sister, and then fear your mother might be taken away.

"People from the church and neighborhood dropped off meals," Eleanor said. "But we wouldn't have made it without Father Tim. He was wonderful, bringing us groceries and driving us to school."

"I don't understand. Why did Father Tim's help cause a problem between Mom and Ruby? Because of Eric?"

She eyed me warily before reaching into her diaper bag and pulling out the crumpled letter I'd found on my mother's nightstand.

My pulse jolted. "Why do you have the letter?"

"I drove to Mom's house after leaving the hospital that first night—after you were so adamant about contacting Tim."

"Why?"

She licked her lip. "I was afraid."

"Afraid of what?"

As way of explanation, she unfolded the letter and read it to me.

My Darling Nadine,

I'm sorry I upset you when we last spoke on the phone, but it's time, sweetheart. Time to tell them the truth. Time to tell them about the choice you made, and the choice I made to help you.

"Choice?" I asked, interrupting. "What was the choice?"

Eleanor's face tensed. "Let me just finish reading it, okay?"

"Okay."

I know you're afraid, but you don't have to do this alone. I love you, and I'm here for you.

I wasn't able to tell you this on the phone, but

Ruby's daughter is trying to find you. She's plan-
ning a party for her mother's seventieth birthday,
and she wants both of us to be there.

I have no doubt this beautiful and capable
woman will succeed, even without my help. That's
what I was trying to tell you before we were ...
disconnected.

I know you're angry and scared, but please
don't shut me out. Please don't ignore me. I'm not
the enemy.

All my love,
Tim

My sister handed me the letter and I reread it, wondering what it all meant. "Why wouldn't Mom want
Ruby's daughter to find her?"

Eleanor brushed a speck of dirt off Jude's head. "After the accident, but before you were born, I heard
Father Tim and Mother arguing about the baby. He
said he loved Mother and only wanted what was best for
her."

"And ..."

Eleanor hesitated before staring straight at me with a
frightened expression. "And they were talking about
adoption. Father Tim wanted Mother to give you up for
adoption."

My breath caught. "What? Why?"

"I don't know. Maybe he thought she wouldn't be able to take care of a baby. Maybe he wanted to give the baby to Ruby in compensation for Eric's death. Or maybe there was another reason."

"Are you sure?" I asked. "I spoke to Father Tim on the phone. He seemed kind and concerned about Mom. I can't imagine him taking away her baby."

"Yes, but he adored Eric. He spent just as much time at Ruby's house helping her and Mr. McCoy as he did us. People process grief differently. Maybe his argument with Mother about adoption was his way of coping. All I know is, after I overheard their conversation, I stopped trusting him. I feared he might take you, and then help the doctors send Mother away."

I covered Eleanor's hand with my own. "You were just a child. I can only imagine how scared you must've been."

She closed her eyes, nodded, and pulled her hand away.

"He can't hurt us," I said. "Regardless of his intentions back then, he can't hurt you now."

"I know." She sounded raw and uncertain.

I tried to lighten the mood by saying, "Trust me, Eleanor, nobody wants to adopt a woman with two rambunctious kids."

She managed a weak smile but remained disturbed. "Did something else happen?" I dared to ask. "Did Father Tim ever try to hurt you or—"

"No," she insisted. "No, nothing like that. Up until I heard him arguing with Mother, I adored him. As an adult, I can understand he was just acting in our family's best interest, but as a kid ..." She shuddered. "As a kid, I was scared to death. I was afraid if he could convince her to give the baby away, he might be able to convince her to ... to give *me* away."

"*Oh, Ellie.*" I rubbed her back, searching for the right words to comfort her. "Everything worked out okay. Mom kept me, and she kept you, and despite everything, we're still a family."

She nodded and we sat in silence, watching Aubrey instruct the boys on how to make a river leading from a large boulder to the sea. The children's cheeks were flushed, and all three of them had removed their jackets. Eleanor must've been severely shaken because she didn't even comment on Aubrey's bare arms.

I looked at the letter and read it again, dying to know what was meant by the choice. "You said Father Tim ruined Mom and Ruby's friendship. What did you mean by that?"

She watched a large vulture cross the sky, its big black wings spread wide. "I always thought he promised the baby to Ruby, and she got mad when Mother kept you … but maybe there was something else."

"Yeah, maybe," I said, hoping I'd be brave enough to ask Father Tim about it when he arrived.

Chapter 27

*A*FTER THE HORRIBLE *accident that took so many loved ones, I had no idea how I was supposed to go on with my life. I had children who needed me. The boys were fifteen and thirteen, and Eleanor just nine. My unborn baby was due in October, but I couldn't function. Couldn't even find the will and energy to get out of bed. I think nowadays they have medication for depression like mine, but in 1985, everything my doctor gave me put me to sleep.*

I spent days lying in bed, crying and sleeping. I barely ate, and I lost so much weight, I probably would've starved to death had Eleanor not brought me meals. At night, I wandered through the dark and lonely house feeling empty and completely lost. I'd crawl back into bed exhausted just as dawn was breaking.

In the morning, Eleanor would come into my bedroom with a tray of food. "You have to eat, Mother. If not for you, at least for the baby."

Guilt ridden, I'd force myself to take a bite, vowing to try harder. But the truth was ... I didn't care about myself or the baby or anything but trying to find a way to reverse time and prevent the accident from destroying our lives. If only I'd stopped Ruby and Harold from going on the retreat. If only Jude hadn't taken Angela and Eric to look at that crib on the other side of town. If only Jude had seen the stop sign.

After the funeral, Father Tim came to the house daily, but I barely spoke to him. I didn't want him pestering me about not attending church. And I certainly didn't want to hear about God's will. How could God's will include taking Jude, Angela, Eric, and my unborn grandchild? How?

One night, I sat in the dark kitchen thinking about the housewife in Dallas who'd driven off the cliff and ended her life. In the depths of my depression, I prayed for the courage to kill myself. I didn't want to live anymore. Didn't want to struggle through the next thirty years without Jude. A mother should never have to bury a child, but losing both my daughter and my husband was too much. And Eric ... Oh, Lord. My heart broke over and over for the loss of Ruby's sweet, precious little boy.

Gazing out the window toward Ruby's back porch, I sucked in a quick breath as I saw the flicker of light from a cigarette.

Ruby was smoking again. We'd all smoked on occasion in college but had quit after the Surgeon General announced the link between smoking and lung cancer.

But now, my fingers itched to hold a cigarette. Like a child's special blanket or a sweater knit by your own mother, smoking was a way to soothe a deep-seated pain. Not that anything could even begin to soothe our pain.

Barefoot and wearing only my nightgown, I opened the back door and crossed the rough and wet grass. With both hands, I held up my belly, heavy with a baby I imagined weighed a hundred pounds.

Stepping onto my best friend's back porch, I felt as if I'd traveled a thousand miles. I hadn't seen Ruby since the day we buried all three of our loved ones. Father Tim had suggested one funeral, and I'd agreed, not wanting to endure a separate mass for each lost soul.

"Ruby?" I whispered, my throat dry.

She blinked but didn't answer. She'd always been trim, but now she'd lost so much weight her body looked brittle. Her usually shiny brown hair hung listless and uncombed at her shoulders.

"Ruby, I'm so sorry." My eyes burned, but I blinked hard, refusing to cry in front of my dear friend who'd lost her only child.

She looked up with red, puffy eyes and took a long drag on the cigarette before turning away and blowing out the smoke. I held my breath, willing her to say something. Anything. But she remained silent. A deep tension pressed down, and the scars on my heart burned.

Not knowing what else to do, I quietly slipped into the

chair beside her. Running a hand over the wooden armrest, I recalled the day Ruby and I had bought four of these chairs at the county fair. Two for her porch and two for mine. Since we couldn't fit more than one chair in my car at a time, we'd returned three times for the other chairs, laughing at the absurdity of it all.

"Ruby, do you remember when—"

The hollow expression on her face stopped me. "I'm sorry," I said. "I'm so sorry."

She ground out the cigarette on the patio, then rose and disappeared inside her house without a word. The screen door banged shut, and my heart shattered. I'd always associated that sound with good memories—Ruby coming to see me with homemade brownies, fresh-squeezed lemonade, or some juicy piece of gossip. Would we ever be friends like that again?

Squeezing my eyes tight, I offered up a silent prayer. "Lord, I'd do anything. Anything. Just tell me what to do to make things right. Guide me, please."

I stayed on Ruby's porch until the sun rose, then I dragged myself across the overgrown grass, neglected since Jude's death. I crawled into bed, pulled the covers over my head, and slept until someone entered the bedroom.

Opening my eyes, I expected to see Eleanor, looking down with a worried and disapproving expression. Instead, Father Tim stood beside me, holding a breakfast tray. "You need to eat, Nadine."

My stomach protested at the smell of eggs and coffee. Even the plain toast didn't appeal to me. "I saw Ruby last night."

His shoulders relaxed. "Good. The two of you need each other. Especially now."

I shook my head. "She wouldn't talk to me. She just went inside her house."

Tim placed the tray on the nightstand. Sitting beside me, he offered a sympathetic smile. "Give her time. You both need more time, then—"

I sat up and leaned against the headboard. "What if this doesn't get better with time?"

He clasped his hands together tightly in his lap. "It will. I promise. God has not abandoned you."

"Are you sure about that, Father?" My voice was full of bitterness. "Where was God when Jude died on the night of the accident? Where was God when they all died?"

I wanted Tim to fight back with words like "our inability to understand God's divine plan" or "all things work for the good of those who love Him."

Instead, he hung his head and didn't speak for a long time. Finally, in a soft voice, barely audible, he said, "When that tragedy happened, my darling Nadine, God wept."

I swallowed past the large lump in my throat. The small part of my soul that still held a small kernel of faith split wide open. I yearned to believe it was true. Yearned to cling to it.

But the rest of my soul—the dark, angry, ugly part— reared its wicked head. "I'm having a difficult time believing that, Father. Honestly, I don't think God even remembers who I am."

He nodded and said nothing. I was grateful he didn't quote some Bible passage or tell me about a thirteenth century saint who'd endured an even worse situation than mine.

Standing, he looked down at me with sadness and compassion. "I'm going to drive Eleanor and the boys to school while you eat this breakfast. Then you're going to take a shower and get dressed. When I return, we'll go for a walk. You need to get out of this house and breathe some fresh air."

I started to protest, but he held up his hand. "I know your heart is broken. Mine is, too. Jude was a good man and one of my dearest friends. I loved Angela and Eric as though they were my own children. But we have to go on, Nadine. We have to pick up our cross and move forward. You can't continue living like this."

I blinked and met his gaze. "What if I can't go on?"

A single tear slid down his face. He quickly wiped it away with the back of his hand as though ashamed to find it there. "You have to find a way. For the sake of your children. For the sake of this unborn baby, and the sake of your precious friend, Ruby. And for my sake, whose soul is breaking seeing you like this. You have to move on."

Guilt and sorrow crushed me. He was right, but that didn't make it any easier, or answer the question as to how I was supposed to move forward.

Chapter 28

I AWOKE IN the morning to find Kyle standing in front of the coffeemaker, dressed for work. He opened his arms, and I walked into them, resolved to accept the things I couldn't change.

"Okay," I said. "If it's really important to you, I won't stand in your way."

"What? Having my morning coffee?"

I swatted his belly. "No, the fellowship."

He gripped my shoulders and leaned back so he could see my face. "Are you serious?"

"Yes. You can do the fellowship or another residency or whatever it is you need to become an OB if that's what you want."

He stared at me. "What's going on? Why did you suddenly change your mind?"

"You're a good husband and a wonderful father. The only reason I said no is because I'll miss you. I hate having you gone all the time. It's lonely, and I just want you home, but I know you love me and would never cheat on me."

"Of course I'd never cheat on you. Why would you even mention that?"

"Jim slept with Vilda."

Kyle's face fell. "I was worried about that."

"You were?"

He squeezed my shoulders before releasing them. Grabbing two mugs from the cupboard, he poured us each a cup of coffee. "It was just a feeling I had. Jim and Eleanor don't seem to enjoy spending time together."

"I know."

"Anyway, you don't have to worry about that with me, okay? I swear. Delivering babies has given me a whole new perspective on the female anatomy down there."

"Down there?" I laughed. "Is that an official medical term?"

He grinned. "You know what I mean."

I took a sip of my coffee, savoring the first taste of the day. "Has it ruined how you feel about *my* female anatomy down there?"

He laughed and patted my hip. "Baby, nothing could change how I feel about your girlie parts."

"Good. Then I guess we'll be hanging out in residency a little longer."

He eyed me cautiously. "You're sure?"

"Yes, but I'm coming with you. Even if all we can afford is a one-bedroom apartment with a communal bathroom. I'm not going to live apart from you for an entire year."

"I wouldn't let you."

I hid my expression in my coffee mug and refrained from pointing out he'd been the one to suggest it.

AFTER KYLE LEFT for work, I decided to do something I hadn't done in a long time: attend church. If there was ever a time when I needed God in my life, it was now.

I endured the usual frustrating routine of trying to figure out what to wear. After trying on a dozen outfits, I finally settled on a simple dress with tights and boots. The boys couldn't find their church shoes or church pants, so they wore jeans, matching polo shirts, and their least dirty pair of sneakers.

In the sanctuary, we sat in the back pew, where Eleanor and her kids joined us. Aubrey looked adorable in a ladybug sundress and a sparkly black sweater.

"I was saving it for spring," my sister said, "but I chose to embrace my chaotic life and let her wear it today."

I smiled. "She looks cute, and so does Jude." Jude

wore a little navy blue sailor suit with tiny anchors on the snaps.

Dan, Darlene, and their kids waved as they marched down the aisle, headed for the first pew where they sat each Sunday, claiming their kids behaved better in the front. Kyle and I had sat with them once. Logan and Zane were much younger, and it had been a nightmare. Unbeknown to us, Logan slid his shoes under the modesty railing, where a lector had tripped on them on his way up to the podium!

The music began, and as we rose for the opening hymn, I saw Michael standing several rows ahead of me. A familiar, curvaceous woman with short blonde hair stood next to him.

"It's one of Mom's nurses from the hospital," Eleanor said.

She was right. *The five-o'clock-somewhere nurse.*

Aubrey leaned over. "Her name is Christy. She likes strawberry ice cream, unicycles, and collecting sand dollars."

"Good to know," I said.

My phone vibrated with a call from Kyle, but I sent it to voicemail, assuming he'd leave a message or text if it was an emergency. Maybe he'd already talked to Dr. Forman about the fellowship and was now slotted to begin tomorrow. If that were the case, I would stay in

Turtle Lake until things were settled with my mother.

Sticking my phone in my purse, I forced myself to concentrate on the readings and sermon. My mind strayed, however, to Michael and Christy. What was going on between the two of them? They weren't touching as far as I could see, but they were sitting close to each other. At one point, she turned and studied him, but Michael didn't react. He probably couldn't see her through that horrible mass of hair. Obviously, Christy had a crush on him, but how did my brother feel about her?

My mind drifted from thoughts of Michael and his love life to what Eleanor told me yesterday down at the lake. She must've lived in terror, thinking any minute she'd lose her mother or unborn sister.

I thought about some of the nine year olds I'd worked with in speech therapy. A few of them were hardened by life, but most of them were innocent. A couple still believed in Santa Claus!

Maybe Eleanor had misunderstood the conversation about adoption between our mother and Father Tim. I couldn't imagine a priest who'd been such a huge part of my parents' lives trying to convince my mom to give up her baby. Then again, if she'd been so depressed she couldn't get out of bed, who knows what they talked about.

Still, something about Eleanor's story didn't sit right with me. What was the answer?

Faith, the voice whispered for the second time.

My eyes darted to the stained glass window above the altar. I stared at the cherub angels flying in the billowy clouds of heaven. "I'm trying," I whispered. "I'm trying."

AFTER CHURCH, ELEANOR and I took the kids outside and met up with the rest of our family. The boy cousins ran to play at the church's park, but Aubrey stayed behind not wanting to get her dress dirty.

Dan placed an arm across his wife's shoulders and looked at Michael with amusement. "Were you sitting with one of Mom's nurses from the hospital?"

Darlene, Eleanor, Aubrey, and I spoke in unison. "Christy."

Dan's eyes broadened, but Michael casually stroked his beard as though it were a pet. "It's no big deal, we just happened to run into each other this morning. She usually attends Saturday night, but she went to a barbecue last night."

Darlene patted Michael's arm. "She *happened* to show up this morning because she wanted to see you. You understand that, right?"

Michael shook his head. "No, it's not like that. She's a pretty girl, but she's not interested in me that way. We're just ... well, not friends, but acquaintances."

Aubrey squinted in the sunshine. "Do you like her?"

"Of course," Michael said. "Don't you? She's a good nurse and takes great care of Grandma and the other patients."

Aubrey rolled her eyes. "Oh, Uncle Michael. That's not what I mean, and you know it."

We all shared a smile just as my phone rang. Father Tim's number appeared on my caller ID, and my heart lurched.

"Answer it," Eleanor demanded, peering over my shoulder.

"Hello?"

"Autumn, darling. It's Father Timothy O'Connor. I'm already at the hospital. A lovely doctor gave me a ride from the airport, but I'd like to see your mother. Shall I wait for you in the lobby?"

"Yes," I sputtered. "We'll be right there."

"Okay, dear. Looking forward to seeing you."

I hung up the phone and glanced at my sister, unsure of what to say to the others. Eleanor cleared her throat. "That was Father Tim. He came to see Mother."

"Father Tim?" Michael looked puzzled.

Dan nudged his brother. "Father Tim. From the

parish in Seattle? Remember?"

"Oh, yeah," Michael said.

"He's not the same Tim who wrote the letter to your mother, is he?" Darlene asked. "Did you ever find out about that Tim?"

I didn't know how to answer the question, but once again, Eleanor came to my rescue. "We should go. I'm sure Father Tim is anxious to see Mother, and I don't want to keep him waiting."

"I'm coming, too," Michael said.

Darlene placed a gentle hand on Dan's arm. "Why don't you go with your brother? I'll take the kids home and wait for you there. Eleanor? Can I take Aubrey with me?"

"Yes, thank you." Eleanor's voice wobbled, clearly disturbed by the idea of seeing Father Tim again.

Darlene smiled at me. "I'd offer to take Logan and Zane, but I don't have enough room in my car."

"That's okay," I said. "You've watched them enough lately."

With that settled, we headed to the hospital where we found Father Tim pacing the lobby. He wore all black except for the white clerical collar around his neck, and although he was the same age as my mom, he seemed much older. When he saw us, he smiled, causing his entire face to transform into the goofy-looking kid from the Elvis movie.

He shook Dan's hand before pulling him into a manly embrace. "You're all grown up, son."

He greeted Michael the same way, but when he spotted Eleanor, tears filled his eyes. "Little Ellie ... and your baby."

"This is Jude," Eleanor said, lifting the carrier.

The priest clasped his hands and pressed them to his mouth. He smiled down at the baby and spoke with approval. "Jude. A fine, strong name for a fine, strong baby. He's very handsome."

Eleanor kept her face stoic, but she nodded, and I wondered what was going through her mind. Did Father Tim's presence bring back all the difficult memories of her childhood?

When the priest finally turned his attention to me, I felt uncomfortable and offered my hand. "Father Tim, I'm Autumn. Nadine's youngest. Thank you for coming."

He gripped my hand with both of his and held on tight. There was an intensity in his eyes I didn't understand. "Autumn, dear ... oh, Autumn."

I swallowed the lump in my throat, not sure why I was so emotional at meeting him. I introduced Logan and Zane, then we all headed upstairs to see my mom.

WHEN WE REACHED the room, we found my mom's physician Dr. Henry, speaking quietly to her. "Your mother helped me with some personal issues," he explained, walking toward us. "I was just telling her how everything worked out."

I nodded, easily imagining my mother doing something like that. She was a good listener and full of sage advice.

Father Tim stepped past us and made his way to the bed. "*Oh, Nadine.*" He sank in the chair and lifted her frail hand to his cheek. "Sweetheart ..."

I stood, mesmerized. The love in his voice was so tender and sincere, I could scarcely breathe. I didn't think it was a romantic love, but it was pure and true, nonetheless.

My siblings followed Dr. Henry out to the hallway where Logan and Zane were playing hopscotch on the tiles, but I stood still, watching Father Tim bow his head and move his lips in quiet prayer.

"Autumn," my sister called, shifting the baby and motioning for me to join everyone.

I glanced one last time at my mom and Father Tim before leaving the room. "What's going on?"

The door had been propped open, but Eleanor closed it with her free hand. She gestured toward Dr. Henry. "He spoke with the other doctors, and we need to talk about the fact that maybe it's time."

"Time?" My voice shook with comprehension.

Eleanor met my gaze straight on. "It might be time to think about removing the feeding tube and letting her go."

Everything inside me froze. "No!"

Dan placed a hand on my shoulder. "I know this is tough, but we'll make her comfortable. She won't experience any pain."

But I will. I will. I will.

Michael asked a question about the procedure, and everyone started talking as if we were scheduling nothing more serious than a dental appointment.

My chest clenched tight as panic shot through me. I couldn't believe my siblings were speaking so casually. Had everything already been decided?

"Wait a minute," I said. "Father Tim just arrived. We can't end her life. Not yet."

Eleanor shook her head. "We haven't made a decision; we're just talking about it."

"Well, my decision is no!"

"Since Father Tim is here," Dan began, as if I hadn't spoken, "we can ask him to give last rites, and if she passes, maybe he'll stay for the funeral."

"No," I repeated, appalled my brother could even think such a thing.

The doctor nervously looked at Eleanor. "Perhaps we could go to my office and discuss this in private? Or maybe you'd prefer to speak to the neurologist?"

"That won't be necessary." Eleanor used her no-nonsense doctor tone. Despite the baby on her shoulder and spit-up sliding down her back, she was all business. "Thank you for your time, Dr. Henry. I'll talk to my sister and get back to you."

I'll talk to my sister? I hated being dismissed as if I were just the youngest kid with no right to an opinion. This was my mother they were talking about. This was her life!

Kyle rounded the corner, dressed in scrubs and a long white lab coat. He looked so professional and handsome and safe, I wanted to throw myself in his arms. Have him hold me and tell me everything was going to be okay.

"What's going on?" he asked, eyeing our group suspiciously.

I shot daggers at Eleanor and Dan. "They want to remove the feeding tube."

Kyle's expression faltered, and he peeked through the little glass window in the door. "Is that why you called the priest? For last rites?"

"No," I protested, my voice trembling. "That's not why he's here at all."

I gripped Kyle's arm. "Tell them to stop. Tell them there's no rush, and we don't have to make this decision today."

Eleanor answered before Kyle could say anything. "I know this is hard, but Mother wouldn't want to live like this."

I recoiled. "You don't know that. She's pro-life! She believes in life."

The doctor flinched at my anger. I was causing a scene, but I didn't care. Adrenaline surged through me, and my whole body shook.

"Mommy, what's wrong?" Logan squeezed my hand and looked up with frightened eyes, making me feel guilty. Placing a reassuring hand on his shoulder, I apologized.

Michael squatted so he was eye level with both boys. "Hey, do you two want to come downstairs with me and get some ice cream?"

Zane jumped into my brother's arms. "Yes, I do. I do. Can I get chocolate?"

"Of course," Michael said. "What about you, Logan?"

Logan looked at me, then at Kyle, who forced a smile and nodded. "It's okay, son. Go with Uncle Michael so Mom and I can talk with the doctor."

Logan stood on tiptoes to peer through the window

at my mom. "Can I say hi to Grandma first?"

"Later, okay?" Kyle said. "After your ice cream."

Logan nodded, then left with Michael and Zane. A fierce silence pressed down on our group. When nobody spoke, I took the opportunity to repeat my disagreement. "It's wrong to give up on Mom so easily. We can't end her life like this."

Eleanor straightened. "We're not *ending* her life, just removing the feeding tube."

Fury grabbed me, shaking my body and accelerating my pulse. All the tenderness and understanding I'd felt toward my sister over the past few days vanished. "People die when they don't eat. Removing the feeding tube is giving her a death sentence. Don't you understand that?"

"Sometimes—" Kyle began.

I glared at him and didn't let him finish. "I can't believe you're taking their side."

"I'm not taking anyone's side. I—"

"I'm through talking about this," I shouted. Spinning around, I flew down the hallway, distancing myself from Kyle, my family, and the horrible fact they were probably right.

Chapter 29

*A*FTER *FATHER TIM* gave me strict instructions to finish my breakfast, he left my bedroom and helped the children get ready for school. I tried to eat the toast, but it tasted like cardboard and scratched my throat. Even the coffee didn't appeal to me, something I could usually stomach in the worst of situations.

Pushing the tray away, I crawled under the covers and listened to the sounds of my children, rushing around the house to find their backpacks and shoes. Eleanor yelled at her brothers for being loud and irresponsible. Dan shouted for her to mind her own business.

The front door opened and slammed shut. Pulling the covers around me, I sobbed uncontrollably into my pillow. It all hurt so much. Nothing, nothing could be more painful than this. How in the world was I going to survive?

At last, exhaustion overtook me, and I fell into a deep sleep filled with outrageous dreams. I dreamed of Jude, Angela, and Eric flying around the world with Elvis on electric guitars. I tried jumping up to capture them, but *they flew out of my reach, laughing.*

At one point, I followed them into the church, where they disappeared, leaving me alone with a small group of people preparing for a wedding. Looking up, I found Ruby standing near the altar. She wore a beautiful lavender dress, and her face beamed with pride as she helped the bride adjust her veil.

Leaning over, the bride kissed Ruby on the cheek and smiled. "I love you, Mom."

I gasped and my hand shot to my heart. Who was this girl? Had Eric actually lived? Was this his future wife? Had Ruby gone on to have more children? How was this possible?

And suddenly, it became perfectly clear.

The bride was Ruby's daughter!

Tears of joy streamed down my face. Ruby had picked up the pieces of her fragile life and had gone on to have a daughter!

A daughter!

Both Ruby and the bride turned toward me. Slowly, I came to my feet, gripping the pew in front of me for support. "Ruby."

She smiled and nodded. "This is Faith—my daughter."

The bride lifted her face and locked eyes with me. A jolt hit me because she looked like she could be one of my own. In addition to Eleanor's high cheekbones, she had Angela's red hair and green eyes. Jude's eyes.

And suddenly I knew. I knew how I could make things right. How I could atone for this awful mess and restore my relationship with Ruby ... and perhaps survive this tragedy.

I awoke with a start, sitting straight up. My eyes darted around the room until they landed on Tim, standing at the end of my bed.

"Are you okay, Nadine?"

My heart pounded, and I struggled to catch my breath, but yes, I was okay. Better than okay. "I know what to do. I know what I need to do."

A quiet smile tugged at his lips. "Okay. I'll make us some coffee while you take a shower and get dressed. Then we'll talk about it."

I shook my head, not wanting him to leave. Then before I could lose my nerve, I told him about my plan for redemption.

My plan to give Ruby my baby.

Chapter 30

*A*FTER STORMING OUT of the hospital, I sat on a bench outside, realizing I couldn't leave without my purse, which I'd left in my mom's room, or my children who were with Michael, eating ice cream.

Even though it was cold enough for a jacket, the sun shone above me. I pulled my sunglasses out of my pocket and put them on. Leaning back, I breathed in the fresh air, grateful winter would soon be over.

Before we knew it, the red bud trees lining the streets of downtown Turtle Lake would come into bloom, announcing the beginning of spring. Announcing it was time to leave winter behind and begin anew.

If my mom died, she wouldn't be here for spring, her favorite time of the year. She wouldn't see the boys grow up, hold baby Jude, or watch me get my master's degree.

How was it possible that just over a week ago she'd flirted on the phone with her doctor? Swam in the pool with her grandchildren and enjoyed lunch on the back patio with the boys and me?

An older woman, around the same age as my mom, approached the bench. "Do you mind if I sit here?"

"Oh, of course not." I scooted over, despite the fact there was already plenty of room for her.

"I'm waiting for faith," she said.

I smiled. *Weren't we all?*

Shaking her head, she withdrew a tube of lipstick and a little mirror from her purse. "I'm sorry. Faith is my daughter. She's parking the rental car. We just flew into Texas and my mind is scattered. I hate getting old, but I suppose it's better than the alternative."

She laughed nervously, and something inside me twitched. I turned to study her, noticing that like my mother, she had dark round age spots on her hands. She was thin with short, gray hair. Large sunglasses covered most of her face, but she seemed familiar.

I wanted to ask why she'd come to Texas, but before I could, Kyle and the boys burst out of the hospital, calling my name. They headed toward me and I stood. Logan swung my purse through the air like a weapon, while Kyle carried Zane, who was crying.

"I've got to get to work, and Zane just threw up," Kyle said, his voice urgent. "I cleaned him off in the bathroom, but he stinks."

Zane lunged at me, and I caught him, despite his repulsive stench. Kyle scooped up Logan and placed a hand between my shoulder blades. "Come on, I'll help you to the car before I go back to work."

As the four of us left, the woman on the bench called out to us. "I hope he feels better."

I'd forgotten all about her, but I peeked over my shoulder and waved. "Thanks."

We walked toward my car, Zane weaving his sticky hand through my hair. "I love you, Mommy. Do you love me?"

My heart melted. "Of course I love you, Stinky Monster." He gave a muffled giggle and buried his face deeper into my neck.

When we reached the car, Kyle helped me buckle up the boys before giving me a huge hug.

"I stink," I protested, trying to step away.

"I stink, too." He leaned against the car, pulling me with him. Closing my eyes, I sank into his chest. He'd been wrong. He didn't smell bad at all. In fact, as I inhaled his pleasant aftershave, I was convinced that nobody smelled better than my Kyle.

"I'm not going to take the fellowship," he said in a raspy breath.

"What?" His statement seemed so out of the blue, I thought I misunderstood.

"Not to psychoanalyze myself, but I think I have this fear of not being good enough. Of not being able to give you and the boys everything you deserve."

"*Kyle* ..." I leaned back and looked him in the eye, wanting to assure him it wasn't true.

"I'll tell you more about it at home, but back there ... after you left, Dan and Eleanor both agreed to hold off on making any decisions until you were ready."

"They did?"

He nodded. "You know, I missed out by not growing up in a family like yours. You and your siblings work things out. You stay together and take care of each other. I never had that ... it's probably why I push people away. Even you. Why I'm afraid of just working next year."

"I don't understand."

He took a deep breath. "What if I'm not good enough? What if when we have more time to spend together, you get sick of me?"

"*Kyle.*" How in the world could I convince him he was enough? That I honestly loved him and wanted to be with him?

His phone rang, but he silenced it without looking at the caller ID. "So, would you be okay if I accepted the position at the clinic, and we just lived a normal life? If I was home at night and on the weekends?"

"I'd be thrilled, but are you sure? I don't want you to give up your dream for me."

"Yes, you do."

I laughed. "Okay, full disclosure. I do. But does that make you mad?"

"No."

"And you're not going to regret it?"

"No." He brushed back my hair. "You've sacrificed for me and my career. Now I want to do the same for you."

My heart filled with so much joy, I thought it would burst. I threw my arms around him and held on tight. "I love you."

"I know you do, and I love you, too."

Frantic knocking on the car window broke our magical moment. We both looked down to see Zane pointing at Logan, who was throwing up.

"Oh, no!" I ran around to the other side of the car and opened the door. "He must've caught what Zane has."

"I think this is my cue to exit," Kyle said, but he didn't leave. Instead, he stayed and helped me clean up the car and our son.

Half a tub of baby wipes later, Kyle held open the driver's side door as I slipped into the seat.

"When I get home tonight," he said, "I'll take your

car to get shampooed. It might be late, but I'll do it, okay?"

I smiled up at him and rested my hand on his leg. "Thanks. Do you want a lift back to the hospital?"

He glanced at the boys, sitting in the back seat and grinned. "In the throw-up mobile? No, thanks. I think I'll walk."

I grunted a laugh. "Yeah, I don't blame you."

With all the windows rolled down, I waved good-bye to Kyle and drove home.

AFTER BATHING THE boys, I settled them in the living room with blankets, bowls, and lots of towels. I turned on the TV and went into the kitchen to wash the dishes.

Even though my siblings had agreed to wait until I was ready, it didn't change the fact that we were probably going to lose my mom. Everything inside me ached at the thought of not having her in my life. She was such a great source of comfort and inspiration, not to mention the best grandmother in the world.

I checked on the boys and saw that while Logan had fallen asleep, Zane was sitting up, drawing.

"What are you drawing?" I asked, strolling into the living room.

Immediately, he slammed the book close and shoved

it under his blanket. "Nothing."

His actions set off every one of my internal alarms. "Zane, what is that? Show me."

"It's nothing," he insisted.

He had a bad habit of drawing in Kyle's medical books or library books. One time, he even took my checkbook and colored little notes for all his Star Wars figures.

"Come on, Zane. Show me."

Tightening his grip on the book through the blanket, he shifted his eyes to the left. "It's mine."

"I just want to see it," I said, pretending I didn't know he was lying.

Reluctantly, he handed me the book. I leafed through the pages and saw his artwork, which was pretty impressive for a little kid. Unfortunately, the first half of the book contained my mom's handwriting. I turned to the first page and noticed it was recently dated and read, *Dear Angela, Dan, Michael, Eleanor, and Autumn.*

"Can I have it back now?" Zane asked, using his polite voice.

My blood froze. "Grandma didn't give this to you, did she?"

Guilt flashed across his face. "I found it. It's mine."

"Where did you find it?"

He hung his head. "In her desk."

"This isn't yours, and you shouldn't have taken it. I'm very disappointed."

He puffed out his lip. "But I miss her, Mom."

I narrowed my eyes. Was he being serious or just manipulative? "I know you do. I miss her, too, but you can't take things that don't belong to you."

"But I didn't draw on the pages she used."

I nodded and found a Spiderman notebook and orange Longhorn pen on the coffee table he could use. "Here, promise me you won't take things that don't belong to you."

"I won't." He took my hand and placed something round and solid in my palm. "Will you give this to Grandma for me? Tell her I'm sorry, and I hope she gets better soon?"

I looked down to see his prized dinosaur egg. "Oh, Zane. That's sweet of you. Are you sure you don't want to keep it?"

"I'm sure."

I couldn't help but grin and ask the question, "What if it hatches in the hospital?"

He smiled and leaned forward to whisper in my ear. "I know it isn't real, Mom. I just like pretending it's a dinosaur egg."

I wrapped my arms around his wiggly body and squeezed him tight. "Baby bear is growing up!"

"I'm going to kindergarten next year, you know."

"I know."

With that settled, I took the dinosaur egg and book into the kitchen and placed them on the table. I made myself a cup of coffee and debated whether or not to open the journal again. The first sentence made it seem like my mom was writing a letter to my siblings and me. Did that justify reading it?

On one hand, I didn't want to violate her privacy, but what if she'd had a premonition about the accident and these were her last wishes? Wouldn't it be best for us to know what she wanted in the event of her passing?

Convinced I had my mother's best interests in mind, I opened the journal and began to read.

Dear Angela, Eleanor, Dan, Michael, and Autumn,

I need to tell you something that will change how you feel about me. While this news will have the greatest impact on Autumn, I know it will also come as a shock to you older kids. I simply ask you, my children, to keep an open mind and try to understand why I did what I felt I had to do. Why I felt I had no other choice.

I hope in time, you'll be able to forgive me.

All my love,
Mom

Chapter 31

A SENSE OF *peace filled me after dreaming about Ruby and her daughter. For the first time since the accident, I had a purpose in life. A reason to get out of bed, eat, and take care of myself.*

Father Tim disapproved of my plan, insisting it would only end in heartbreak. "My heart is already broken," I told him. "This is a way to provide healing for all of us."

"You're making a mistake. You're not thinking," he said.

He didn't understand that after weeks of living in a fog, I was finally thinking clearly. Over the next several days, Tim and I spent hours talking about the adoption. Despite his compassion for my situation, he refused to support me.

At one point, Eleanor caught the two of us arguing. I tried to reassure her everything was fine, but of course it wasn't. I was planning to give away her sister, which sounded horrible when I thought of it in those terms.

One overcast afternoon, Tim and I sat at the little table

in my kitchen drinking tea while the children were at school. The Seattle rain pelted against the window, and I pulled my sweater a little tighter. I'd just finished trying to explain my decision for the hundredth time.

He dropped a cube of sugar into his teacup and stirred it vigorously, the spoon clanking noisily. "Of course I understand. Especially if you feel God spoke to you in a dream. I gave up sex, a wife, and children because God spoke to me. But we have to be careful about not confusing God's desire for our lives with our own stubborn will."

"So you think I'm just being stubborn? You don't think God gave me this vision?"

He sighed heavily and lifted his tea cup to his lips but put it back down without taking a sip. "I didn't say that."

A tense silence followed in which we both stared out the window, watching the rain. It'd been an unseasonably cold fall, even by Seattle's standards, and I envied my parents for having moved back to Texas. I wondered if moving south would help the constant depression that hovered over me. Maybe I was simply doomed to feel sad forever.

"If you actually go through with this, and everything is fine with the adoption," Tim began, "how are you going to handle seeing your daughter being raised by another woman?"

My heart lifted because maybe I was finally getting through to him. "Don't you see? Ruby isn't just another woman, she's my best friend. She's like a sister to me."

"I just don't know, Nadine. All my instincts tell me you'll regret it."

I took a slow sip of my tea. "If Ruby refuses to take the baby, then I'm asking you to give my daughter to another deserving family. It hurts to admit this, but I'm not in a position to care for another child. I've got Eleanor and the boys who need me. I can barely take care of myself right now, let alone an infant."

He reached out and covered my hand with his. "Sweetheart, there are organizations that can help you. The church can help you."

I shook my head. "I don't want to be on your charity list."

"It wouldn't be like that." He closed his eyes, and I braced myself for another lecture. "Let's just see how things go after the baby is born. Maybe when you see her and hold her, you'll change your mind."

"No. I don't want to see her. And I definitely don't want to hold her. I just want you to make sure she gets to Ruby. Promise me."

"I can't make promises like that."

I jutted out my chin. "Then I'll find someone who can."

Whether it was the tone of my voice or divine inspiration, he finally stopped trying to change my mind and agreed to accompany me to the meeting with his brother. At Ray's office, I sat next to Tim on the couch and explained *how I wanted to give my baby up for adoption.*

Ray frowned and looked at Tim before turning his attention back to me. "Are you sure this is something you want to do? Many women in your position feel differently after the baby is born."

"In my position?" I said with a snort. "Do you have many clients who've lost their husband, their daughter, their grandchild, and their best friend's son?"

The lawyer tapped a pen against his legal pad. "Of course not, but I have clients who find themselves in difficult situations. I just want you to understand all your options."

My options? Did I even have options?

Ironically, I had sat with Jude and Angela in this very office, on this very couch, discussing Angela's options. All the anguish over our unwed daughter's decision to keep her baby had been pointless. That innocent child had died along with her mother.

Pushing away the pain, I wrung my hands together and gathered my strength. "I want to sign the papers before I deliver, so everything will be in order. And I want this to be a closed adoption, but you have to assure me Ruby McCoy will get my baby."

Ray sat back in his chair and studied me as though questioning my mental health. "If you know Ruby is the adoptive mother, then this won't be a closed adoption."

"Only on her part. I'll know the truth, but she won't."

I rubbed a hand over my enormous belly. I'd never been this large with the other pregnancies, and although my doctor insisted everything was fine, and there was no need to do a sonogram or further testing, I couldn't help but worry.

Ray leaned forward. "Mrs. Kingsley, you don't want to do this. Such an arrangement might not even be legal."

"I'll pay you," I said. "Whatever it costs. Jude left me a fortune in life insurance, and you can have it."

Tim tensed beside me but said nothing. His brother gazed out the window onto the busy street. So many cars and people raced back and forth. What was the point of all this hurrying around? Didn't they know everything they cared about could be lost in an instant?

Had I known how quickly my life would change, I would have slowed down and taken the time to enjoy life. I would have held on to Jude and been more loving toward Angela. I would've given Eric more attention and told him how much he meant to me.

Scooting to the edge of the couch, I pleaded with Ray. "I need to do this. I'm going to do this. If you can't help me, I'll find someone else, but I'd prefer to use your services. I trust you." I squared my shoulders, hoping to appear more confident than I felt.

Ray ran a hand through his thinning hair and looked at his brother. "Father Tim? How do you feel about all this?"

Tim exhaled slowly, and I feared he would try to talk me out of it again. Instead, he took my hand and gave it a reassuring squeeze. "Nadine has spent an enormous amount of time thinking and praying over this decision. While it's not something I recommend, or even agree with, I won't stand in her way."

I breathed a sigh of relief.

Ray crossed his legs. "I won't be involved in anything that's illegal or could jeopardize my agency's reputation."

My body felt lighter, and I moved a hand over my belly just as the baby let out a whopping kick. "Of course not. But this baby is not mine to keep. She belongs to Ruby. I believe that with all my heart."

Ray nodded, and I thanked him for helping me, but he held up a hand. "I'm not saying yes. Just that I'll look into it. Give me a few days to make some phone calls."

I nodded enthusiastically. "Okay, but please understand I'm not keeping this baby, and I don't want to see her. I can't see her. At least not until she belongs to Ruby. Please promise me that."

"But if Ruby doesn't want her—"

"She will. I know she will. I don't know what will happen with her marriage, but if you tell her there's a little baby who needs a good home, I know Ruby will take her."

The lawyer crinkled his brow. "And you're certain it's a girl?"

"Yes. That's what God told me in my dream."

Chapter 32

MY MOTHER'S JOURNAL read like a fast-paced novel. She'd met my father in high school and had instantly fallen in love with him. They'd faced obstacles but had overcome them to create a beautiful life together.

I read the pages in one sitting, and when I finished, I could hardly believe what I'd learned. Eleanor had misunderstood the conversation about adoption between Father Tim and our mom.

It was *our mother*, not Father Tim, who wanted to give me away.

She'd wanted to give me to Ruby, and honestly, I didn't blame her. She'd lost so much, and suddenly she was a single mother with three kids to raise. No wonder she didn't think she could handle another child.

In the end, however, she'd kept me. So what changed her mind? Seeing me in the delivery room? Holding me for the first time?

I leafed through the journal, searching for answers that weren't there before realizing several pages had been removed. My mom must've used a ruler and a razor blade to take them out, but why? And where were they now?

I ran a finger over the smooth edges. Did these missing pages contain the reason behind my mom's decision to keep me, or was there more to her secret?

Closing the notebook, I took a sip of my coffee, which had grown cold. Father Tim had been a good friend to my mom after my father died, and I felt foolish for ever believing they'd been romantically involved. Judging by the journal, he was obviously dedicated to the vows of his profession.

When my phone rang, I was so absorbed in my own thoughts I jumped. Glancing down, I saw it was Father Tim. "Autumn, dear. How are you? Eleanor tells me your boys have a stomach bug?"

I looked at Logan and Zane who were both sound asleep on the couch. Thankfully, neither one of them had thrown up since getting home. "I think they're feeling better. Hopefully, the worst has passed."

"Wonderful. Thank you for contacting me about your mother. I'm grateful I saw her, despite the situation."

"Of course. I know you were good friends, and ...

well, I saw the letter you wrote. About her choice?"

"Yes," he said, solemnly.

I walked over to the sink and dumped out my coffee. "I was wondering … could you tell me about her choice? Was it just the fact she was going to give me up for adoption then changed her mind?"

He was silent for a moment. "You know about that?"

"Yes," I said, not admitting I'd read the journal.

"I'll tell you everything, but I'd like to speak in person. May I come see you?"

I looked at my boys and realized this was probably the best idea. I certainly wasn't going to wake them up in order to meet Father Tim at a coffee shop. "Sure. But you don't have a car."

"Not a problem, darling. And Ellie gave me your address."

Darling … the word reverberated in my head. Did he call everyone darling? He certainly seemed fond of the endearment. "Okay, Father, I'll see you when you get here."

"See you shortly. And Autumn?"

"Yes?"

He cleared his throat. "I'm bringing a friend of your mother's with me. Her name is Ruby, and she's here with her daughter—Faith."

ENERGIZED WITH EXCITEMENT, I quickly cleaned the kitchen then rushed around the house with a laundry basket, filling it with toys, clothing, and various clutter. I stashed the laundry basket in the closet and checked my refrigerator. Hopefully, Father Tim, Ruby, and Faith wouldn't want anything to eat because I had nothing to offer but a few hot dogs and leftover macaroni and cheese. Tomorrow, I had to go to the grocery store.

The boys were sleeping when the bell rang. Neither one of them budged as I opened the front door to find Father Tim standing on the porch with two women.

Ruby was the older lady from the hospital, and I embraced her, wondering how I'd failed to make the connection. She pulled away and pressed her hands to my face. Tears pooled in her eyes. "Oh, Autumn. It's so good to see you."

"It's wonderful to meet you!" I assumed Father Tim had told her about my mom, and that was why she'd come to Texas.

Ruby smiled that same smile from all her pictures. She was lovely, and I desperately wanted to understand what happened to end her friendship with my mother.

Ruby gestured to the woman beside her. "Autumn, this is my daughter Faith."

My heart stopped as I gaped at the other woman. "Faith?"

Faith gave a tentative smile that slowly rose to engulf her entire face. My knees wobbled, knowing the truth in my heart before my mind could comprehend. "You're Ruby's daughter?" I asked, shocked and confused.

"Yes, I am."

"I don't understand."

She smiled again and reached into her purse to retrieve an envelope written in my mom's handwriting.

I sucked in a quick breath. "I found that envelope on my mom's desk in a stack of letters marked outgoing."

"Did you read it?" she asked.

"No. It was sealed, so I put a stamp on it and stuck it in the mailbox with the utility bill."

Ruby placed an arm over her daughter's shoulders and smiled at me. "Perhaps we should come inside and have Faith read your mother's letter."

"Yes, I think that would be best," Father Tim said.

"Of course." I opened the door wide and led my guests past the boys and into the kitchen where we sat around the table, my mother's journal and Zane's dinosaur egg sitting in the center.

Then Faith read the letter.

Chapter 33

Dear Faith,

You are probably wondering why an old lady has sent you pages from her journal. I assure you, I'm not crazy. I'm just trying to find a way to best explain something I did several years ago.

Your mother Ruby is my best friend. I say "is"—even though we haven't talked in thirty years—because I have never replaced her. Not a day passes when I don't think about her. And you.

Please read these pages I wrote for my children. I don't want to interrupt your life or that of your mother's. But I've kept this secret long enough, and now it's time to face my fears and allow the truth to come to light.

All my love,
Nadine Kingsley

ON THE DAY *I went into labor, I rose early and cooked breakfast for Eleanor and the boys. Working in the kitchen calmed me and gave me hope everything would be okay.*

Eleanor woke first and joined me at the stove. "Are you feeling all right, Mother? Do you want me to finish cooking breakfast?"

Eleanor had always called me "Mother." Never Mama, Mommy, or Nadine, like Angela had done during one of her rebellious phases. Just Mother. Even in preschool, it was, "Mother, did you know caterpillars turned into butterflies?" and "Mother, guess who got four gold stars today?"

"Mother?" Eleanor repeated.

I forced a smile as a small contraction rolled through me. Today would be difficult, but once the baby was born and the paperwork signed, life would improve. "I'm fine, honey. Actually, I'm feeling good today, just a little uncomfortable. Go get ready for school, then come back to the kitchen and we'll eat breakfast together."

Eleanor stood her ground, not believing a word I'd said. Following the accident, she'd assumed the role of a parent, something I regretted. But starting today, things would change.

Eleanor would be sad to learn her new baby sister had died during childbirth, but Ruby would have a new baby, and we would all begin to heal from the tragedy of the past few months.

Or maybe not.

Maybe I'd move the children to Texas where my parents now lived, and we'd start a new life. Away from Seattle and all the memories. Away from Ruby and the daughter I was leaving with her.

After the children left for school that morning, I called Father Tim to tell him I was in labor. He came over immediately and drove me to the hospital. "It really is for the best," I said, as he pulled into the hospital parking lot.

He held an expression of resignation but said nothing. Tim had been one of Jude's best friends since high school, and he'd spent numerous hours praying with Ruby and Harold over their marriage. Surely, he understood how this was for the best.

But as I entered the labor and delivery ward, I never imagined how things would work out. Never imagined my plan would fall apart, and I would live with the consequences the rest of my life.

Childbirth at forty-one was much more difficult than it'd been in my younger years. While the contractions started slow, they rapidly increased, one on top of the other with no rest in between. I struggled to catch my breath, terrified my womb was tearing in half.

After the baby was finally born, I collapsed against the pillow. Exhaustion overwhelmed me. The baby cried, and my chest clenched. I squeezed my eyes tight and focused on the image from my dream of Ruby standing next to her daughter in the church.

Father Tim placed a gentle hand on my shoulder. "It's a girl, just like you said."

I opened my eyes and nodded, relieved it was almost over.

"Would you like to hold her?" one of the nurses asked.

"No!" Even to my own ears, my voice sounded sharp and uncaring.

The nurse shot Tim a look, but I turned away, refusing to see the judgment in her eyes. Nobody in this room could possibly understand what I'd been through. They couldn't possibly understand the reasons behind my actions, and what compelled me to follow through with this painful plan.

Nausea took ahold of me. I closed my eyes and concentrated on my breathing, which was becoming more difficult. A strange, icy cold fear wrapped around my windpipe and suddenly, I was suffocating. I gasped and thrashed about, but I couldn't breathe. Couldn't get the air into my lungs.

"Nadine?" Tim called. "Nadine? Are you okay?"

The room spun, and I clenched the bed sheets. I tried to suck in air. Tried to gain control.

Intense pain stabbed me over and over in the gut. I called for help, but the words got stuck in my throat and wouldn't come out.

"She's not breathing," someone shouted.

An enormous weight slammed down on my chest, and I looked to see if something had fallen on top of me, but nothing was there.

"Where's the cart?" the doctor yelled.

Tim grabbed my shoulder. "Hang on, Nadine. Hang on."

I shook my head because I didn't care about hanging on anymore. What was the point? The baby was safely delivered, and my other children would be better off without me. "I'm ready," I said, surrendering to the pain. "I'm ready."

"She's fading!"

"Don't let go," Tim screamed, his eyes fixed on mine.

But I did. I let go and felt a rush of air as I fell from the cliff I'd been hanging onto since the accident.

HOURS LATER, I opened my eyes to a dark and silent room. Shifting in the hospital bed, I winced at my stiff and sore body. A man dressed all in black slept in the chair next to my bed. Was he the grim reaper, come to take me, not to heaven but hell?

My eyes adjusted and I breathed a sigh of relief. "Tim," I whispered.

The priest's eyes shot open and he jumped to his feet. "Nadine, thank God." He clasped my hands and brought them to his lips. "You scared me to death."

My throat was dry and cracked, but I pushed past the discomfort to ask the question that was most on my mind. "What happened?"

He squeezed my hands tighter. "You almost died. You did die, technically. Do you remember?"

I inhaled deeply, so grateful for the gift of oxygen. I remembered the delivery. Remembered the nurse asking if I wanted to hold my baby, and then ... I let go.

Tim poured a glass of water and handed it to me. I took several gulps before speaking. "What about the baby? Did you give her to Ruby?"

He hesitated. "Nadine, darling, we need to talk."

"I don't want to talk about this. I signed the papers. I gave her away. I told you ... " But even as I said the words, I felt my resolve weakening. Was I seriously going to see this through?

Tim nodded solemnly. "We followed your instructions, and everything went well."

"Ruby accepted the baby?"

He smiled sadly. "She was overjoyed."

"And Harold?"

"He cried when he held her. He called her a gift from God. I think he believes this baby will heal his marriage. He loves Ruby, you know. He just ... stumbled."

Peace flooded my heart. I'd made the right decision after all, and in time, my soul would heal as well. "They don't know where the baby came from, do they?"

Tim shook his head. "Not right now. But they're going to find out."

"No," I insisted. "They won't. I'll tell everyone my baby didn't make it. Ruby lost so many babies, she won't give it a second thought. People lose babies all the time. You have to trust me on this—"

"Nadine, listen to me." The lines around his eyes deepened, and when he spoke, his voice shook. "There was another baby. You have another daughter."

"What?"

"You gave birth to identical twins."

"Twins?"

He nodded and my mind whirled with endless emotions – joy, fear, anxiety, elation, confusion …

"The first baby was fine," Tim explained, "but the second one had complications. She's in the neonatal intensive care unit. There were some problems with her lungs, but she's going to be okay."

I swallowed hard, imagining my baby, all by herself in the nursery, feeling abandoned. Suddenly my arms ached with the need to hold her. To hold this baby I didn't even know existed. This miracle. "Can I see her?"

He nodded and stood to get the doctor. Panic filled me, and I almost yelled for him to come back, but I didn't.

After what seemed like hours, but was probably only a matter of minutes, Tim returned with a nurse who helped me into a wheelchair. My heart pounded with anticipation as she pushed me down the hall to the nursery.

"There she is," Tim said, pointing to an incubator surrounded by machines and tubes. At first, I didn't see her among the technology of the day. But then, in the middle of everything, lay a tiny newborn. Tears pricked my eyes, and I clutched the collar of my gown. "That's her? That's my baby?"

The nurse wheeled me forward and launched into a detailed explanation of my daughter's medical needs. I tried to pay attention, but all I could think about was the fact that this was Jude's baby. Jude's baby ... and she needed me.

All my logic and well-thought out reasons of why I couldn't raise another child crumbled. This was my daughter. Jude's last gift, and I wanted her more than anything in the world.

The nurse explained how I should hold the infant skin to skin. I tried to listen, knowing it was important, but all I could think about was my desire to keep and protect my baby.

When I had her safely in my arms, pressed against my chest, I breathed in her sweet scent. My breasts tingled, and every part of me was willing to lay down my life for her.

The nurse left and Tim sat beside me. "What are you going to name her?"

A large tear slipped down my cheek, landing on the

baby's face. She scrunched her eyes but didn't cry. I brushed off the wet tear with my fingertip and smiled. "What about Autumn? I've always liked that time of year. It's full of new beginnings and hope."

"It is," he agreed.

We sat in peaceful silence, both of us gazing at the baby. Then Tim asked the difficult question. "What about her twin sister? The girls are identical. Ruby will know. She'll find out."

"I just want to do what's best."

Father Tim offered no answers, but he placed his hand on the baby's head, closed his eyes, and offered a blessing. I closed my own eyes and prayed for peace, direction, and healing.

Chapter 34

*C*OMING HOME FROM the hospital was one of the most difficult things I ever had to do. Jude had taken such good care of me after the birth of each child, but this time, I came home alone. I didn't even have my newborn, Autumn Marie, since the pediatrician had insisted on keeping her longer.

Leaving the baby at the hospital felt as though someone chopped off my arm. A part of me missed the first baby, but having twins was so unexpected, I couldn't wrap my mind around it. Besides, Faith was with her mother where she belonged.

That first night home, sleep eluded me. Tossing and turning in bed, I realized Tim was right. If I stayed in Seattle, Ruby would discover the truth, and that wasn't something I could let happen. Seattle had been my home for a long time. I couldn't imagine leaving, but staying was impossible.

The move would thrill my parents, of course. The kids would be upset, and Tim would disapprove. Still, what else could I do? I had to leave and try to make a new life where nobody could discover what I'd done.

With a plan in motion, I finally slept until the morning when Eleanor entered the bedroom, holding a tray of coffee and toast. Yesterday, she'd come to the hospital to see her baby sister. "We're really going to keep her?" she asked, fixing me with her gaze.

"Yes, of course."

She'd nodded and returned her attention to the baby. But her question stayed with me, and I wondered if she knew about Autumn's twin.

Now, in my bedroom, Eleanor opened the curtains. Bright sunlight streamed into my darkened sanctuary and I blinked. It was time for me to stop wallowing in my misery and take care of my children.

Tossing back the covers, I sat up and threw my feet over the side of the bed. My body still ached from childbirth, and my heart remained damaged, but I was ready to get out of bed and move forward.

Eleanor stared at me. "Can we go to the hospital and see Autumn today?"

"Of course."

She breathed a sigh of relief, making me feel guilty for all my shortcomings as a mother. I walked into the bathroom and brushed my teeth. In the mirror, I gaped at my pale, sunken face. Then I looked myself right in the eye and said, "Nadine Rose, you're going to survive. You're going to *take the remaining shards of your life and meld them together to make a new life. A life that will never compare to what you once had, but a life that your children deserve. A life that would honor Jude and Angela."*

"Mom?"

Michael's voice startled me. He stood just outside my bathroom, looking rumpled and in desperate need of a haircut. He'd outgrown his pants, and I wondered when he'd gotten so tall.

I smiled sadly. "Did you sleep in those clothes, sweetheart?"

Embarrassment flashed across his face, and he smoothed a hand over his stained and wrinkled shirt. "Eleanor didn't wash my clothes, so this is all I have."

Shame overtook me. He was depending on his little sister for clean laundry? How had I allowed things to get so bad? "I'm going to teach you and your brother how to do laundry this afternoon when you get home from school. You shouldn't have to depend on others for clean clothes. Go gather all your dirty things, including your sheets."

He looked uncomfortable and turned his gaze to the floor. One big toe poked out of a hole in his sock.

Stepping toward him, I brushed back his hair. "I'm sorry about everything. About how I haven't been here for you. It's going to get better. I promise."

He shrugged. "Can you tell Eleanor to stop inspecting my lunch every day? I can make a sandwich without my little sister's help."

I frowned, saddened that Eleanor had taken on so much during my depression. "Of course."

Instead of sending my children to school that day, I kept them home with me, needing their presence. I made blueberry pancakes, and we ate a leisurely breakfast together before tackling the laundry and putting our house back together.

A sense of hope filled me as I cleaned the refrigerator, wiped the counters, and swept the floor. There was something uplifting about engaging in household chores after neglecting them for so long.

Next, I collected all the flowers sent by friends and parishioners. I brought them to the kitchen sink and dumped out the dirty water. The dead flowers went into the trash, but I managed to salvage enough to make one healthy looking bouquet that I placed on the center of the kitchen table.

Standing back, I admired my work. The windows needed a good washing and Dan's vacuuming wasn't the best, but it was a start. While the dishwasher and washing machine hummed away, the kids retreated to their rooms, afraid I might assign them more chores. I smiled at the normalcy of it all.

I looked through the kitchen window and stared at Ruby's house. What would she say if I marched across the yard, knocked on the back door, and demanded to see the baby?

I shook my head, knowing I needed to forget about her. That baby—Faith—belonged to Ruby. I had enough kids to worry about ... enough problems of my own, and Ruby needed that child.

Suddenly, Ruby's back door opened. I held my breath as she stepped onto the porch with the baby in her arms. My chest clenched, and I made an unfamiliar wheezing sound.

I had to see the baby. Had to hold her. Drawn by instinct, I stepped outside and strode across the grass. I had no idea what I would say or do, but staying away was impossible.

At the edge of the porch, I hesitated, waiting to be acknowledged. Ruby looked up, and I feared she might go back inside without talking to me. To my relief, she pulled back the blanket so I could see the infant's exquisite face. "Faith, this is Nadine Kingsley ... my best friend."

Tears filled my eyes. There was so much I wanted to say, but I remained silent as I closed the distance between us. "She's beautiful ... so beautiful. May I hold her?"

Ruby pressed the baby to her chest, causing the noose around my heart to yank tight. I breathed deeply, willing myself to let it go. This was not my baby. Not my baby. If her mother didn't want me to hold her, that was okay.

Hesitantly, Ruby passed the baby to me. My heart pounded as I took the infant and gazed into her eyes. Father Tim had been right. She was perfect.

Silently, I sent her a secret message. Remember me, sweet one. Remember me and be good for your mama.

Ruby placed a hand on my forearm. "I'm sorry."

I shook my head, unable to speak past the lump in my throat.

"That night you came over... I'm sorry I left. Until Father Tim gave me Faith, I could barely get out of bed. My doctors heavily medicated me, but this baby gave me back my life—gave me hope I could go on."

I nodded, knowing exactly how she felt. It was the baby, not me, who'd helped Ruby. No matter what happened, I couldn't do anything to jeopardize Ruby's relationship with her daughter.

Gazing down at Faith, I knew this would be the last time I'd ever see her. I studied her every feature, taking in her upturned nose and perfect little cheeks. I was torn about leaving Seattle, but what else could I do? Staying would only lead to more heartbreak. If I wanted to help Ruby, she could never know the truth.

"Tim told me you named your baby Autumn Marie," Ruby said, interrupting my thoughts. "I like that."

I smiled. "Coming home without her has been difficult, but she's going to be okay."

She placed a hand on top of mine. "I'm so relieved. And so happy our daughters will grow up to be best friends, like you and me."

I nodded, wishing it could be true. "And Harold? Is he okay with another baby?"

Ruby's eyes moistened. "Yes. And I'm trying to forgive

him. I'm trying to remember without that night of indiscretion, I never would've had Eric."

She paused and wiped her eyes. "Even though losing our son has been excruciating, I'm so grateful for the years we had together. So grateful he was part of my life. And now I have this little bundle of joy ..."

Chapter 35

*M*Y GUESTS AND I continued sitting around the kitchen table until Faith finished reading the missing pages from my mom's journal. My twin sister looked across the table at Father Tim, then to Ruby on her right, and finally to me. "It's incredible, isn't it?"

"Yes," I agreed.

Although Faith weighed about thirty pounds more than I did, the similarity between us was unnerving. We shared the same eyes, same nose, same chin. Our hair had the same reddish hue, but while mine was long, hers was cut in a stylish bob.

I'd been wearing my sunglasses when I spoke with Ruby on the bench at the hospital; otherwise, I'm sure she would've recognized me. Looking at Faith was like looking in a mirror.

Zane entered the kitchen, rubbing his eyes. "I'm thirsty, Mom."

"Do you want a sip of my water?" I offered.

Keeping his head down, he nodded as though shy and walked over to where I was sitting. I hugged him and handed over my water bottle, reminding myself not to drink after him unless I wanted to get sick. I placed a hand on his forehead, relieved he didn't feel hot. Hopefully, it was just something he ate or a short-lived virus.

He looked around the room, then buried his face in my shoulder. "What are all these people doing in our house?"

Father Tim, Ruby, and Faith smiled, and I made introductions, reminding Zane he'd already met Father Tim at the hospital.

"I know." He stared at Faith for a long time. "You kind of look like my mom."

Faith smiled. "Do I?"

I ran a hand through Zane's thick hair. "She looks like me because she's my sister. My twin sister."

His eyes widened, and he gave Faith a little wave. She waved back, then I pulled him onto my lap and he snuggled against me, tucking his head under my chin. I would never wish for my kids to be sick, but there was something wonderful about their snuggles when they didn't feel well.

"Did my mom say anything else?" I asked Faith, gesturing to the letter.

She nodded and continued reading.

When Autumn was released from the hospital, the children and I moved to Texas. I told them we were only going for a visit, but I'm certain they suspected we weren't returning.

I found a job teaching music at the elementary school, and we bought a beautiful two-story house, surrounded by Texas live oak trees in the small town of Turtle Lake. The community welcomed us, and while they knew about our tragic loss, they didn't know everything. We made a clean start and built a life here.

Regardless, you and your mother are always on my mind and in my heart.

Faith, I'm so sorry if my choice caused you pain. I'm sure it did—especially when you tried to locate your birth mother several years ago, and she didn't want to be found. Please know everything I did was out of love and what I believed was best for you, your mother, and the rest of my children.

As I enter my seventies, I feel a desire to make sure my affairs are in order. I'm planning on living for a long time, but I no longer wish to carry this secret. It's too heavy a burden.

I deeply miss your mother's friendship. Father Tim said you would like me to come to her birth-

day party. If after reading this you feel the same way, I'd be honored.

All my love, Nadine

Faith looked up at me and smiled. "It's still such a shock. Neither my mother nor I had any idea."

I studied Ruby carefully. "You didn't suspect Faith was related to my mother? Dan said I look like Angela."

Something I couldn't identify flashed across Ruby's face, but she didn't get a chance to respond because Logan entered the room, asking if Faith was really my twin sister.

"I am," Faith said. "And you must be Logan."

"I'm six and Zane is four," he said proudly, lest anyone confuse the issue of age. He opened the bottom cupboard beside the sink and removed a plastic cup, which he filled with water by standing on his tiptoes to reach the faucet.

I turned back to Faith. "Did you ever suspect you were a twin?"

She nodded and pressed a hand to her heart. "Maybe not a twin, but I always felt something important was missing. Something just out of my reach."

I pressed a hand to my own heart, thinking about my personal struggle with feelings of loneliness. I remembered hearing God say, "Faith." Had He meant a belief in Him, or was he referring to my sister? Or maybe both?

"My favorite movies have always been about twins," Faith said. "*Parent Trap, Big Business* …"

I laughed. "Me too. And I love those stories on the news about twins or lost siblings being reunited."

Nodding in agreement, she held out her hands to Zane, who slipped off my lap and climbed into Faith's.

"He's been sick," I said. "Are you sure you want to hold him?"

She pulled him close. "I don't mind. I work as a speech pathologist in the hospital, so I have a pretty high immunity."

My jaw dropped. "I'm a speech pathologist, too."

We smiled at each other, and I could hardly wait to find out more about her.

Logan wandered over to the table, set down his cup, and leaned against me. I wrapped my arm around him and kissed the top of his head. "Are you feeling better?"

He nodded.

I smiled at Ruby and asked why she'd never tried contacting my mom. Ruby fiddled with the latch on her purse. "I wanted to see Nadine, but we didn't have cell phones back then. I figured she'd call me when she was ready. Although we parted as friends, I mistreated your mother after the accident. I was too caught up in my own grief, and I've always regretted that."

I nodded with understanding. When I'd read about Ruby going inside the house without speaking to my mother, I'd been angry. Sure, Ruby had lost a son, but my mom had lost a daughter *and* her husband. Now, I felt compassion for Ruby and all she'd endured.

"After adopting Faith, I visited my own parents in Florida," Ruby said. "When I returned, your mother had already sold the house and moved. I had no idea where she went."

"That must've been such a shock," I said.

"I was devastated. We'd been best friends since the second grade, and suddenly, Nadine was no longer part of my life." Ruby's voice cracked, and she retrieved a tissue from her purse. "I'm sorry."

Faith reached past Zane and placed a hand on her mother's arm. "It's okay, Mom."

Ruby dabbed at her eyes, trying to regain her composure. "I'm just devastated by all the time I've wasted. And now she's lying in that hospital bed …"

Zane leaned toward me. "Mom, is that lady sad about Grandma?"

I nodded.

He reached across the table, grabbed his dinosaur egg, and handed it to Ruby.

She gave a little laugh. "This looks like a turtle egg."

Zane opened his mouth in surprise. "Yes, it is a turtle egg. You can have it."

"I thought you were going to give it to Grandma," Logan said.

Zane's expression darkened, but Ruby said the right thing. "How about we share it?"

"That's a great idea," Zane said. He jumped off Faith's lap and announced he was going back to the living room to watch TV.

"Me, too," Logan said.

After they left, I found an unopened tin of Danish Butter Cookies in the pantry. Faith arranged them on a plate while I prepared drinks for everybody.

When we were all seated at the table again, Ruby spoke. "Since we're being honest, I need to confess something."

"What is it, Mom?" Faith asked.

I held my breath, wondering if there was more to my mom's secret. Ruby sighed and addressed her daughter. "I came to see Nadine when you were about six. You had so many questions about your adoption, and I just needed to talk to my best friend. Perhaps I suspected something—especially since you looked so much like the Kingsley family—but mostly, I wanted to see Nadine. I missed her so much."

Everyone remained silent as Ruby continued her

story. "I didn't tell Nadine I was coming. I just showed up and sat in my rental car outside her house, waiting for her to come home. When she pulled into the driveway, all the kids piled out of the car—Dan, Michael, Eleanor, and ..."

Ruby paused and looked directly at me. "And I saw you, Autumn. You raced into the house, your little pigtails bouncing ... and I knew what your mother had done. I knew why she'd left and had never called. At that age, you and Faith were absolutely identical, and it scared me to death."

"Why were you scared?" I asked.

Father Tim took a cookie from the plate. "You were afraid Nadine might want Faith back."

"That's right," Ruby said.

Faith enveloped her mother in a hug. "Oh, Mom. I'm so sorry you had to go through that."

Ruby patted her daughter's back. "That's okay, honey."

Straightening, she returned her attention to me. "All the kids, including you, Autumn, helped Nadine carry the groceries into the house. You all seemed so happy. I didn't want to disrupt your life, or mine, so I left. I came home to Faith and Harold, and we made a life for ourselves."

"Did you ever tell Dad?" Faith asked.

Ruby nodded. "We spent time in counseling, vowing to be honest with each other. He agreed it was best not to say anything, so we put our hearts and souls into our marriage and kids."

"Kids?" I interrupted.

"Harold and I were able to adopt two little boys. Faith has two younger brothers."

Happiness swept through me. After reading my mom's journal, I knew how much Ruby had yearned for more children.

And now with everything out in the open, she'd have me as an additional daughter.

———◆———

ELEANOR, MICHAEL, DAN, Darlene, and all the kids came over to the rental to say hello to Ruby, Faith, and Father Tim. We ordered Chinese food and sat around talking long into the night. Despite the fact my mother's accident and subsequent coma had brought us together, a festive mood pervaded the house.

True to his word, Kyle returned from work, met our guests, then took my car to get washed and shampooed. Afterward, he showered before joining us in the living room.

Father Tim led us in a prayer for our mother that brought everyone to tears. I wasn't ready to let her go yet, but I found myself able to put her fate in God's hands. Whatever happened, I knew would be in his Divine Mercy.

When Kyle and I climbed into bed that night, he held me tight and chuckled to himself.

"What's so funny?" I asked.

"I seriously can't believe there are two of you."

I smacked him on the arm. "I know. It's crazy I have a long lost twin sister."

"Maybe next year, when we're living a normal life, you could fly up to Seattle and spend a few days with Faith. Get to know her and Ruby."

I pressed up on my elbow and stared at him. "Do you mean that?"

He nodded and ran a strand of my hair between his thumb and forefinger. "Definitely. It's your turn now."

I studied him carefully. "Kyle, what really changed your mind about the fellowship? Just seeing my family in the hospital, or was there something else?"

He cupped the back of my head with his hand and pulled me toward him. I resisted and shook my head. "No, not until you tell me."

"Come here," he beckoned. "Let me kiss you first, then I'll tell you."

I laughed. "It doesn't work that way. Tell me first, then you can kiss me."

"Okay." He sat up in bed and adjusted the pillows behind his back. "You know I have a lot of admiration for Dr. Forman."

"I wasn't aware of that," I said in a serious tone.

He flicked my knee with his finger, making me laugh. Then the line between his brow furrowed, and he spoke in a sober voice. "I viewed him as a father figure. Someone to emulate, but this morning ... he showed me pictures of his kids, who live back in Australia with his ex-wife. I'd assumed they were grown, but they're only a few years older than Logan and Zane."

Kyle ground his knuckles into his chest. "Seeing those pictures made me sick to my stomach. He's completely missing their childhood, and he doesn't even realize it. I tried to explain it to him, but ... he doesn't care. He's so focused on his research and career that he's losing out on the best part of life."

Kyle's eyes met mine. He tugged me toward him, and I put my head on his chest. "You and the boys mean everything to me, Autumn. I'm not going to do anything to jeopardize that. But more importantly, I want you to be happy, too. I know I sometimes forget to consult you and consider your feelings, but I'm going to work on that. I'm going to stop putting up walls between us, and ..."

"What?" I asked, sitting up so I could see his face.

He took a deep breath and exhaled slowly. "I never told you this, and I'm sorry, but I had a sister. A younger sister. She was adopted out of foster care, and I wasn't. I lost track of her, but I'm going to find her."

"Oh, Kyle." I was shocked he'd let me into his past like that. I had so many questions, but for now, I wrapped my arms around his chest and held on tight. "I love you, and I'll do whatever I can to help you find her."

"I know you will."

IT WAS EARLY in the morning when we received the call. My phone rang, jarring me out of a deep sleep. At first I thought it was my morning alarm, but then I squinted at the caller ID on my phone.

Eleanor!

"Oh, no!" I said in a strained voice, violent fear rushing through me.

Kyle sat straight up in bed. "What's wrong? Who's calling?"

I handed him the phone, unable to face what Eleanor had to say. *Please, God. No. Please, please, please.*

Kyle spoke to my sister in a calm and steady voice. "Okay," he said, giving me no indication of what was happening. "We'll be right there."

Chapter 36

*T*HE MORNING SUN shining through the window made it difficult for Nadine to keep her eyes closed. She tried turning over but found her body stiff and sore. Blinking several times, she opened her eyes and took in the unfamiliar surroundings. Where was she?

"Nadine?" A man who resembled a much older Father Tim leaned over her bed. "Nadine, darling? Can you hear me?"

That's right, she'd had the baby, and then something had gone wrong. Her mind churned as though clogged with clay. She tried to put all the pieces together. Tried to remember.

She'd had another little girl. Twins! And then she'd moved her family to Texas. She wasn't a young woman anymore. Her children were raised. She had grandchildren.

She'd gone to the grocery store, flirted with Dr. Henry, and then what? She couldn't remember what happened or why she was here, but judging by the rails on her bed and the strong smell of antiseptic, she was in the hospital.

Had she gone in for surgery? No, that wasn't right. At least, she didn't think so. She'd received the letter from Father Tim, telling her about Ruby's daughter looking for her. Then she'd written down her life story and ...

Her thoughts stalled as more and more faces appeared around her bed: Dan, Darlene, Michael, Eleanor, Autumn, Kyle, her grandchildren, and a woman who looked so much like Autumn, they could be twins.

Twins?

Nadine sucked in a sharp breath and tried to speak. Eleanor offered a glass of water. "Not too much, Mother. How are you feeling? Do you remember anything?"

Nadine guzzled the water then focused on the stranger in the room. Could it be? Could she be here? "Faith?"

"Yes." The woman had a pleasant smile. Autumn's smile. "You know who I am?"

Nadine nodded and tried to reach up to touch her daughter's face, but she could only lift her arm a few feet high.

A warm hand clasped hers. "Nadine, honey, it's me,

Ruby."

"Ruby?" Nadine couldn't stop the tears streaming down her face, nor find the strength to brush them away. "Ruby, you're here."

"I should've come a long time ago."

"I'm sorry," Nadine whispered.

Ruby shook her head. "You have nothing to be sorry for. You gave me the greatest gift anyone could've given me. You gave me a daughter, and she's amazing. Thank you. Thank you."

Nadine looked at Faith, afraid she might see resentment in the young woman's eyes. Instead, there was only love and understanding.

A doctor, not her Dr. Henry but someone much younger, pushed his way through the crowd and shined a flashlight in Nadine's eyes. "Mrs. Kingsley, can you see me?"

"Not with that blasted light in her eyes!" Eleanor snapped, shoving his hand away. "Honestly, my mother just came out of a coma. She hasn't even had her morning coffee yet, so back off, okay?"

"Oh, yes, Dr. Fairchild. I was just checking her vitals."

"Well let's try to be a little less invasive about it," Eleanor said.

Nadine smiled, grateful her assertive daughter's personality hadn't changed. "The baby?" she asked.

Eleanor grinned and pressed a hand to her flat stomach. "I had a little boy, and when he's not screaming his head off, he's incredible. He's got Dad's eyes and he's—"

"He's right here," said a nurse. Her name tag read *Christy,* and she lowered the bundle in her arms so Nadine could see her latest grandchild.

"He's beautiful."

Eleanor smiled proudly. "I named him Jude. After Dad."

Nadine breathed a sigh of contentment. She was surrounded by family and friends. For the first time in her life, all her children were in the same room. One might argue Angela wasn't present, but Nadine would disagree.

With all the love in this hospital room, she felt certain Angela, Jude, and Eric were present in spirit.

A feeling of complete contentment washed over her as she embraced the life she'd been given ... and the life still to come.

Dear Reader,

Thank you for reading *A Mother's Choice*. If you enjoyed it, please consider leaving a review on Amazon, Goodreads, or wherever you purchased this book. The review doesn't have to be long. Just one or two sentences giving your honest opinion would really help me out by allowing new readers to find me.

Like Autumn and Kyle, my husband and I married before medical school, and like many couples, we struggled to balance family with a demanding profession. We've been blessed with six gorgeous children, and their cute antidotes provided the inspiration for many of the details in the lives of Logan, Zane, and Aubrey.

Jules Dahlager, one of Alaska's most beloved artists and my great grandfather, gave me the idea for the hidden messages in Jude's postcards. I love using the magnifying glass to decipher his secret notes to his future wife Eva. If you'd like to see some of the postcards, please visit me on my website or join me on Facebook.

The best way to keep up with my new releases is by subscribing to updates at my website.

Again, thank you for reading my book, and I look forward to hearing from you. If you enjoyed *A Mother's Choice*, keep reading for a sneak peek of my book *Forgiving Natalie*.

Kristin Noel Fischer

Convicted felon Natalie Jones once gave her heart to Gage Merona. Now her heart belongs to eight-year-old Dash, the son Gage doesn't know about. Determined to face the criminal charges against her, Natalie moves Dash across the country to meet his father for the first time.

Although Dash is Natalie's whole world, her plan for redemption involves the heartbreaking task of leaving him with Gage. Will Natalie be able to forgive herself for what she must do? Will Dash?

And what happens when emotions between Natalie and Gage rekindle? How will Gage react when he learns the actual truth of what happened all those years ago?

"Forgiving Natalie is an unforgettable love story about forgiveness and second chances. An intense read, this latest Kristin Noel Fischer book will stay with you long after you finish the last page."

"Perfect for fans of Karen Kingsbury and Diane Chamberlain."

Chapter 1
Natalie – 2017

To-Do List

1. Sell everything.
2. Drive to San Francisco.
3. Introduce Dash to his father.
4. Leave Dash with his father.
5. Return to Chicago alone.
6. Go to jail.

"It's Alcatraz!" eight-year-old Dash shouted from the back seat of the rental car. "Do you see it, Mom?"

Shuddering, I tightened my grip on the steering wheel and focused on driving across the Bay Bridge. Maybe bringing Dash to San Francisco was a mistake. Maybe this time a list wouldn't solve my problems and I should just turn the car around and go back home to Chicago.

Except, after selling everything, I no longer had a home. No longer had anything but Dash, his dog, and a determination to face my past instead of run from it.

Through the rearview mirror, I watched Dash pull his labradoodle, Roxy, onto his lap and point out the window. "This is San Francisco, Roxy. Our new home. Do you see all the buildings? Do you, girl?"

In response, Roxy began barking and racing across the back seat from one window to the other. I pressed my fingertips to my temple. The dog's constant yapping drove me crazy.

Still, I was grateful Dash had her. Everybody needed a faithful companion when on the verge of a major change in life.

"How long until we get to our new house?" Dash asked once Roxy stopped barking.

I turned on my blinker to exit I-80. "The rental is just a few minutes away, but we're not scheduled to meet the landlord for another hour. I thought while we still had the car we'd drive down to Fisherman's Wharf and find a place for Roxy to run around."

"Do you mean use the bathroom?" asked Dash, never one to mince words.

"Yes, that's exactly what I mean."

"I thought so. I have to go, too. Hey, look. There's the Ferry Building."

Glancing to my right, I spotted the historic clock tower as Dash began spouting off everything he knew about the Embarcadero, which was a lot. Before leaving Chicago, we'd checked out several library books and had watched hundreds of YouTube videos about San Francisco. If things didn't work out with Dash's father, I joked to myself, Dash could always earn a living by becoming a tour guide.

Yet, as my son continued talking, I once again questioned the sanity of my decision. Would I actually be able to follow through with my plan? Would I actually be able to leave Dash with Gage?

The thought of being separated from my son was unfathomable. Dash was my whole world, and I'd do anything for him, which was why I had to turn myself in and go back to jail.

I couldn't live with this constant fear anymore. I couldn't continue having panic attacks every time I encountered a cop or saw the flashing lights of a patrol car.

"There's Coit Tower, Mom."

I looked to my left and swallowed hard. Years ago, Gage had kissed me on the top of that tower. He'd told me he loved me and that we'd be together forever. Unfortunately, *forever* turned out to be much shorter than either one of us had imagined.

As if reading my mind, Dash said, "Do you think my dad's ever been to San Francisco?"

The knot in my stomach tightened. Dash's questions regarding his father had increased lately. Hopefully, that was a good thing, given the fact that Gage would soon have full custody of the son he didn't even know existed.

What would Gage say when I told him about Dash? Would he despise me for keeping his son a secret? Would he refuse to acknowledge Dash as his own? Of course, none of that compared to what Gage would say when I told him why I needed to go back to Chicago.

Hands trembling, I reached for my water bottle, only to discover it was empty. Placing it back in the cup holder, I swallowed past my dry throat and continued driving.

In an ideal world, Gage would patiently listen as I explained everything. While he might disapprove of my actions, he would at least try to understand and be supportive.

Most importantly, he would embrace the son who grew more like him every day. He would welcome Dash into his life and promise to take care of him while I was gone.

"I think Roxy and I are going to like San Francisco," Dash said, his voice full of hope and enthusiasm. "I can't wait to get started on my new life."

Glancing back at Dash, I forced a smile. If only I

could borrow some of his optimism as I started my new life without him.

Forgiving Natalie
Available Now

Acknowledgments

I almost didn't include an Acknowledgments, not because I wasn't grateful for everyone who helped me produce this book, but because I was afraid I might leave someone out. If I did, please forgive me. I am truly blessed to be surrounded by so many supportive people.

First, thank you to my husband who's been a constant source of encouragement and support. Thank you for cooking us wonderful meals, helping me brainstorm book ideas, and believing in me. You're the best!

Thank you to our children: Frankie, Joey, TJ, Ben, Beth, and Sarah. You've always respected my writing time and been excited for me each step of the way.

To Barbara O'Neal, thank you for offering your voice class that taught me to believe in myself. To all the Mobsters in the Class of 2013, I love you, girls, and I'm so grateful to have you in my life!

Thank you to my original beta readers Joe Fischer, Phil and Jeanne Smith, Margo Hays, Sandy Carroll, Kendal Keith, and Sherri Graf. You read this book back when it was called *The Girl in the Painting*. Now it has a new title and no painting, but I hope you enjoy it even more.

Thank you to my recent beta readers Chris Campillo and Cerrissa Kim. This book would not be the same without you two.

I am deeply grateful to my wonderful editors, Valerie at Loud Lit Chicks and Jessica at The Editing Chick. Thank you Arianne, Jennifer Oliver, and Chrissy from EFC Services, LLC, for your invaluable help with proofreading. Thank you Paul at BB eBooks for formatting. All errors in this book are entirely my own.

Thank you Kim Killion for my gorgeous cover, and Cheryl Rae for my fabulous website.

A giant shout out goes to my 2013 Golden Heart sisters! I feel honored to be counted among so many talented writers. Thank you for your incredible support and advice.

To my ARWA chapter mates, I love you all! A special thanks to Emily McKay and Robyn DeHart who first introduced me to RWA, taught me GMC, and encouraged me to *write the next book.*

Finally, thanks to Jeanne and Phil Smith, aka Mom and Dad. You provided me with the best example that persistence and hard work pay off in the end. I'm so fortunate to have your love and support. Thanks for reading all my manuscripts and helping me become a better writer.

Love

Kristin Noel Fischer

Author Bio

Kristin Noel Fischer was born on the island of Guam and has always loved the water and sunshine. Growing up, she spent endless hours fantasizing about touring with the Harlem Globetrotters or becoming a circus performer. In fact, her childhood daydreams were so vivid, she seriously worried about her overactive imagination. Little did she know, despite her horrible spelling, she was, simply, a writer.

After high school, she lived in Costa Rica and later Japan, where she journaled extensively about her experiences. She worked as a nanny in Boston before obtaining a degree in Biology from Washington State University. Kristin now lives in Texas where she enjoys biking, yoga, and spending time with her husband and six kids.

Made in the USA
Middletown, DE
18 July 2020

13112248R00213